PAMELA BINNINGS EWEN

SECRET OF THE SHROUD

a novel

Printed in the United States of America

ISBN: 978-1-4336-7115-9

Published by Broadman & Holman Publishers,
Nashville, Tennessee

www.BHPublishingGroup.com
www.pamelaewen.com

Dewey Decimal Classification: F
Subject Heading: CLERGY—FICTION \ HOLY SHROUD—
FICTION \ MYSTERY FICTION

1 2 3 4 5 6 7 8 • 13 12 11 10

IN LOVING MEMORY OF
MY FATHER,

Walter James Binnings
and
the WWII crews of PT 279
and PT 281

The shroud is an icon written in blood: the blood of a man who has been flagellated, crowned with thorns, crucified, and wounded in his right rib.

—Pope Benedict XVI
Turin, Italy (May 2, 2010)

CHAPTER ONE

New York City, August 1955

The child fell, pulled to the earth by gravity at the rate predicted by Newton, velocity increasing 32 feet per second, each second he fell. Leo Ransom looked up at the baby's sharp, shrill cries of terror. The little body seemed almost to float; even so, some part of him calculated the rate of the fall. Before entering the ministry, Leo taught piano at the Julliard School, focusing almost entirely on Bach's music, especially his mathematically precise techniques of ornamentation. Leo loved calculations and numbers.

Leo lurched forward, stretching his arms up toward the tiny body, but it seemed to gather speed, rushing past him to the sidewalk. It landed at his feet. *God have mercy.* He froze, then crossed himself as lifeblood spread around him and upon him like scattered light. Stunned, newly ordained, uncertain, he looked up in disbelief, craning his neck, and saw two boys peering down from the roof of the fourteen-storied building. When they spotted Leo, the heads disappeared.

Leo blinked, not sure what he had seen. Cars and buses ground to a halt, and for a moment an eerie silence settled around him. Then Leo heard feet pounding on the pavement, and the street came to life. The ground seemed to shift beneath him, but he willed himself to hold steady.

Suddenly the door of the building burst open, slamming against the dirty brick wall; and a small boy, not more than eight years old, exploded onto the street. Tears streaked through the grime on his face, and his breath came in great gasps as he halted and stood rooted to the spot, his eyes fixed on the little body lying on the sidewalk.

Later, each time Leo recalled this moment, he pictured a tableau, like an old sepia portrait—a closed circle containing himself, the boy, and the dead child—suspended, flat, and still.

The boy tore his eyes from the body and stared at Leo. He remained quiet, even after a woman in the distance began to scream.

✣ ✣ ✣

Police and ambulances converged on the scene. Leo reported having seen two children peering over the low brick ledge on the roof when he looked up at the sound of the baby's screams.

"Are you certain?" the policeman asked.

Leo sat on the ground now, cradling the rigid boy who had burst from the building. One hand cupped the boy's head against his chest. "Yes," he said. The boy was gangly, with long bones for such a young child, unmoving as Leo rocked with him back and forth. His clothes were worn, slightly oversized, but almost subconsciously Leo noted that the shirt and pants were carefully darned in several places.

Leo glanced up, and the policeman gave him a questioning look. He pressed the child closer to his chest and nodded to confirm his words. "I'm absolutely certain."

"What's your name, Father?"

"Ransom," he replied. "Leo Ransom." He glanced at the child in his arms, then at the small body still lying on the sidewalk, now covered with a white cloth, surrounded by medics, policemen, and a man in a rumpled business suit who seemed to be in charge.

"You know the . . . ah . . . the baby?" the policeman asked.

"No." Leo shook his head. "I was just passing by." His voice broke. He swallowed and went on. "The screams . . . I heard . . ."

"He's almost three years old," whispered a small voice. The policeman slid his eyes to the boy.

Over the child's shoulder Leo saw the small body being lifted onto a stretcher. Gently, he placed a hand at the side of the boy's face to block his view of the frantic scene.

"How do you know that, son?"

The child hesitated, then raised his head and stared at the policeman. When he finally spoke, his tone was strange, tight and flat. His fists were clenched, ridged tendons stretched the length of his forearms. A tiger coiled to spring, Leo thought.

"He's Sam. He's my brother."

The policeman watched the boy for a moment.

"What's your name?"

"Little Guy."

"Little Guy." The policeman sucked air, then blew out his cheeks as he pulled a small notebook from the breast pocket of his short-sleeved blue shirt. "Okay. We'll come back to that." He stooped down to eye level with the boy.

"Were you on the roof?" he asked in a low voice.

The boy nodded, mute.

The policeman thought about that a moment. "Then how did you get down here so fast?" he finally asked.

The boy's chest rose and fell. An ugly flush crept up his neck and along the sides of his face, and his eyes filled again with tears. He seemed to gasp the answer. "I ran."

The policeman's gaze swept up the fourteen-storied building, then he looked back at the child in disbelief. "You ran down all of those stairs in that short time?"

The boy nodded once again, and a small sob escaped. He stared at the policeman and shuddered.

"Why?"

The boy looked away. After a moment he said, in that same strange, flat tone, "I thought that . . . maybe . . . I could catch him."

✣ ✣ ✣

Months later Little Guy sat beside his mother on a long wooden bench in a small courtroom. The ceiling was high, but the stark white walls seemed to close around him. On the other side of him was Father Ransom. *Father Leo,* he remembered. Little Guy caught his mother's eye and managed a weak smile.

Streaks of flinty light filtered through dirty windows high up in the courtroom, near the ceiling. The room was packed with spectators, reporters, some friends of Little Guy's mother and a few people who seemed to know the two boys, Jesse Reardon and Malo Sanchez, the killers, sitting at a long table in front of the room, to the left, just inside a low, wooden railing. Another long table inside the railing on the right was piled high with books and papers. Two men dressed in dark suits sat at this second table, drumming their fingers, making notes with pencils on a tablet before them as they talked. Little Guy had seen them all before.

Father Leo had remained with Little Guy through the long ordeal of staring spectators, questioning policemen, ambulance drivers, and doctors on that day . . . the day that Sam died. When his mother arrived at the hospital, Father Leo had explained . . . passing by . . . Sam . . . the boys . . . Little Guy. He'd prayed with Mother, stayed with them.

Sitting in the courtroom, Little Guy struggled to forget that day, but pictures flashed into his mind, then disappeared and reappeared like pop-ups in a haunted house . . . people crowding, pressing, crying. The wailing ambulance—one for Sam, one for him. Father Leo's black suit with the thin white circle around his neck. His mother's heaving sobs, leaning on Father Leo. Some things were sharp and clear, faces looking down at him with pity and, just behind, a white sheet covering Sam—it was soaked in blood—and a nurse who brought hot chocolate.

Finally, after a long wait, Father Leo had bundled Little Guy and his mother into a taxi and took them home. Little Guy shuddered, hating to think of it even now—walking into the apartment in the late afternoon when light turns dull and gray. Without Sam the rooms were empty, damp, and cold. Father Leo stayed with him until he'd fallen asleep.

Now in the courtroom Little Guy felt ice blades slice through his stomach and shuddered. His mother slipped her arm around his shoulders and pulled him close. Little Guy looked up at Mother, then at Father Leo. Since that day, the day that Sam had died, Father Leo visited his mother and him several times a week, bringing treats for him and, once, flowers for his mother. After the flowers his mother began taking him to Father Leo's church on Sunday mornings. It was the Apostolic Church, Father Leo said. God's house.

There was a big gold cross inside the church, up at the front under a window with colored glass, and the cross gleamed in the light on sunny days. Sometimes Father Leo played the piano just for Mother and him after everyone had left and the place was empty, dark, and cool. Church wasn't so bad, Little Guy decided. Besides, he liked having someone to call "father." His own had been gone for years—just disappeared one day. He'd been sitting on the stoop in front of the apartment house, down near the sidewalk, when his father had come hurrying out the front door with a small brown suitcase in his hand. When he'd spotted Little Guy, he'd given a large sigh; and even though his father had grinned down at him, Little Guy remembered how cold he'd felt at the sound of that sigh.

His father sat down next to Little Guy on the stoop, fished a silver dollar from his pocket, and flipped it from one finger to the next, over and under, like he was thinking hard.

Then with another sigh he'd handed it to Little Guy. Little Guy still had that dollar.

He'd held the coin in the flat of his hand, examining it. "What's this for?" he'd asked.

"Won it at the races," his father said with a strange, sad smile. "It's yours to keep. Remember this son," he'd added as he pushed himself up from the step. "There's not a lot in life that you can count on. But that dollar coin there—it's got real silver in it. That's something real enough—you can always count on that. I'd give you more, but your mama took the rest, and that's all I've got today." He'd chucked Little Guy underneath his chin and smiled again, tipped his hat to the back of his head, turned, and walked away. Little Guy had watched until his father rounded the corner and he couldn't see him any more.

Every day for weeks and weeks Little Guy had waited on the stoop for his father to come home. Finally one day he'd understood. His father wasn't coming back. He'd wrapped the silver dollar in some tissue paper then and put it into a small brown box that he tucked at the back of his underwear drawer; right next to the round, white "I like Ike" button.

And now Father Leo came to visit. Little Guy wondered if he'd ever stay—take his father's place. He banished thoughts of his own father, angry thoughts. Sometimes Father Leo sat with his mother in the kitchen for hours, just like a real father might. They spoke in low, serious tones over cups of coffee; and he noticed that sometimes the tips of their fingers touched across the table while they talked, just lightly, as if resting there. When occasionally the talk came around to

Sam and God, he'd listened, trying to understand. Once he'd asked Father Leo where God was. "Why can't I see him?"

"He's invisible," Father Leo had said after a moment.

The boy thought this was probably a trick, but he kept the thought to himself. Father Leo had patted his arm and smiled.

This courtroom reminded him of Father Leo's church, Little Guy mused as he looked around. Except the church was dark, and this room was bright. Both places were closed in, though, with a funny, musty odor. An old, stale smell. Both places reminded him of Sam. *But Sam was dead.*

Just before coming to the courthouse for the first time about one week ago, Father Leo sat with Little Guy at the kitchen table, wearing a grave expression as he told what to expect that day, that Little Guy would see the boys who had dropped Sam from the roof. His brown eyes sloped down at the corners, and bushy brows drew together as he talked while he tapped his fingers on the table like he was playing a piano. Little Guy had tried to smile as if he didn't care, fixing on those long, thin fingers; but his eyes blurred, and his lip trembled.

"Sam lives with God now," Father Leo said gently. "He's in a happier place. God will take care of him."

An image of Sam's little body falling from the roof flashed before Little Guy, and he'd turned his eyes to Father Leo. "What if he doesn't?" he'd asked.

"Doesn't what?"

"Doesn't take care of Sam."

Father Ransom had smiled and put his hand on Little Guy's shoulder. "Of course he will, son. God's with us all the time. He loves us. He'll take care of Sam."

Little Guy hesitated as a rush swooped from his head to his feet and turned his stomach upside down. He caught his breath, fighting the nausea as he thought of Sam falling. *Why did Sam have to die?*

He must have spoken out loud because Father Leo's hand had tightened on Little Guy's shoulder for an instant and his smile died. After a moment he said, "God has reasons that we can never understand, Little Guy." His voice was firm, resolute. "It's a *fact* that Sam's in a happy place now. He's with God."

Little Guy dropped his eyes and thought about Father Leo's words. How could this be true? Sam, dressed in a little blue-and-white playsuit, with his baby-silk hair carefully parted and brushed to one side, lay alone in a box in a graveyard just across the river, outside the city. Little Guy had seen him put there. It occurred to him that Father Leo might be wrong about God and Sam. But he pushed the thought aside. What if Father Leo became angry and left—like his father had left him? What if he stopped visiting, stopped calling Little Guy "son"? So Little Guy tucked the corners of his mouth into a smile and nodded.

The bench was hard, and Little Guy had been sitting still in this courtroom for a long time. He shifted his buttocks, and his mother rubbed his shoulder in an absent manner. He looked up at her, but she stared straight ahead with her lips pressed together. He sighed, then straightened as a door in the back of the room opened, a loud unintelligible announcement was made, and a large man dressed in black robes entered. His mother stood, and Little Guy slid from the bench, shuffling his feet.

A week ago, when he'd first seen this man dressed all in black like Father Leo, Little Guy thought he was a priest.

His mother had shook her head. "This is a judge," she'd whispered. "He's here to decide how to punish the boys that dropped Sam from the roof. It's his job."

Little Guy stared at the judge and hoped that the killers would be beaten to death. That's how he thought of Jesse and Malo . . . the *killers.* Or that they'd be left to starve on an island filled with tigers and poison snakes. Alone.

When the judge took his seat behind a large wooden desk high above everyone else in the room, Little Guy's mother sat back down, and he followed suit. He reached only to his mother's shoulder, and he had to tilt his head up to see the judge. This was an important day, Mother had said. When the judge began to speak in a solemn tone, Little Guy waited to hear Sam's name, but instead the judge used the same old words that Father Leo used in church on Sundays, words like *remorse, society,* and a long one—*redemption.* Little Guy's thoughts began to drift while the judge went on, his voice humming, rising and falling in the distance, settling into a rhythm.

Pictures of that day skittered through Little Guy's mind, and he squeezed his eyes tight to shut them out. Still they came. Two killers. Malo's hateful laughter as Jesse held Sam's little legs, dangling him upside down from the edge of the roof. Even now he could feel Malo's iron grip twisting his arms behind his back while he struggled, fighting, begging them not to hurt his baby brother. He could hear them laughing when he'd jerked free, moving toward Sam.

Memories struck in flashes now, like bolts of lightning from the past piercing darkness. Images formed, then disappeared. But suddenly in the courtroom Little Guy heard . . . no *felt* . . . the scream that rose from his bowels that day. *Let him go!* The words rang through his mind as the agony of that moment—the pain of it—hit him; and he doubled over, dropping his head onto his knees. The courtroom spun. His mother bent toward him, rubbing his back in small, worried circles.

Jesse holding Sam. "Let him go?" Jesse had laughed. Then he'd given Little Guy a long look. "Did you say to let him go?"

Too late he'd realized the mistake. Little Guy groaned, remembering. Shards of light ripped through his mind. He couldn't breathe as the hateful voice repeated the question. *"Did you say to let him go?"*

The white light flashed. He saw himself tearing down the narrow stairs, dark and dirty . . . slipping on a concrete landing wet with something sticky, the smell of sweat and something else, something sickening as he was chased by the mocking words.

Did you say to let him go?

His mother pulled him upright, slipped her arm around him, and held him fast against her. She was soft and warm. Little Guy forced his eyes open with a deep, shuddering breath and stared at the backs of the two boys that killed

Sam. A woman sat with them. Cold fear crawled through him as he watched her. He'd seen her before; she'd made him sit in the big chair next to the judge while she asked questions. Her smile was tight, and her eyes were hard. When she'd walked over to him, stalking, he'd shrunk from her. Jesse and Malo had watched him, and he glimpsed Malo whispering something to Jesse, who snickered.

From the chair he'd searched the crowd behind the railing for his mother. His eyes blurred as he found her, sitting there with Father Leo, and Malo had laughed again. When the woman began asking questions in sharp staccato bursts, Little Guy's heart pounded; and he shifted in the chair, moving closer to the judge. His tongue stuck to the roof of his mouth, and he found he couldn't answer.

"The judge will protect you, son," Father Leo had told him. "That's what he's here for. He's a good man."

At Little Guy's frightened look, Father Ransom had patted his shoulder. "I promise, son." That was one week ago, and he'd held on to those words, repeating them to himself in the dark just before he fell asleep each night. He had thought of Father Leo's promise each day as he woke and looked to the empty bed across the room he'd shared with Sam.

Then yesterday, the day had come. Father Leo had promised, and the promise gave him courage to go into the courtroom and to walk up to the chair all by himself. He had relaxed a bit when he saw that the chair was near the judge.

But he was surprised.

"Up there on the roof," the lady had begun in a quiet voice. "What did you do when you saw that your little brother was in danger?"

Flashing lights blinded him. He couldn't breathe.

"Little Guy?" Her voice was lower this time. "Little Guy?"

He looked up at her, not understanding.

"I asked, What did you do when you saw Sam in danger on the roof?" She moved toward him, and her voice turned to steel. "Did you try to help your baby brother, Little Guy?" She waited. "Little Guy?"

His tongue was thick; he couldn't speak. Against his will the pictures came again. A flash of light . . . white sunshine . . . hot up on that roof. Sam crying, crying.

Her voice came from far away. *Did you say to let him go?*

Himself lurching away from Malo with a surge of strength. Reaching for Sam. Grabbing, pushing, fists flying, punching. And then . . . Jesse's round eyes gaping at him. And Jesse's empty hands.

He gasped. The room whirled.

From far away Little Guy heard the judge's stern voice. "Answer the questions young man."

The judge's words came to him in a stream of pulsing beats, low and ominous like far-off drums. Confused, he couldn't think . . . didn't want to think . . . to remember any more. Twisting around to look up at the judge: "I tried to catch him; tried to catch him." His voice broke, and tears ran down his cheeks. "It wasn't my fault. I tried to catch him," he cried.

A man helped him down from the chair, carried him from the room, sobbing. Everything turned black. When he awoke, his mother was by his side. And Father Leo.

"It's all right, my boy," Father Leo whispered. "The judge will see they're punished—Jesse and Malo. It's *their* fault, not yours." Little Guy gave him a close look, wanting to believe.

"I promise, Little Guy."

Suddenly his mother tensed beside him. The memories disappeared, and he looked up. The judge had stopped talking and was putting on his glasses, tucking them carefully behind each ear. Then he picked up a piece of paper that lay on the desk before him, cleared his throat, and began to read aloud.

"The defense has presented evidence in this case raising a valid question: which one of the three boys was the proximate cause of the child's death. Or to put it another way, which boy actually caused the child to fall." The judge glanced with a frown over the top of his glasses at the two men before him in dark business suits, then at the crowd behind the railing.

"It seems the actions of the child's older brother may have contributed somehow to the tragedy," he went on. His mother's arm around him tightened, and she drew in her breath. "The extent of his responsibility for the child's death is undetermined, and in fact," the judge took off his eyeglasses and wiped them carefully, then settled them back upon the bridge of his nose, "we will probably never know what really happened on that rooftop."

Jesse seated at the table just in front of the judge, turned to scan the rows of spectators behind him. His eyes swept past Little Guy and his mother with disinterest, then assuming a bored look, he jammed his hands into his pockets, slid down in his chair, and gazed out the windows.

"Society has failed these two boys. They're victims as well." The judge's voice grew loud and stern. Little Guy saw him nod toward the killers. "They've never had an opportunity to learn the difference between right and wrong. No one has ever taught them how to behave. No one has looked out for them or cared for them." His voice rose. "Not their teachers, not welfare workers, not friends, not family . . . *no one.*" The judge paused for an instant and scowled over the silent room.

"Therefore, given all the circumstances, I cannot in good conscience grant the state's motion to try these boys as adults under a charge of first-degree murder." He fixed his eyes on the two men in dark suits. "They will be tried as juveniles, and the court proposes to the prosecution that a lesser charge, such as manslaughter, would be more appropriate for consideration."

At a cry from his mother, Little Guy's head swiveled. Her mouth contorted, twisting as she stared up at the judge, and tears spilled. Father Leo reached for her hand and, folding it between his two, patted it. People around them began to rise, talking in hushed whispers as they picked up coats and bags and hats, preparing to leave.

Little Guy's stomach roiled with fear. His eyes snapped to the judge, who was removing his glasses, wiping them with a corner of his full, black sleeve. Little Guy watched as he looked up and laughed at something one of the men in dark suits said. The man said something to the woman, and she smiled, too.

Father Leo bent toward Little Guy's mother. "There's a trial yet to go through, Rebecca," he whispered. "You must be brave. It will turn out right in the end."

"No!" Her painful cry shot through the room, piercing Little Guy. The judge looked up and frowned. Little Guy's eyes shifted from Father Leo to his mother, to the killers, and then to the woman with them. The woman who had tormented him yesterday. She wore a bright smile now.

Father Leo stroked Mother's hand again.

"It *won't* be all right, Leo," he heard his mother say as she released Little Guy from her grip. "The judge doesn't care about Sam, or Little Guy, or me." With her knuckles she rubbed the tears from her eyes. Little Guy stared at his mother. Until Sam died, he'd never seen her cry.

"You know as well as I do those two thugs will be back on the street in a few years." She spat the words. "They're old enough to murder my baby," suddenly her voice broke, "but not for real prison."A bitter laugh was cut short by a sob. "Think of it! Manslaughter! Why, they'll be free in a couple of years." She paused, swallowing; her hands flew up, and she lunged forward, hiding her face. "I should never have left my boys alone to wander the streets." Little Guy saw her shoulders heave.

"Rebecca," Father Leo said, bending over her. "You're not to blame! Think clearly. You had no choice. You were working."

She moaned. "I can't bear this. I just *cannot* bear it."

Little Guy turned her words over in his mind. She *couldn't* be right. His eyes slid back to the judge. What had happened?

The judge glanced at his watch and rose, still chuckling, and in that instant Little Guy understood. There would be no beating; there would be no island prison with tigers and snakes for Sam's killers. Little Guy gave Father Leo a sideways glance; Father Leo had promised the judge was a *good* man.

His mother's voice broke through her son's building rage. "How can this be? It's insane." She turned to Leo and collapsed against him, sobbing. "You're a priest! How could your God let this happen?"

Little Guy fixed his eyes on the back of his mother's head; looked at the coils of red-gold hair that stuck to the nape of her neck in the heat, looked at Father Leo's hand smoothing those curls while she wept.

"And, worst of all," he heard her gulp as she lifted her head and looked up at the priest, "Did I hear right? Did the judge say that . . . that . . . *Little Guy might have been part to blame?"* Her voice rose to a shrill pitch, and her hands curled into fists at her side. "Did he say that *my boy* might have caused Sam to fall?"

Little Guy froze. *What did she say?*

He gripped the edge of the hard wooden bench and turned, staring at the woman still standing next to Jesse and Malo at the table in front of the room, and the question she'd asked came back to him. *Did you try to help your baby brother?*

His heart began to race. A sheen of sweat glazed his neck and arms as his heart pounded in his chest. In rapid succession it beat . . . no no . . . no no . . . no no . . . That wasn't right, that wasn't right. He wouldn't think of that.

Did you try to help your baby brother, Little Guy?

Suddenly, with a roaring in his ears, fury surged through Little Guy, a powerful force that struck him as he turned his gaze to the judge. The torrent of hate flowed from him like a vaporous cloud, engulfing the judge, Jesse and Malo, and the woman with them, and the awful accusation. The merciful cloud filled Little Guy as well, swelling within him, shrouding the ugly pictures in his mind. He lifted his chin, gasping for air as he fought for control.

He would not let them see him cry. He would not think of that day. He would not cry. The words ran through his mind: *It's not my fault it's not my fault it's not my fault.*

Jesse turned, and Little Guy's eyes locked with his. He saw a blurred, sneering grin; then Jesse's mouth formed the words that would haunt him all his life: *You said to let him go.*

CHAPTER TWO

New York City, October 2007

Cold wind whipped around the corner of the cathedral and caught the folds of Archbishop Wesley Bright's crimson cloak, causing ripples of silk-shine even in the dull afternoon light. It was the indigo eyes that drew him. As he stood at the top of the wide limestone stairs leading to the sidewalk, there, just past the cameras and the waiting crowd held back with thick velvet ropes, the eyes of a small child standing near an old wooden cart piled high with flowers caught and held him.

How strange that he could see those eyes from such a distance; as if the little girl stood right before him. Then Wesley shook himself and lowered his chin just a bit as he'd been taught, to take the edge off, to make himself more personable. He remembered to smile, crinkling his eyes, letting the breeze ruffle his light brown hair as he strode down the steps toward a dark town car waiting on the street below, stopping occasionally to shake a hand that snaked across the ropes.

The archbishop's assistant, Emily Scott, waited at the door of the car, watching him work the crowd with a confident, sure touch. She smiled as he descended toward her. *Wesley.* Wes. Even though he was old enough to be her father, once in a while, in her mind, she allowed herself to call him by this name.

She focused her attention on business now, trying to view the archbishop critically, objectively, as the media would do. Despite her smile, a light crease between her brows deepened as he descended the stairs. He . . . maybe the church . . . she wasn't sure just who . . . but *someone* had hired a media-relations consultant who said the archbishop walked with too much bounce, overconfidence—although Emily knew the spring in his step was merely energy. But the consultant had insisted, getting rid of what he'd called "that cocky stride," the pacing and his countenance. She pressed her lips into a thin line as she thought of the hired consultant with his Armani suits and slicked back hair—the lizard, she'd called him—a man used to working with CEOs and investment bankers, she supposed. The archbishop had laughed at the nickname . . . *lizard.*

"Bless you," Wesley murmured to an elderly man who reached from the crowd to touch his arm. His eyes scanned the old parchment face, the rheumy eyes, as he took the hand and held it, fighting a vague undercurrent of repulsion while the television cameras ground away. He did not blink as flashbulbs popped around him before he let go of the bony hand. Wesley was proud of his ability to reach out to ordinary people, to bring a bit of grace and comfort to the poor.

As his foot touched the concrete sidewalk, a strange frisson stirred him. Wesley stopped, turned, and found himself looking down at the little girl. Enormous eyes stared back at him from a porcelain face. Except for the eyes, the child's features were small and fine. He quickly took in her blue woolen dress that hung just above tiny, sandaled feet. Thunder rolled in the distance as the thought registered. Sandals, in this weather? She stood beside the wooden flower cart, and her head barely reached the top. The child looked familiar somehow. He gave her a sharp look.

The girl gazed back with wide, questioning eyes, as if she also knew him, then extended her arm, thrusting out a small bouquet of flowers. A car horn honked, and she jumped, turned toward the sound, and whirled back again, fixing her gaze on him as if by this means she could steady herself. She whispered something, and despite the din of noise from the crowd and the traffic, he could hear her voice, but the language was foreign, and he couldn't understand.

The little girl's intense scrutiny made Wesley recoil. His gaze dropped to the flowers in her hand, and he felt a surprising surge of relief. Ah, just another child with flowers. With a wide smile, turning slightly toward the bank of cameras, Wesley reached down for the bouquet, at the same time placing his left hand flat upon the top of her head. Emily touched his arm. "The car's waiting. It's going to rain."

Gray clouds had gathered, and they seemed to sink into the city, misting between the tall buildings amassed on the island of Manhattan. Wesley glanced at the sky, then back to the child who still stared at him with that intense look.

"It'll make the front pages," Emily said as Wesley turned toward the waiting car. The lizard would like that. The crowd surged closer, and she placed her hand on the middle of the archbishop's back, pressing him toward the town car.

"What did you say?" he asked, letting her steer him forward.

"The picture with the child. The little flower girl." Emily stepped aside, shielding the archbishop as the driver opened the car door for him. "It's a good shot for the morning papers."

"Yes," Wesley murmured in a pleased tone as he ducked into the car. "But she's a strange little thing. So solemn."

Emily glanced over her shoulder as the driver slammed the door behind Wesley, then hurried around to the other side of the car, dodging traffic on Fifth Avenue. The archbishop was not yet protected by an entourage—no convoy of cars, no blocked-off streets or police escorts. Not yet, but it wouldn't be long, she reflected. With his all-inclusive, clear-eyed acceptance of diverse views, already he was the most popular spiritual leader in the country. Single-handed he'd rescued the Apostolic Church from the grip of the idea that Jesus was divine; from the lethargy and those old judgmental first-century myths and legends that, as he liked to point out, had caused such turmoil through the centuries.

Opening the door, Emily slid in beside Wesley, sinking into the soft leather and resting her head against the soft-cushioned back of the seat. Crowds like this were unsettling.

She wondered absently how they had known the archbishop was in the cathedral today.

As the car began to move forward, Wesley turned once again to look back at the child. She stood motionless, staring after him with that grave look. The car picked up speed, sweeping down Fifth Avenue. The little girl disappeared from sight, and Emily leaned forward to confer with the driver.

Wesley smoothed back his hair with both hands and let his thoughts drift, observing himself as the crowd must have seen him. He pictured a man of distinction in the prime of life, fifty-nine years, with a fine shaped head and a pleasant expression, standing in front of the great Gothic cathedral.

The cathedral, this fine symbol of power, was a new acquisition orchestrated by him only a few years ago on behalf of the church. He sighed at the thought of the drawn-out difficult negotiations with the Vatican, but the scandal of pedophile priests in the United States that had surfaced in the last few years was expensive for the Catholic Church, and finally he'd prevailed.

The delicate architecture of the building, with its slender spires and flying buttresses, had always reminded him of a sand castle. His mother had taken him once to the Jersey shore when he was a boy, and he'd built such a sand castle, drizzling the sand through his fingers, layer by fragile layer. But in the end, the tide had washed it away. *How appropriate,* Wesley thought, smiling.

He leaned back and masked his satisfaction, conscious of the eyes of the driver in the rearview mirror.

✣ ✣ ✣

She watched the big car pull away from the curb, following it with her eyes until it disappeared in the traffic. When she could no longer see it, her gaze skimmed the street, the tall glittering buildings, the big people crowded around her.

"I'll buy those from you."

The child looked up but couldn't make out the strange words. The woman's face was friendly, but she seemed unreal, far away. The girl stiffened, and her chest fluttered inside.

"How much are they—that bunch there?" The woman held her eyes on the girl as she pointed to a bouquet of flowers in the cart. "How much?" she asked again.

The child stared without answering.

"Oh my," the customer said softly.

Just then an elderly woman burst from the crowd and hurried to the cart. "$4.50, please," she said in a brusque tone, as she reached into the cart for the flowers and handed them to the customer.

The woman opened her purse and fished out the money, still looking at the child. "She's a beautiful little thing," she said as she took the bouquet.

"Oh. The child?" The old woman looked around as if surprised to see the little girl still there. "Yes, I suppose she is."

"Is she yours?"

"No. I don't know who she is." The old lady shrugged and dropped the money into a deep pocket of her well-worn coat as she spoke. "She tended the cart for me when I slipped away to see the archbishop up close. I don't think she can speak." She bent down and smiled. "Can you speak, child? Cat got your tongue?"

The little girl gazed back in silence. The old woman chuckled as she straightened and turned to see the customer moving away. The crowd had dwindled; the cathedral steps were almost empty now.

"Ah well," the old woman said, glancing at the sky. "This has been a good day, all in all." She turned to the cart and pushed the flowers to the center. When they were safely away from the slatted edges, she set herself between the handles and leaned forward, bending her elbows to lift them. "Do you live around here?" she asked. The little girl did not answer.

"Perhaps you cannot hear, as well?" A crack of thunder caused her to jump. She threw the child a worried look and hitched the handles over her shoulders, grasping them with both hands. "You'd best be getting on home now, dear." At the child's blank stare, she sighed. "Home," she barked, louder this time. Tugging the handles, she moved forward, dragging the weight of the cart behind her. "Run along home, now. Shoo! You'll get wet," she called, glancing back over her shoulder.

A drop of rain fell on the girl's face, and she wiped away the water with the heel of her hand as she gazed around with huge dark eyes. She stared again at the tall buildings surrounding the church. They seemed to disappear in the heavy mist, reaching into the sky. The clouds were the color of slate now, and wind gusted around her with sharp, cold bursts. The street was slick, streaked with water and colored lights, and rain glossed the tops of black umbrellas bobbing past.

The little girl crossed her arms over her thin chest, and shivering, she began to cry. But as tears rolled down her cheeks and mingled with rain, warm air slowly swirled around her small form, sinking through her flesh, warming and filling her from limb to limb. A tingling sensation rose through her legs, her arms, her chest, her neck, and at last, she dissolved.

The old woman blinked and stopped. The child had disappeared right before her eyes! One second she was there; the next, she was gone. Her fingers tightened on the handles as she peered back through the rain. Finally she shook her head and shrugged, moving forward once again, pulling the cart behind her and wondering where the little girl had gone.

The uniformed driver held an umbrella high as Wesley dashed from the car, herding Emily before him up the stairs of the three-storied town house that he preferred over the old rectory attached to the cathedral. Carriage lanterns flickered at each side of the door as Wesley's housekeeper, Miss Honeman, held it open for them. Yellow light from the foyer streamed around her and seeped out into the cold, dark evening.

For ten years Miss Honeman had managed to make herself necessary to the archbishop. She knew to fold his newspaper just so, leaving the editorial page face up so that when he came down in the morning for breakfast he'd have something to hide behind until he'd had his first cup of coffee, hot and black. Her hair, streaked with gray, was stretched into a tight knot, low on the nape of her neck. A black dress covered her gaunt frame, and in turn the dress was covered by a starched and pressed white-bib apron. His Grace had protested the apron, she was fond of saying, but Miss Honeman insisted on the formality while she was in the rectory.

As Wesley and Emily ducked into the hallway, the driver lowered the umbrella and shook the rain from it, then followed. Miss Honeman pulled the door closed, and her eyes slid past Emily as she gave the archbishop a warm smile.

"Bad weather, Your Grace?" Miss Honeman said. Her eyes dropped to the small bouquet of flowers still clutched in his hand. "What have you got here?"

Wesley handed over the flowers, then shrugged out of his wet cloak. Miss Honeman caught the vestment with her other hand, wondering why he'd worn it home. Someone's idea of a photo opportunity, most likely.

Wesley nodded at the bouquet she now held. Despite the miserable fall weather tonight, the flowers looked like springtime. "Given to me by a little girl at the cathedral," he told her.

Miss Honeman looked at the flowers. "They're lovely," she said. "I recognize the chrysanthemums, but not the others. Very unusual. I don't believe I've ever seen any quite like these."

Emily greeted Miss Honeman without taking off her coat. She set a briefcase on the floor and removed a folder.

"The fund-raising reports," she said to Wesley. "Do you have time to go over them with me?"

He sighed and held out his hand.

"The archbishop's tired, Emily," Miss Honeman said in a brisk tone. "His dinner's almost ready. Put it in the study, please." She eyed the water dripping from Emily's coat onto the wooden floor as she spoke. "Are you staying? Or would you like the driver to wait?"

Wesley gave Miss Honeman a grateful look.

"I'll only be a minute," Emily said, hurrying down the hall to the study. She called back to the driver to wait.

The driver nodded and, at a look from Miss Honeman, settled into a corner near the door.

When Wesley turned into the library, Miss Honeman followed. A cheerful fire blazed, bathing the small room in an amber glow. A burgundy carpet patterned with intricate designs of blue and beige covered most of the hardwood floor. Polished mahogany bookcases climbed the walls on either side of the fireplace, and just in front were two blue leather armchairs, each with its own small, round, marble-topped table.

"Ah," Wesley sighed in a contented voice. "The first fire of the season. That and a glass of claret will make a perfect evening." He sank into one of the armchairs and closed his eyes, relaxing as the fire warmed him.

"Claret, Your Grace?" Miss Honeman asked, frowning. This was something new. "Wouldn't you prefer a white wine?"

"I'm off," Emily called from the door.

Wesley waved in her direction without opening his eyes. "Not tonight, Miss H," he said, sliding down into the soft leather. "It's been a long hard day. And a cold rainy night needs a glass of claret, I believe." Rain beat against the windowpane, making him drowsy. He loved the sound of rain, but Miss Honeman turned on some music. It was a Mozart concerto, a slow sensuous blend of piano and clarinet, his favorite.

"Very well," Miss Honeman murmured, and looking down at the flowers in her hand, she disappeared into the kitchen to see if she could unearth a bottle of claret. The archbishop did like fine things. She smiled to herself, filing away the new information: claret on a cold, rainy night.

Pillowed in his chair before the fire, Wesley sighed again. In the distance he heard a deep rumble, a long roll of thunder through the universe that reminded him of drums. Warmth from the fire drifted around him, driving away the thought as his muscles yielded one by one. His lids grew heavy, and a gray mist plumed through his mind as the door between two worlds opened in the twilight sleep. Here faint images formed, the sketched outline of a child's form, barely visible in the swirling mist. Something was there—he *felt* the presence—and still he heard the drums. At last the ghostly vision disappeared, and he drifted deeper into sleep.

Emily waved to the driver as she leaped from the car and ran under a canopy to the door. Despite the driving rain, a doorman in a dark blue uniform with gold braid on his cap patiently held the door open for her. He smiled and touched the bill of his cap when she entered the lobby, then looked both ways down the sidewalk before closing the door behind her.

"Wet one, Miss Scott," the doorman said walking to the small desk in the lobby.

"I love rain at night," Emily answered.

He smiled as he ran his fingers across the mail alcoves in the wall, stopping at one in the middle. He pulled out some envelopes and a magazine and handed them to Emily. "Everyone does if they're inside," he said.

She nodded without looking up and walked to the elevator, sorting quickly through the envelopes as she entered and pushed the button for the twentieth floor. The elevator shifted with a jolt and rose while she gazed at herself in the smoky mirrored door. Her reflection was hazy, giving the effect, she thought, of an old impressionist painting. She brushed her dark hair back from her face, but it had already begun to dry and slipped through her fingers like fine silk.

The apartment she entered was small, and the building was old. The sound of rain patter on the window penetrated, and as she flicked on lamps one after the other, Emily was happy at the thought of being inside, safe and warm on such a night. The lamps cast a soft light over the cozy room. In one corner was a small piano, a spinet that had belonged to her mother. She glanced at it with a shadow of regret. She'd used to play but these days never seemed to have the time.

Shedding her coat, Emily went into the kitchen, poured a glass of chilled white wine, and wandered back into the living room. She put the glass down on top of the piano and sat on the small wooden bench placed before it. For an instant the sound of the rain on the window lulled her, and the thought of bed and a good book was tempting. Then she shook herself. No time for that. She needed to schedule the archbishop's interviews with the media this week, several television and one with a reporter from the *Post* who had called him a breath of fresh air. She'd have to confirm first thing in the morning.

Wesley. Emily picked up the glass of wine and took a sip, letting herself think of him for just a moment as Wesley—a man, not as the leader of the largest church in the nation. Sometimes he reminded her a little of her father, always taking a stand on principle. They were both rebellious men. "Just you and me against the world, princess," Dad had said each time things went bad. She looked again at the rain and the warm, cozy feeling dissolved in a puff.

She guessed Dad had been fired from just about every job he'd ever had. Mom hadn't liked to talk about it much. Emily's hand closed tight around the stem of the wine glass as she thought of those years at home. Mom trying so hard to make him happy. Dad growing closed and bitter, mean as the years went by.

Not really mean, she admonished herself. *Curmudgeon* might be a better word. You had to look beneath the surface with complicated people like Dad, like the archbishop.

Emily's chest felt tight remembering the days that Dad came home with that look in his eyes each time they'd let him go; a lookof . . . contempt, maybe? Who do they think they are anyway, he'd mutter. Then he'd disappear into a little room filled with books and half-finished manuscripts, and for weeks until another opportunity came his way, the house filled with smoke from his pipe and rattled with the clanks and twings of the old typewriter that announced the end of each line with a bell-like ping. Dad refused to use a computer.

The first time he was fired, he'd flipped his hand. Plebes, he'd called them—plebeians. "I'll find another day job soon enough," he laughed. "Anyway, I'd rather write."

Mom had given him a worried look. "But lots of great writers kept a day job and wrote at night, dear, or early in the morning. Anthony Trollope for one." At a glance from Dad, she'd grown silent.

Year after year his books and stories and poems came back in the mail, and after a while—Emily learned to recognize the squared packages wrapped in brown paper—his laugh turned sour, and the headaches began—headaches that lasted for days, that only stopped when he drank. Once she'd seen him weeping. Large silent tears sliding down his face as he jerked his head up with wide, surprised eyes when she'd opened the door to the bedroom. Neither one of them had ever mentioned this, however; but it was then she knew it was up to her to pull him through. And she never could.

She rubbed her eyes, then pressed them hard with her knuckles. Think of the good times. When she was five or six or ten, in the evening at bedtime, Dad read to her, Pooh Bear and Peter Pan at first, and later on Tennyson and Shelly, Dickinson and Keats. She loved the rhythm of the old words as they lulled her to sleep. But once, when she was twelve . . . Emily frowned, trying to remember exactly what he'd said.

"It's the shadows in the words that matter, Princess. Tennyson knew that. Poetry teaches us to think, clears away the clutter, gives us room to grow: *'Free space for every human doubt, that the whole mind might orb about,'* is how he put it."

He'd downed his drink with a flip of his wrist, and his chin had slowly dropped to his chest as he repeated the words over and over until he fell asleep. That was the last time he'd read to her, she realized with a wistful smile. She'd memorized the words.

Dad fought shadows all his life, and they were deeper, darker now.

She'd tried. God knows she'd tried to help. Now Dad was like a cactus; *but,* she told herself, *his thorns hid something bright, shining, and strong.* When he was sober, he was charming, even funny. He'd been angry at first when she'd come home to tell him—and Mom, of course—about her new job with the archbishop.

"Religion is hypocrisy," he'd slurred into his scotch. Her heart had sunk.

"I needed money one time for a ride," he mumbled. "Youngster. No job. A few dollars is all I asked. Went into a church. Couple'a dollars, and he said no."

"Who, Dad?" she'd asked, touching his arm, aching to see her excitement for the new job reflected in his face.

He'd patted her hand, then jerked his arm away. "That . . . that . . ." He slammed his glass down on the table and glared at her as if trying to remember what he was going to say. "That priest!" he finally spat. "That hypocrite. He said no." His head slumped onto his chest. "Who do they think they are anyway? Hypocrites. All of them. All of 'em."

But the next morning when he'd sobered up, he picked up a book Emily had left on the table. It was the archbishop's most recent and controversial book, and he'd loved it. "Feisty little clergyman," he'd said to Emily, and she'd thrown her arms around him, holding him until he'd pulled away.

Her throat constricted at the memory. She tensed. That was the last time she'd seen Dad sober. She rarely went home nowadays, just called Mom once in a while, mostly on Sundays. Poor Mom.

Get a grip! she told herself. *Mom's made her choices. And it's too late for Dad. Don't think of that. Think of the good things, think of the future, think of Wesley.*

She gazed at the rain sliding down the windowpane. It wasn't the archbishop's looks that attracted her so, she reflected. He was nice looking, but much older. *Probably as old as Dad.* She winced and dismissed the thought.

Think of the good things. It was the archbishop's . . . perhaps you'd call it *élan,* his *charisma.* She tilted her head and sipped the wine. It was the way he crinkled his eyes when he smiled, the way he spoke to her—*to everyone,* she admitted to herself—as if you were the only person in the world that he wanted to be with right at that moment. Like Dad, before he changed.

Emily was still astonished at the good fortune that led her to this job. She'd been working in the publicity department of the archbishop's publishing house, and they'd hit it off right away. Wesley Bright was only a bishop at that time, with some best-selling books attacking the most fundamental Christian principals. He was so casual, so comfortable in his rebellion, unlike Dad, that at first she'd wondered how on earth he managed to remain in the church at all, much less as a bishop.

Before this job Emily had never thought much about religion—shackles of the mind, Dad had called it. Out of curiosity she'd taken a comparative religion course at NYU in her first year of college. All religions have a great flood, she'd learned, and resurrection stories and messiahs and other divines.

She laughed out loud recalling the end run Wesley Bright had made around the stiff church hierarchy two years ago. He was so outrageous and courageous! Like Dad used to be. Despite the groans of the establishment, Wesley was called by congregations across the country to fill a new and powerful position, presiding archbishop of the Apostolic Church. The populist revolt was effective because it was backed by withholding across the country of pledges and donations to the church.

But even so the archbishop still had his work cut out for him. Churches would have to be consolidated, local prelates must still be persuaded to embrace his spiritual philosophy that was more attuned to the modern lifestyle than the old worn-out doctrines, like miracles, or someone rising from the dead.

"Embrace the moment," he liked to say. "Don't waste time with a gamble on some vague idea of eternity. *Now* is all we have."

The archbishop seemed to like Emily, and her duties had expanded over time. He was on the verge of reaching a new pinnacle of power and influence, Emily mused. The latest traffic count on his Web site was astounding, and the cathedral office was routinely inundated with e-mail from fans. Suddenly he was in demand for national talk shows on television and radio and for interviews in major newspapers across the country.

Emily watched the rain and mulled this over. If she stayed focused and worked hard enough, perhaps he'd find her indispensable.

She ran her fingers over the piano keys and gazed through the window. Ridges of water rolling down the glass-reflected colored lights from the city outside. She smothered a slight, melancholy feeling. She'd broken off a relationship with a young lawyer she'd dated for several years on and off—her first *real thing*—because this job was so demanding; he'd resented the time it took.

Her slight depression disappeared, and Emily grimaced at the recollection. She preferred books anyway; like Dad, she could get lost in poetry or a good nineteenth-century novel. Besides, Wesley made other men seem almost childish by comparison. She picked up her glass, swirled the wine and took a sip, fixing her attention on the fragrance and fruity flavor as it slid down her throat.

But sometimes she was lonely. What would it be like to share this rainy night with Wesley? To lie in bed with him. She caught herself and shook the thought away. Still—she was thirty, getting older every day.

A siren rose from the street below. Emily smothered the feeling that something might be missing from her life and forced herself to mentally sort through the archbishop's schedule of interviews for the coming week instead. Time was the problem. Her time belonged to the archbishop.

❖ ❖ ❖

The next morning Emily raced down Second Avenue, turned right on Fifty-first and headed toward the cathedral. She glanced at her watch and saw that she was late. Four more long blocks, and she should have been there ages ago. The archbishop was punctual and demanding; if she was late, nothing would excuse her. On a wall to her right, Emily saw a colorful poster advertising an exhibition of the Shroud of Turin this month at the Metropolitan Museum of Art, and it reminded her that she needed to mention this to the archbishop in case the subject was raised in one of his interviews. This was the first time the Vatican had permitted the Shroud to be exhibited outside of Italy, and people in New York were waiting in long lines for tickets. It was sure to come up.

As she approached the light at Fifty-first and Lexington Avenue, Emily saw a beggar huddled on the sidewalk near a stone wall streaked with grime. Without thinking, she found herself edging nearer the street as she passed the man, or woman—whatever it was—leaving a wide space between them.

"Hey!"

Emily stared at the light.

"Hey!" the voice said again.

Emily turned and glanced down at the shabby heap on the ground near the wall. "Me?"

"Yeah! Got ten dollars for a vet?"

"Ten dollars!" Emily wasn't sure she had heard correctly. "Did you say ten?"

A chuckle rose from the center of the heap. "Yeah. Well. How about a quarter?"

Emily smiled at the insolent tone. From the corners of her eyes, she saw the light turn green. She hesitated, then wheeled around, and walked over to the heap. Dropping down in front of it, she found herself level with a pair of eyes that glinted back at her.

"Smart move, lady," the beggar said gruffly. "Skirt's too short to be standing over me like that."

Emily gave him a sharp look. His face was suntanned but smooth and unlined. His eyes were clear, and his gaze was steady. Despite the rags he wore, his dark hair was combed neatly back from his forehead. He was no more than thirty-one or thirty-two, she guessed, about her own age. Quickly she took in the mangled body below this face, to confirm what her eyes had first seen. Both of his legs were gone, and his torn brown pants were folded under the stumps. The man's torso was borne by what looked like a small wooden crate on wheels. He seemed to have anchored himself to it with a rope that crisscrossed and tied around his waist.

"Vet?" she said, as she fished in her purse. "Was it the Gulf War?" Not Afghanistan or Iraq certainly. He was too old for those. A cigar box was placed in front of him for change, and beside it was a book and a rumpled paper bag, thin from use. His lunch, she guessed. Emily pulled a ten dollar bill from her wallet and dropped it into the box.

The beggar ignored her question and reached into the box as she snapped her purse shut and started to rise. He picked up the bill, examined it, then held it out to her.

"That's a ten, lady." His voice was hard. "You should be more careful, but this is your lucky day. I'll trade you for a dollar."

Emily looked at him in surprise and squatted back down again. "I *know* it's a ten. I figured if you had the nerve to ask for that much, you must need it."

The eyes narrowed for an instant, then he folded the bill and slipped it into his shirt pocket, pressing it against his chest. "Thanks. I can use it," he said in an offhand tone.

Emily studied him. "What's your name?" she asked.

He looked startled. "TeeBo. John Jay Thibodeaux, *comin at'cha.* TeeBo's for short." He slanted his eyes at her and spelled it. "T–h–i–b–i–d–e–a–u–x."

"I don't hear the X. Is it French?"

He gave a sardonic laugh. "Sort of. I'm from Empire, Louisiana. Right down at the mouth of the Mississippi."

"What happened?" Emily nodded to the stumps of his legs.

He shrugged and leaned forward, bracing his hands flat on the pavement, then shoved the cart back against the wall. Settling back, he glanced at Emily as if surprised to see her still there. "Clean up mission after the Gulf War. The kind of thing that doesn't make the news."

"I'm sorry," Emily said.

"No need," the beggar told her with a shrug. He looked off, fixing his eyes on the busy traffic along Lexington Avenue. "You bleeding hearts are all alike. I'm healthy as a mule."

"U'mmm." She eyed him doubtfully.

A fleeting look of irritation flicked across his face, then disappeared. He studied the legs walking by. "How I see it is I'm one lucky son of a gun," he added.

"Lucky?"

TeeBo gave her a sideways look. "Yeah. I could've been killed." A quarter dropped into his box, and he scooped it up quickly. "Gotta keep an empty box," he explained, pocketing the coin.

Pity engulfed her. Emily stood, shifting the strap of her purse so that she could open it again. The beggar's voice stopped her.

"Forget it." His voice turned harsh. "We're even. I got your ten bucks, and I didn't look up that skirt."

Without thinking, Emily danced back a few steps; and he laughed, a short barking sound that rolled up from the center of the heap. A smile crept across her face, then suddenly she glanced down at her watch. No more time to spend here.

"Okay, TeeBo. We're even," she said, turning away as the light changed to green.

"Hey! What's your name?"

"Emily," she called over her shoulder as she started to run.

CHAPTER THREE

Jerusalem, AD 33

"No!" the woman hisses, grabbing at Hanna's tunic. "It's nearly Sabbath."

The man jerks the little girl back. "She'll be home in no time, Joanna," he says. His voice is harsh, and a wave of guilt surges through him, knowing that his younger sister has no choice—in Judea in the reign of Tiberius, she's only a woman.

The woman stares at her brother's angry eyes and shrinks back into the door of the small house. His hair, dirty and matted, hangs loose to his shoulders. His beard is ragged, untrimmed, and his clothes are torn and shapeless. He sways as he glowers back at her, as if he's tired, as if he hasn't slept for days. She realizes suddenly that she doesn't really know him. It's been years since she married and left home.

"Why?" she demands. She peers over his shoulder, hoping to spot her husband, but he's nowhere in sight.

Her brother glances around. In the distance she hears the jeering crowd, the ominous drumbeat. "If they're looking for you . . ." she pauses, realizing that Hanna is listening. "Is it dangerous?"

"They're not searching for a man with a child. She'll be all right." He averts his eyes. "Besides, they think we've already left the city."

"Please," she says helplessly.

He softens. "I'll keep her close, Joanna. No harm will come to her."

She has no choice. He'll take the child with him in any event. "Hold on to her," she says, smothering a flash of resentment as she smooths Hanna's hair.

He nods and pulls the child to his side.

"And bring her home quickly." Tears swim in Joanna's eyes as she watches her brother turn and hurry away, pulling Hanna along behind him. The city is jammed with visitors for the Passover holiday. They sleep in villages on the hills around Jerusalem at night and swarm into the center of the city like angry wasps each morning.

Joanna watches until the tall man and little girl round a corner at the end of the narrow, dusty street and disappear from sight, conscious that she has no way of knowing that he'll take proper care of Hanna. For two years he's been traveling back roads and villages with that strange rabbi. And now. *Now he's hunted, along with the others that arrived with the teacher.* Joanna sighs, tucks a loose strand of hair into the braids wound around her head, and turns back into the dark room, feeling small, invisible, and helpless without her husband by her side.

Hanna stumbles as she struggles to keep up with Uncle. She's never met him before today. He slows and turns, hunching over her as they pass two soldiers from Antonia, the fortress on the Temple Mount. They're Romans. "Hurry!" he orders in a quiet voice. Her head tilts up to him, and suddenly he smiles.

She stares uncertainly, and he loosens his grip on her hand. "Don't worry, Hanna," he says. "You're safe with me."

Hanna thinks about his words as they walk, and the next time he looks down at her, she smiles back and curls her hand in his.

She's so small! He slows his pace so that Hanna can match his step. Joanna's daughter! How was it possible? It seemed only yesterday that his sister was a child.

More soldiers. He draws Hanna close as they near and forces himself to remain calm. The rumbling of the drums grows louder now. The soldiers look past him and hurry on, their eyes scanning doorways and dark narrow alleys leading into the street. He knows they're on guard for the slightest sign of trouble. The city is stirred up, a scorching hotbed of rebellion.

He pushes the girl before him as they slip through a dark, small passageway onto a busy street. Here men are gathered in angry groups, peering in the direction of the sound of the drums as they press back against the stone buildings. He slips in among them, pulling Hanna with him to the front of the shoving, heaving crowd, holding her close so that his body protects her. The other men don't notice Hanna.

The drums grow near, and the noise reverberates against the walls. Suddenly, a soldier, one from the garrison, appears around the corner of a building. An animal roar rises from the spectators. More soldiers follow, and among them are three men. Two wear only loincloths; the third is dressed in the shredded remains of a bloody robe. It crosses his mind that this is not a sight for Hanna, then he chases the thought away. Too late now.

The crowd jeers and laughs as the prisoners stumble toward them, bending beneath the weight of heavy wooden beams carried on their shoulders.

"Who are they?" Hanna whispers.

"Hush! They're prisoners."

Several of the soldiers move ahead of the prisoners now, to clear the way. Hanna loses her balance as one of them shoves her, and quickly Uncle jerks her back to him. "Here!" he hisses, shielding her from the forest of legs around her. "Stand close to me."

She leans back into his worn cloak, reassured by the strong, hard muscles of his legs, and glances up. The smile is gone. His expression is strange and tight, his face pale against the dark, unkempt beard.

As they move forward, one of the prisoners suddenly halts, crouching beneath the beam as it rocks on his shoulders. He struggles to hold it steady. Uncle's fingers grip Hanna's shoulders. A soldier knots his hand around the *flagrum,* the scourge used on prisoners and gladiators, then whips it down, slashing into the muscles of the prisoner's back. The sound of the three leather thongs, tipped with dumbbell-shaped pellets, crack as they cut through the flesh.

The child closes her eyes and trembles, pressing against Uncle's legs. When she opens them again, the prisoner is struggling to stay on his feet. His back is bent, bowed and covered with blood, and he holds still for a moment as if mustering strength. Finally the tendons in his neck and arms swell, he straightens, swaying, and moves slowly forward. Again the lash snaps down and he stumbles.

Hanna flinches. She can hear him breathing just in front of her—shallow, painful gasps, as if the air were filled with splintered glass. As she draws in her own breath and holds it, waiting, the shouts and jeers around her slowly fade, until at last the only sound she can hear is the prisoner's rasping breath and the crack of the cruel scourge.

The prisoner sways again beneath the weight of the beam, sinking to his knees. A flash of pain crosses his face, and his eyes close. Filled with dread, she cannot look away. His head drops and the whip cuts across his shoulders, already ribboned with blood. The sight jolts Hanna and she shrinks back, pressing against Uncle's legs. Dust stirs around him from the street, and the beam rocks and twists as the prisoner kneeling before her fights to steady it. His muscles are taut as he strains; long sinews carve his thighs, jutting through a tear in his robe, skin gleaming with sweat and bright blood.

Get up! Hanna cries inside, overwhelmed at the piteous sight.

"Get up!" she shouts aloud. *Please, please get up.* She longs to reach out for him, to touch him, but Uncle grips her, holding her tight so that she cannot move. Tears fill her throat as instead she braces for the sound of the whip.

Slowly the prisoner lifts his eyes to hers.

Spellbound, Hanna stares into eyes that say he knows her well, that she is his. One is swollen, almost closed. The eyes shine into her, like rays of light, a warm and living smile. He is glad to find her standing there, she knows, and he's not at all surprised. He expected to find her just there at that spot. They are alone together now, just the two of them. The crowd of rough, shoving men, the dust, Uncle, the soldiers and their whips, the noise and hatred—all disappear as she drifts in the warm light of the prisoner's gaze.

Hanna leans toward the kneeling prisoner. Uncle feels the movement, and his fingers dig into the muscles of her small shoulders, holding her.

"Hanna!" he warns.

But Uncle's words are lost, submerged beneath another voice like music streaming through her mind. The prisoner holds her with his eyes, looking deep inside, sinking into her as he whispers in her mind. *You have a destiny, child,* the silent music sings. *A duty to fulfill.*

The thought swells until it fills her as she listens. Is the voice real? Or was that just a sigh?

Again the words flow through her mind. At once heard and felt, the voice is sweet and soft and gentle—*a destiny, a duty*—and his eyes hold hers while she drifts.

CHAPTER FOUR

Little Guy ambled down the sidewalk. Ever since Sam died almost three years ago, Mother had tied him in knots with demands. She made him go to church every Sunday—a grim, depressing place. She'd even made him stay and help Father Leo clean up after the service last week. He grimaced, thinking of Father Leo. His mother was always trying to impress Father Leo. And the priest was always in the way, touching Mother when they spoke, giving her private little smiles like his real father used to do.

It was all too much. He was sure Father Leo was the reason for all his mother's new rules. No roaming the streets. No sitting on the stoop in the afternoon after school. Call the minute he got home. But he had to walk home from school because she was at work. She was always at work these days, it seemed, and usually this small freedom cheered him up. Sometimes he stopped along the way for a few minutes.

Thinking of the empty apartment, Little Guy grew more irritable. As usual, Mother wouldn't be home for several hours. She was a secretary for a teacher, a professor at the university downtown. It was an important job, she'd told him. Most nights she brought home things to do, and he'd sit with her while she typed and typed and he finished his homework. "Extra money," she'd said when he complained it took up all her time.

But on this warm spring afternoon, his feet dragged. She insisted he go straight home after school each day. Rules, rules, rules. He sighed. Oh well, it wasn't really Mother's fault. He supposed it was because of Sam falling off that roof. He understood. Tried to, anyway.

But Little Guy didn't want to go home on this sunny day and sit alone in the small, empty apartment. And he was sick of grown-ups telling him what to do—tired of his teachers at school, tired of Father Leo who visited his mother and him almost every night these days, lurking around, giving him worried looks when he wasn't in a good mood and didn't feel like pretending. Talking about God and all.

Anger buzzed through him when he thought of grown-ups like his teacher and Father Leo who thought they knew everything. And the ones that left you to fend for yourself too. Like his father who was God knows where under the sun, and for that matter, God himself. God, who Father Leo *said* was taking care of Sam. Little Guy swished some saliva around his mouth and spat on the ground, inspected it, then fixed his eyes on a policeman at the corner and spat again, further this time; and that made him smile.

To his right a low iron fence separated the sidewalk from a small park near the apartment he shared with his mother. His army-green canvas book bag was growing heavy; and when he came to an entrance to the park, on a sudden whim Little Guy veered through the gate. He followed a dirt path, kicking pebbles and small hard clods of dirt absently as he walked, until he came to a narrow slat-board bench painted dark green, slung his book bag onto the bench, and collapsed beside it. For a while he sat, feeling languid, his legs splayed before him, watching three boys who looked about his age play soccer on the other side of the park.

The sun was hot and sweat rolled down his neck. After a moment he slipped out of his jacket and tossed it on top of his book bag. A bee buzzed past his ear, and he flicked it with his hand, then swiveled to watch it. When he lost sight of the bee, his gaze shifted back to the children. The sun lulled him with its warmth, and after a few minutes he leaned against the back of the bench, feeling drowsy. Across the soccer field the boys shouted at each other. The din of the city faded as his chin dropped to his chest; his lids grew heavy and slowly closed.

A short time later he woke with a start. The bee buzzed around his ear again, and Little Guy swatted it. Something sharp stung his hand, and he jerked it back. The bee was gone, but now the tender center of his palm began to throb. He examined the hand and found a bright red spot beginning to swell. The pain intensified. He reached down for his book bag, and a shadow fell before him.

Little Guy looked up into the face of Jesse Reardon.

He stared, speechless, at the boy who'd dropped Sam from the roof. Jesse's eyes were slits, his nose was crooked on one side, as if broken, and a bright new scar ran from his temple near his right ear down to his jaw. His pale, pocked face was framed with dirty hair greased back over his ears, except for one thick curl dangling on his forehead.

Jesse stared back at Little Guy. As recognition dawned, a red patch crawled up his throat, mottling his face. His eyes narrowed; his lips drew back flat across his teeth, and suddenly he laughed, a sharp, wheezing sound interrupted by a cough. Little Guy saw that some of his teeth were missing, and some were brown and rotting.

Little Guy tensed, but Jesse was on him in an instant, one hand gripping his shoulder, immobilizing him.

He swatted Little Guy's head just behind his ear. "Where you goin', little boy?" he leaned down and whispered. His fingers dug into Little Guy's shoulder. "This must be my lucky day. Here's you and me, all alone in this park." He glanced up and scanned the area quickly, then bent until he was nose to nose with Little Guy. "Do you know how long it's been since I been in a park, punk?" His breath was foul, like the smell of a dead animal rotting in hot sun.

Little Guy tried to jerk away his shoulder, but Jesse tightened his grip. "I thought you were in jail," Little Guy said in a low voice. The words escaped before he could retrieve them.

This seemed to infuriate Jesse. He slapped Little Guy's head again with the flat of his free hand, then released his shoulder, straightened and looked down with a sneer. Little Guy shrank against the back of the bench, trying to ignore the sharp pain radiating from the side of his head into his shoulder, and held very still.

Spotting the book bag, Jesse knocked it off the bench and gave it a kick. “What’s in this thing?”

“My books. For school.”

Jesse picked it up and hurled the bag into the bushes.

Little Guy forgot himself. The books were expensive. “Don’t do that!” he cried, pushing himself toward the end of the bench, away from Jesse.

“Books for school?” Jesse sneered, following him. “You little punk!” he shouted in a shrill voice. Bending down, he punched Little Guy’s shoulder with his fist. His voice grew shrill. “You been reading books while I’m doing time ’cause of you? Do you know how long I been locked up ’cause of you?”

Fear gripped Little Guy and he trembled, fighting images of that day. The day that Sam died. His head hurt and his stomach churned. *Did you try to help your baby brother?* Against his will the question he’d been asked on the witness stand at trial churned in his mind. He could feel the hot sunlight on the roof as it burned his skin, smelled the stink of garbage and beer and hot tar, heard Sam’s cries, Jesse’s raucous laughter, Malo’s snicker behind him.

“Because of me?” he stammered with a catch in his throat.

Suddenly Jesse hunched and lurched toward him. “You creep—little fruitcake mama’s boy!”

Little Guy’s stomach erupted. With the force of an explosion he spewed vomit over Jesse’s arms and chest, his legs, his feet.

Jesse shrieked, made a fist, and drew back his arm to punch Little Guy, then suddenly doubled, arms flailing, racked by a vicious cough. He fell forward and caught himself, gripping the back of the bench as he coughed.

Little Guy bolted. Behind him Jesse's hoarse voice shouted through an explosion of coughing, choking bursts of hate: "I'd a never dropped him but for you, you stupid punk. You PUNK! YOU PUNK YOU CREEP YOU. I'd a never dropped him!"

✣ ✣ ✣

He watched his mother and Father Leo from the corners of his eyes. They sat together on the couch laughing at something they were reading while he worked on his school assignment across the room at a table near the window. She'd been distraught when she'd arrived home from work and he'd told her about the encounter with Jesse, embellishing the story a bit in his favor. She'd put balm on the bee sting and ice on his shoulder, and she'd smiled at him in a way that made him proud.

But now, with Father Leo, she seemed to have forgotten all about him. Little Guy was conscious of a vague, growing dislike for the priest. His shoulder ached, and an earlier inspection in the mirror had revealed the beginning of a large bruise. Now that he thought about it, he still had a headache as well. He tensed irritably when Father Leo placed his hand on his mother's forearm and leaned close to whisper something in her ear.

In that instant Little Guy's elbow slipped sideways and brushed a vase on the table. It was one given his mother by his father years ago. The vase rocked, then crashed to the floor. His mother jumped and looked up in alarm. Father Leo's hand lifted from her arm and landed on the couch beside him.

"What happened, son?" Rebecca asked, rising from the couch and crossing the room. She stopped when she spotted the broken bits of porcelain scattered across the floor, and a flicker of emotion crossed her face before she stooped and began picking up the pieces.

Little Guy wrinkled his forehead into a worried look and stooped down beside her. "I'm sorry," he said in a contrite tone, picking up some of the pieces himself and piling them onto the tabletop above him. "I'm really sorry, Mother. It's just . . . my shoulder hurts . . . and my head . . . and my hand." He fell back on his heels and rubbed his shoulder as he looked up at her.

"I'll get a broom," Father Leo said, disappearing into the kitchen.

His mother sat beside Little Guy on the floor and pulled him toward her, holding him in her arms. Gently she stroked his hair. "Don't worry, son. The vase can be replaced." she said. "Poor thing. You're very brave, Little Guy, standing up to Jesse Reardon as you did. It makes me sick to think you had to see him again, and all alone in the park."

Mother was soft, and he nestled against her. "He's bigger than me, but I'm smarter. I wasn't afraid." He stroked her forearm where Father Leo's hand had rested. "I'll work and buy you another vase."

"Brave, brave boy. Forget the vase."

Father Leo arrived with the broom and a dustpan, and Rebecca helped Little Guy to his feet. She stood aside with her arm around him while Father Leo swept pieces of the vase into a dustpan.

"Here, son," he said to Little Guy after a moment, holding the broom out to him. "Why don't you finish up."

"He's not feeling well, Leo," his mother said quickly. "I'll do it."

Father Leo frowned and glanced at Little Guy. "Your mother's tired from work, Little Guy. I think you can handle this chore now, can't you?"

Little Guy flinched and felt a rush of resentment at Father Leo's words. His mother pulled him toward her. "He's not feeling well," she repeated in a sharp tone. "I'll take care of it." Releasing her grip on Little Guy, she took the broom and dustpan from Father Leo and swept up the remaining pieces of the vase without speaking.

"Rebecca," Father Leo began.

"I said, I'll handle this," she interrupted.

Father Leo looked stricken at her sharp tone. Little Guy turned his head to hide a smile and sat back down to finish his homework.

✣ ✣ ✣

Leo's one extravagance was an ebony grand piano that dominated the living room of his small apartment. He lived next door to his church, St. Luke's, one of the smaller in the Apostolic Church's dioceses of New York. The piano had been purchased from Juilliard when he'd returned from seminary, having been ordained a priest in the long line of apostolic succession that began in the first century with Peter, the fisherman who followed Christ.

A bird lifted from the branch of a tree just outside the open window to his left. Leo had been sitting on the piano bench gazing at the tree for some time, thinking of Rebecca, when the movement startled him and the daydreams disappeared. He smiled at himself, gave a small sigh, and turned his attention to the piano. Spreading the fingers of both hands, Leo brushed them lightly across the tops of the white keys before him. But again came the thought: Rebecca.

Rebecca's face rose before him, her somewhat enigmatic smile, the way she tilted her head to the side with her low smoker's chuckle when she was amused. *I'm in love,* he realized. The thought stunned Leo. Love?

Rebecca was smart. Ambitious. Worked her way through secretarial school. Read all the time—good books, the classics, philosophy. *She's too interested in politics,* he thought, not being one to dwell on things like that. But still, he admired the way Rebecca stuck to her principles, no matter what. Tough lady—he smiled, thinking of how her eyes shone when she got excited about some new idea or book or article that she'd read, or something smart that Little Guy had done.

Suddenly he laughed and said the words out loud to hear how they would sound. "I'm in love!" He pressed the keys with surprise and joy—a fugue from *The Well-Tempered Clavier* spiraled through the room with the words: "I'm in love I'm in love I'm in love!"

The Apostolic Church, like its Episcopal siblings and the Roman Church, embraced a catholic theology—the communion of saints and forgiveness of sins, the cross and the resurrection of Christ—it was a formal church. But as he played, Leo's thoughts were trained on one fact that had suddenly assumed great importance. Unlike in the Roman Catholic Church, celibacy was not required of priests of the Apostolic Church or the similar Episcopal Church. Marriage was permitted, even encouraged. Priests could marry and have families of their own.

The thought stopped him cold. He lifted his fingers, letting them hover just above the keys as he stared at the wall in front of him. He could marry Rebecca. He and Rebecca and Little Guy could be a family. His hands dropped back down to the piano with a dissonant crescendo as the new thought solidified and fixed in his mind. Marriage. *Yes, marriage was a possibility.*

Leo looked down at the piano that he loved and thought that perhaps, after all, he could do without this extravagance. If he could sell it, perhaps he and Rebecca—and Little Guy, of course—could take a trip, a honeymoon somewhere wonderful after they were married. But he would wait before discussing this dream with Rebecca, he decided. He'd not try to *make* this happen. Instead, Leo resolved to leave his dream in the hands of God. Rebecca would discover his love slowly over a period of time, long enough to let the raw sting of Sam's death subside a bit, long enough for Little Guy to grow closer to him. *Besides,* he whispered to himself, *I might spoil things by being rash.*

✣ ✣ ✣

Every once in a while Father Leo took Little Guy to a baseball game where they bought hot dogs and peanuts. Little Guy thought that he remembered going to a baseball game with his father once when he was very small, and so, at first, he searched the crowds in the stands, just in case. After a while he stopped looking for his father. Little Guy decided then that he hated his father.

One day, when he was just a few weeks short of twelve years old, during a break in the game while the umpire argued vehemently with a shortstop, Little Guy spotted a boy sitting below him in the stands. A lump grew in his throat. The boy was about the age that Sam would be today, he guessed. Sam, as he remembered him. Sam who was dead.

He stared. The child turned his head, and Little Guy saw that he even looked a lot like Sam. He watched the boy peel a peanut from its shell, then toss the remnants onto the ground beneath the bench on which he sat. Little Guy fought against a sudden wave of depression, trying to banish it from the sunny afternoon. He wondered what Sam would have been like if he were here today.

You said to let him go. The old words burst through his mind, and he squeezed his eyes closed, but still the pictures formed in slow motion . . . Jesse's look of surprise as Little Guy had lurched toward him . . . Sam falling . . . the dark narrow stairs as he raced down to the street.

He swallowed hard. A little voice whispered in his mind: *It's okay. Sam's in heaven. Father Leo said so. God is taking care of Sam, isn't he?*

Little Guy nodded to himself.

But if God's really there, the voice persisted, *if he loved Sam so much, why did he let him fall from the roof? Why did he let it happen?*

He tensed at the new thought. The questions whirled through his mind. He tried to dismiss them, to focus on the game. But suddenly he had to know.

"How do you know that God's in heaven?" he asked Father Leo in a casual tone as he watched the boy who looked like Sam. "How do you know God's taking care of Sam?"

You said to let him go. Jesse's voice rasped in his mind. *I'd a never dropped him but for you.* Little Guy's hands gripped the wooden bench beneath him while he waited for an answer.

Father Leo slid his arm around Little Guy's shoulder. He hesitated, then said, "We just have to have faith in these things, son." He hugged the boy to him as he spoke, pressing the thin body against his own. "Faith. Hope. That's all we really have."

For a moment Little Guy wasn't sure he'd heard correctly. He pulled away from Father Leo, then held his breath and slid his eyes toward the field below, trying to understand what Father Leo had just said. He'd ridden a roller coaster once. Now his stomach lurched, dropping down a steep slope just like on that roller coaster ride. He'd expected a clear, firm answer to his question, something like, well, scientists know this or that, or there's a picture or a map, or something.

"But how do you *know* it's true?" he asked.

"Because the Bible says so," Father Leo said.

Little Guy mulled this over. "How do we know that the Bible's true?" he asked after a moment.

Father Leo shook his head and gave Little Guy a worried look. "It's like I said before," he answered. Taking a deep breath, his words came out all at once. "Faith. We have to have faith that the Bible's true, Little Guy. There's no way to prove such things."

Little Guy frowned. He thought again of Sam in that box underground and tried to replace it with a picture of Sam in heaven with God, but he couldn't. "Okay. What is faith?" he asked.

"What?" Father Leo blinked. Little Guy watched him without moving. Seconds passed before Father Leo said, looking off into the distance, "Well, to have faith means to trust. You just have to trust that it's true."

Trust? He'd trusted his father. He'd trusted the judge at Sam's trial. He'd trusted Father Leo too.

Little Guy shifted away from Father Leo with a slight, almost imperceptible jerk. Father Leo sighed and rested his hand on Little Guy's shoulder. "You're old enough now to realize this, my boy. There's no way to prove little Sam's with God. We must trust God because we know that he loves us. Like a father loves his son."

A dull ache swelled in his chest at the words. Like a *father* loves his son? Little Guy braced his hands beside him on the bench as he fought back a sense of imbalance.

"That's all there is?" he finally asked in disbelief. *"Just trust?"*

"Yep," Father Leo said in a firm tone. A noisy argument broke out again between the umpire and shortstop, and the priest's head swiveled to the ball field below. "Now look at that would you?" he said. "There they go again." His voice was too loud, too cheerful as he released Little Guy and slapped his knees with exasperation. "The ump's an idiot!"

He glanced at Little Guy, but the boy seemed to be engrossed in the game. "Take a look at that runner on first," Father Leo added in a hearty tone, nudging him. "You think he's ready? Not likely!"

Little Guy fixed his eyes on first base while his thoughts roiled and the memories consumed him. He sat very still, trying to breathe, overcome by a new certainty that he was alone in the universe, fighting an urge to scream out that he was sorry, that he hadn't meant to hurt Sam on the roof that day. But still the thought wormed up from the recess of his mind to the surface where it coiled and writhed and lingered. Sam's death *was* his fault. Jesse had said so. The judge had said so. Maybe Father Leo thought so too. He closed his eyes as the abyss rose to meet him, and there he saw Sam, alone in the box, buried underground.

His eyes opened and he glanced at Father Leo. Why hadn't God caught Sam when he fell?

Don't be stupid, a voice hissed inside: *Because he wasn't there.* None of it was true. Father Leo had lied. *God isn't there at all.*

Fear lodged in his chest and grew hard, like a stone. Father Leo had lied. The realization bludgeoned him. Death was the end of everything; it was a dark, wooden box underground. His eyes dropped to the little boy who looked like

Sam sitting on the bench below, and it hit him full force that Sam was gone forever and that someday he too would die.

For all these years Father Leo had lied! Suddenly, Little Guy knew that he hated Father Leo as much as he had hated the judge at Sam's trial, as much as he hated his own missing father. Maybe more. And most of all he hated Father Leo's God who wasn't there.

Some instinct veiled these new thoughts. He needed to think them over when he was alone, these secrets of his. So Little Guy worked to compose a smile and, when he had succeeded, threw a peanut at the umpire standing behind home plate.

Father Leo looked at him. "Great game," Little Guy said in a happy tone that took all of his effort. He glanced up at Father Leo and drew the smile into his eyes.

Father Leo studied him for a moment and seemed pleased. His brow smoothed as he turned back to the ball game. The priest's hair ruffled in the breeze across his smooth, high forehead, above deep-set eyes and a long, thin face. He was young to be a priest, Little Guy supposed, but for the first time he noticed that Father Leo's collar was frayed and his clothes were worn. It seemed to him that Father Leo had somehow shrunk, grown smaller. He averted his eyes as he pushed the thoughts away. He'd think this over later too, when he was alone.

You're never alone, Father Leo would have said.

Not so, Little Guy told himself. Except for Mother and Sam, he'd *always* been alone. The grim thought whistled through him like wind howling off the East River. And Sam? Well, Sam was just dead. Once again the hatred twisted inside of him. Little Guy glanced at Father Leo from the corners of his eyes and clinched his jaw. Someday he'd show Father Leo how it felt to be lied to and abandoned.

He'd show them all.

Leo whistled a tune as he swung along Eighth Avenue. He'd just finished playing with a small ensemble of musicians, a weekly practice among friends, and he was happy. As usual, his thoughts turned to Rebecca and Little Guy, and this made him smile. He pictured the three of them as a family: himself, Rebecca, and Little Guy.

Leo stopped to purchase a newspaper, folded it, and stuck it under his arm as he continued walking. The afternoon with Little Guy at the ballpark last weekend had been a wonderful experience. He'd make a good father for the boy, he knew. And he was sure he'd made progress when Little Guy had asked about Sam during the game. He'd done okay. This thought sobered his mood. He realized that he'd come to love Rebecca's son and wanted to help him; the boy always seemed so lost.

A picture of Little Guy bursting through the door of the building on the day that Sam died popped into Leo's mind. Recalling the explanation he'd given at the baseball game when Little Guy had asked about Sam and God and faith and trust, Leo was certain he'd seen a smile of relief on the boy's face. A bond was growing between the two of them, he knew. Rebecca and Little Guy had even joined the church two years ago. Maybe now the time was right. Someday soon perhaps he'd gather courage to go ahead and ask Rebecca to be his wife.

Working his way through the traffic at Columbus Circle, Leo continued down Central Park West, dodging baby carriages pushed by young mothers and nannies, bicycles, and children on skates. It was already late spring. The air was crisp and cool, and sunlight danced through the trees, throwing dark patterns on the pavement that shifted as the soft breeze rustled branches above.

Thinking of Rebecca and Little Guy made Leo even happier, and his step quickened as he entered the park and sought out an empty bench in a cool, sunny spot to read his newspaper. He recalled the counsel he'd given Little Guy at the ballpark and again felt a rush of pride. Opening the paper, he stared unseeing at the printed page before him.

I've done it, he thought. *Passed the first test. I've done what a priest must do; answered the hard questions for Little Guy, comforted him over the loss of Sam. I've brought a lost sheep into the fold.* The knowledge straightened his back, lifted his chin. Leo ran his finger under the stiff white clerical collar around his neck, smiled with satisfaction, and shook the paper straight, holding it up in front of his face.

Suddenly he knew that the time was right to ask Rebecca to be his wife. He felt it all at once. He'd seen the acceptance in Little Guy's face at the ballpark. Ever since Sam had died, he'd been a friend, a comforter as well as priest for Rebecca and her son. Now it was time to make the three of them a family. At this thought, Leo gave up trying to read. A tremor of excitement ran through him. He would take Rebecca to dinner at a special place this weekend—to a romantic restaurant with soft lights and music—and he would ask her to marry him. Little Guy would be thrilled. Leo had seen love shining from the boy's eyes the last time they were together at the ballpark.

It did not occur to Leo that love and hate are so very much alike.

CHAPTER FIVE

The vast room was filled with people who decorate the pages of slick magazines; she'd met a few of them before. Like silver tinsel on a Christmas tree, they glimmered, dazzling Emily as they celebrated the arrival of a new conductor at Carnegie Hall. She stood with Wesley before a long glass wall of windows, gazing out over the grid of the city down to Wall Street, to the empty space where the twin towers of the World Trade Center once stood. For an instant she closed her eyes against those scenes—the tall buildings twisting, whiplashed from the impact of the planes, engulfed in flames, steel melting in the heat.

A waiter appeared at Wesley's elbow and she turned, watching as he lifted two glasses of wine from the silver tray. Handing one to Emily, he sipped from the crystal glass. Voices hummed around them, and in the background the modern jazz quartet played "The Jasmine Tree," a crisp light tune. He smiled, seeming to enjoy the music.

"Ozymandias . . . two trunkless legs of stone stand in the desert," Emily murmured, turning back to the ghosts of the twin towers.

"What's that?" Wesley asked. She looked lovely tonight in that red dress, he thought. It brought out the highlights in her hair. He felt a surge of pride when she looked up at him, and he was conscious of her admiration—dare he say, adoration? He was pleased with his assistant and with his new status as a social lion in the city; the hostess had insisted he attend—wouldn't take no for an answer, she'd said.

"It's a poem by Shelley that was e-mailed around the country right after 9/11," Emily replied. *"My name is Ozymandias."* Her voice was quiet as she recited the words. *"King of Kings, Look on my works, ye mighty, and despair!"* She glanced back at the lights of the city and sipped the wine.

"I remember," Wesley said, following her eyes to the invisible towers. "He's speaking of Pharaoh in the book of Exodus." At Emily's startled look, he grinned. "You know, plagues, frogs, gnats, locusts, burning buildings." He shook his head. "It's the blind arrogance of entrenched power."

"Hmm. Sad, isn't it?" she said, turning away from the window. "I can hardly bear to look. I keep thinking of all the people trapped in those towers when the planes hit." Emily shook her head. "The depravity of the terrorists is too terrible to contemplate."

"Jihadists," Wesley corrected in a mechanical tone. "And it's not a question of depravity," he went on. "Jihad is sacred to them. They believe they're right too. And who are we to judge?" He paused, studying her. "I know it's difficult to think of things this way, but it's very provincial and self-centered to burden other cultures with our own point of view. We're hated all over the world for that."

Emily frowned.

He gave her a patient smile. "All cultures are interdependent, and the issues are too complex. I think Shelley said it well. How does it go again?"

"Look on my works, ye mighty, and despair."

"Exactly." He nodded. "Shelley was right. Our strength has made us arrogant." The crease between his brows turned to a frown. "When will politicians finally understand that these things are relative? Nothing's absolute, you know." He shook his head. "Right and wrong are matters of circumstance."

His words jolted Emily. Images of firemen covered in soot, exhausted and frightened as they beat their way into the collapsing buildings of the World Trade Center on the morning of September 11, 2001 rose in her mind. With a strange feeling of discomfort, she glanced around. She'd never before questioned his wisdom, but now she touched his forearm and whispered, "Be careful, someone might hear. People are sensitive about 9/11."

He raised his eyebrows and pursed his lips. "Hmm," he said playfully. "I don't take polls on matters of morals and spirituality, Emily." He sipped his wine and looked past her at the milling crowd.

But Emily was worried. The archbishop was in demand as a guest for talk shows now, and that media exposure was critical to his career. It was her job to remind him of this. "Remember what happened to Bill Maher?" she said under her breath.

He lifted her hand from his arm, patted and released it. "My own well-being is not the point, my dear. I'm used to being the underdog, fighting for principle." As he spoke, his voice rose, and faces turned toward them.

He's courageous but somewhat careless, Emily thought. Despite her misgivings, she smiled.

"You *are* a bold man, Archbishop." Emily's head swiveled as the speaker, Merle Camden, a member of the cathedral vestry and an old friend of Wesley's, sidled up. Merle cocked her head to one side, and a smile played around the corners of her red, lipsticked mouth.

"Hello, Emily," Merle said in a cheerful tone as she brushed Wesley's cheek with a kiss. "I just heard the last bit, but I'll be the first to applaud a man with the courage of his convictions."

"Ah, there you are," Wesley said, stepping back, touching the place she'd kissed with the tips of his fingers. He puffed out his cheeks, and his tone turned combative. "If you're talking about my multicultural views," he added, with a half shrug, "all I can say is, when I have a strong opinion on a subject, I often find it hard to be diplomatic."

"What is it that you feel so strongly about?" Merle asked, slanting her eyes at him.

"Our obligation as the most powerful nation in the world to understand other cultures," he answered without hesitation. "Having the courage to wean ourselves from the childish view that things must be done our way, that they're black or white." He lifted his chin, but his eyes shone. "Even in the case of something as dramatic and controversial as 9/11."

Emily smothered a flicker of annoyance as he ignored her warning.

Merle gave him a knowing smile. "Controversy is always provocative, isn't it?" she drawled. She crossed her arms and slumped, resting her weight on one hip. "It's much more interesting to write about new ideas than old ones, I suppose."

He gave her a sharp look. "That's not what I meant."

"No," she said with a toss of her head. "Actually," she went on in an appeasing tone, "your frank views are refreshing." She gave a short laugh. "You're proof that religion and intellect are not incompatible, Archbishop."

Wesley pulled upright, lifted his glass to his lips, and fixed his eyes on Merle as he took a sip of wine. "I trust, Merle, that none of us would run from controversy when it involves our principles."

"Of course not," Merle said. She moved to his side, leaning in to speak to him. "But speaking of controversy . . ." she began.

Emily smothered a yawn while the archbishop and Merle launched into a discussion of the contemporary events called "experiences" just instituted by the Apostolic Church in place of the old Scriptures and prayer services—free-form dancing, meditation with mantras and chanting, self-awareness programs, yoga. There were no more creeds, Communion, or long, drawn-out sermons in the archbishop's church.

Only half listening, she found her gaze drawn back to the spot where the twin towers stood a few years ago. She mulled over what the archbishop had said about the jihadists. *Was such evil really just a matter of perspective?* she wondered. Again unwanted images rose before her: people inside the collapsing buildings, using precious seconds to free strangers from elevators and jammed stairwells while thick black smoke filled the air, tending the injured while glass shattered around them and the heat grew unbearable. What made them do it?

Lighten up! She told herself, shaking off the thoughts. *This is a party.* Emily turned away from the window and her eyes ranged over the pretty room. She should be enjoying herself. This was a far cry from life in the suburbs of Philadelphia where she'd grown up.

"Speaking of controversy, what do you think of the exhibition at the Met?" Merle's voice emerged from the hum of voices around them.

"Exhibition?" Wesley arched one eyebrow.

"I think she means the Shroud of Turin," Emily said.

Merle nodded. "It's sold out, you know."

Wesley grimaced and shrugged. "Not much substance there, my dear," he answered in a bored tone.

Merle smiled at his words. "Mystery's enough," she said with a touch of cynicism. "The public doesn't generally require substance."

"Well, it's a Catholic thing. I don't know much about the subject." Wesley's eyes wandered as he replied. He straightened his shoulders when he saw the elderly hostess of the event bearing down upon him with a familiar-looking gentleman in tow. Her dress billowed as she pushed through the crowd.

"Archbishop Bright," she called, sounding breathless. "I want you to meet someone." Halting just before him, she nodded to Merle and Emily and turned to the man trailing behind, hooking her arm through his in a proprietary manner when he'd caught up.

"This is Robert Mustler. He's here for the *Times,*" she said, smiling at the well-known reporter. "Now see here, Robert. You cannot monopolize the archbishop tonight."

Robert Mustler shook Wesley's hand. "I've read your books, sir, and find them downright intriguing coming from a man in your position. Can you spare just a few minutes for me this evening? I have a deadline and would like your thoughts on some things."

"Certainly," Wesley said, dipping his chin as he turned to his hostess with a practiced smile. "Is there a quiet corner we could use?"

The woman nodded and brushed past Merle to steer the two men toward large French doors at one end of the room. "I have just the place."

Wesley glanced over his shoulder at Emily and gave an apologetic shrug as he was ushered through the door.

"I'm particularly interested in your thinking on the Shroud of Turin, Archbishop Bright," Robert said. "This is the first time it's been exhibited in the United States so far as I know. It's a controversial exhibition, I understand."

Wesley rolled his eyes and slapped the reporter on the shoulder. "Mysteries tend to be controversial, Robert."

✣ ✣ ✣

Miss Honeman moved around the dining room table as Wesley stabbed at a plate of soft scrambled eggs. He shook the morning newspaper into shape with his other hand, then put down his fork, folded the paper in half, and held it up in front of his face.

"Is that an interview of yours, Your Grace?" Miss Honeman asked, noticing his picture on the page. She poured fresh coffee into the cup near his hand as she spoke.

"Yes. A reporter was at the reception last night." Wesley's tone was smooth and low as he scanned Robert Mustler's article. He was pleased with what he read.

"You're getting to be quite a celebrity, I'd say." Miss Honeman set the coffeepot down on a silver trivet and picked up the creamer, drizzling just a bit into the cup before replacing it on the table next to the pot. "It's all those books and television shows that do it."

Wesley shook the newspaper, irritably. Why did the woman hover so? But then, all women annoyed him to some extent, except his mother, bless her, when she was alive. And Emily, he suddenly realized with surprise. He'd toyed with the idea of marriage from time to time—not with anyone particular—he was too busy to invest the time required to find someone appropriate, someone who would be a help rather than a hindrance to his career.

Marriage relationships were so *tentative.* All in all, he supposed he was much better off with a good steady housekeeper like Miss H. The thought of some woman's bright red lipstick on his pillowcase night after night was unbearable. Although Emily was different from the others. She adored him, of course. Like Mother had. He smiled to himself at the thought of how pretty Emily had looked at the party. He'd gotten quite used to having her around, he realized. And she was quick, a good learner. Why shouldn't she be? She had a good teacher.

He snapped the paper again, then folded it into quarters and continued reading. Wesley liked Mustler's style. A *philosopher,* the young man had called him—not bad. His picture stared at him from the newspaper, a photograph that the publishers of his last book had insisted upon. The photographer was well-known for his famous subjects, and Wesley was pleased with the result. Studying the airbrushed face, he wondered if Emily had seen the picture and hoped that she had. After a moment his eyes slid to the next column, and he saw that it was a story on the Shroud of Turin. With a grunt he slapped the paper facedown on the table.

Miss Honeman gave him a puzzled look. "Is anything wrong, Your Grace?"

"No. No, not at all," Wesley answered quickly. "It's just that exhibition at the Met this month." He clucked his tongue with exasperation. "It's such complete nonsense, and it's all anyone could speak of last night."

"The Shroud of Turin? I've been meaning to ask you about that. It's difficult to get tickets. Do you think your office could obtain one for me?"

"Hmm." Wesley picked up his cup of coffee and took a sip. "I suppose that could be arranged if you'd like to go, Miss H," he said irritably.

⁜ ⁜ ⁜

Emily dressed quickly, rode the elevator down to the ground floor, and strode through the marble-floored lobby of her apartment building out onto Second Avenue, nodding to the doorman as he opened the door for her.

"Morning, Miss Scott," he said with a cheerful smile. "Rain's washed the city clean for us today."

Emily took a deep, exaggerated breath. "What's that—fresh air?"

He chuckled, then hurried to the curbside where a taxicab had just pulled up.

It was a glorious fall morning, and Emily felt a rush of anticipation at the start of a new season. Pumpkins. Thanksgiving. Maybe she'd even go home for the holiday this year. Maybe things would be different if she went home.

Turning to her left, she passed a row of small Irish pubs, then waved to the old man selling bagels as she hurried past his colorful cart. No time to stop today. On a lamppost at the corner where she waited for a light, she spotted another handbill for that new exhibition at the Met. *Shroud of Turin,* it said. *"A picture of the resurrection?"*

Right, she laughed to herself. *Show and tell?*

The posters were plastered all over the city, in subway stations, at the corner market, on a fence near the playground. At Fifty-first Emily turned, walking briskly toward the cathedral, forgetting the exhibition as she ticked off the things that needed immediate attention. Not enough time in the day, she concluded. Time was always the problem.

As Emily drew near the corner of Lexington and Fifty-first, she saw that TeeBo still staked out the territory against the wall. He straightened when he saw her.

"Hey!"

She waved as she passed him, as she did now every day. "Beautiful morning, isn't it?" she called, waiting for the light to turn green.

"What's your hurry?" TeeBo asked. "You're a whirlwind. Don't you ever slow down?"

She turned back to him. "Can't stop today, TeeBo. I'm late. Time's the one thing I don't have."

He made a face, an expression of pity. "Wrong," he said. "Time's the one thing *everyone* has. It's how you use it that counts."

Emily shrugged, then opened her purse and dug out a dollar bill. She walked over to TeeBo and squatted down to drop it into the box, when suddenly he grasped her forearm, holding tight. With an exclamation, she tumbled back, landing on the sidewalk, and found herself sitting beside him.

"Sorry," he said in a contrite tone, lifting his hand from her arm. He fixed his gaze on the legs walking past. "I didn't mean . . . , but I thought we were friends now." His voice turned angry. "What do you think I am, a troll?"

She yanked her arm away feeling clumsy. "Don't be stupid!" she snapped. "I'm only trying to help." In the silence that ensued, TeeBo ignored her, giving all his attention to chewing a short piece of straw stuck in the corner of his mouth.

Emily studied the beggar covertly, still rubbing her arm. He had a strong grip. It was obvious that he'd been a tall man before. Hair was a little long and ragged, as if he cut it himself, but neatly combed. His square jaw had a defiant tilt right now, and his back was rigid as he balanced on his cart.

Her face grew hot, and she glanced around, then moved to rise. What was she doing sitting on the sidewalk in the middle of the city? What if someone she knew saw her? But another look at TeeBo's face told her he was still offended. She paused, and suddenly she settled back against the wall. Probably no one would notice her down here anyway. In the city everyone looked straight ahead. And she could afford to be a few minutes late for work once in a while.

The dollar bill was still crumpled in her hand. Annoyed, Emily tossed it into the open cigar box and, following TeeBo's gaze, stared at the moving pedestrian legs. "Besides, I thought we had a deal," she said after a moment.

Still TeeBo ignored her. A minute passed, then he plucked the straw from his mouth, threw it on the sidewalk beside him, and glanced at her.

"I'm sorry," Emily said in a low voice. "I only wanted to help."

"Okay." He averted his eyes, then muttered, "Thanks."

They sat in silence, watching people rush past. *Going where?* Emily wondered, conscious that everyone seemed in a hurry. It was strange sitting next to TeeBo down here. She felt invisible; she'd been right—no one noticed them at all. They were surrounded by disembodied moving parts, legs and socks and shoes, pants and skirts. City eyes were trained to avoid contact, perhaps to look around but almost never to look down to the dirty sidewalk, home of the down and out, the old and maimed—the forgotten shades.

TeeBo picked up the box and fished change from the bottom, scooping up Emily's bill as well. Holding the coins in his fist, he pocketed the dollar bill and began counting the coins. When he had finished, he dropped the change back into the box.

What would it be like to be in TeeBo's place? Emily mused, watching him from the corners of her eyes. *How difficult life must be for him!* She resolved to find a way to help. Maybe she could get the Veteran's Administration to give him a wheelchair or something. Glancing at her watch, she sighed and pushed herself up from the sidewalk. "I'm late, TeeBo. Gotta go."

TeeBo watched her hurry off without a backward glance. When she was out of sight, he stuck another straw between his teeth, leaned back against the wall, and closed his eyes. Women were too complicated. He wished he'd brought a book.

Emily felt Wesley's eyes on her before she looked up. She pushed aside the heavy piece of crystal she'd been cleaning with a handkerchief and smiled. The archbishop stood in the doorway to her office wearing an amused expression.

"I've been watching you, my dear," he said with good humor as he entered the small office and took a seat in a comfortable chair just to the side of her old walnut desk. He squinted at the light that streamed into the room from the window behind her desk, then looked around. Emily's office was always neat, well organized, but somewhat cluttered. The length of one wall was taken up by an overstuffed couch, and a table in the corner held glossy magazines. Behind him was a wall of well-worn books.

"What are you doing?" He nodded toward the crystal on Emily's desk.

"I've been using this as a focus tool." Emily pushed the crystal toward the archbishop, who picked it up, turning it in the light as the prisms flashed.

"Nice."

"It helps me to concentrate during meditation."

"U'mmm," Wesley nodded his approval. Although he had permitted some of the old church traditions to survive after his election as head of the church, titles and vestments and such—the people do like a good show—he'd quickly abolished the meaningless prayers the church had relied on for hundreds of years. He hated those dry old biblical words and ideas stuck in the first century and encouraged meditation with a focus on the here and now instead—thoughts freed from words were less restrictive.

He rubbed his thumb over the crystal in an absent manner, feeling the smooth, many-faceted surfaces. "It's a good idea. I've been meaning to try this myself." He set the crystal down. "I just dropped by to see if there's anything I should review before my interview tomorrow night with Phil Johnson."

"I think we've covered almost everything," Emily said. "This show will give you national exposure. Johnson has an enormous viewing audience, Archbishop."

He nodded. "Right. And I don't want any surprises."

"You'll have fifteen minutes, uninterrupted. That reminds me. I've been wanting to talk to you about that exhibition at the Met." Emily nodded to a newspaper open in front of her. "The Shroud of Turin. Johnson may bring it up."

"I doubt that, Emily," Wesley said in an ironic tone. "Not at the price of *that* airtime. Anyway, don't I recall that the Shroud was revealed as a fake some years ago?"

Emily nodded. "I think so. I believe it was radiocarbon dated and the conclusion was that the linen was manufactured in the thirteenth or early fourteenth century, give or take a few years. It's a forgery, probably a painting." She thumped the newspaper. "Here's an article on the exhibition."

"You mustn't spend too much time on this," the archbishop cautioned. "This shows a window of opportunity. Time and focus; time and focus. Getting my message across, communication. Those are our most important concerns right now."

"You're right," she said, leaning back. "But the Shroud *is* an interesting relic. I saw a picture of it once. Don't recall much about it except that it's a long cloth with images of the front and back of a naked man, as if it was pulled over his head lengthwise." She smiled across the desk at him. "The legend, of course, is that it's the burial cloth of Jesus."

Wesley snorted. "Legend is a good word—says it all. It's obviously painted."

"Wonder how they did it?" Emily mused. "Oh well." She shook her head. "At any rate, you might be asked about it."

"I *have* been asked about it more times than I can count in the last two days," Wesley snapped.

Emily gave a little laugh as she picked up the newspaper. "You should be aware of it, at least. Be prepared for a few questions." She folded the paper into a neat square highlighting the story and slid it across the desk to Wesley. "Here. Read this, it's short—just the basics."

"Must be a slow news day," he muttered. He stuffed the article under his left arm with a shake of his head and stood.

"Johnson won't be a cakewalk," she warned. "He's Republican, conservative, old school, high church, and all of that; but he's smart and he brings in good ratings."

Wesley squinted against the light with a slightly worried look. "Conservative" was probably an understatement for Paul Johnson's show, he knew. He was used to verbal battles, but he'd not yet been exposed to a hostile interview where the stakes were so high. He wouldn't consider it if the show was only a local broadcast.

"Hope I can remember everything, my dear," he said, rolling the article into a cone and slapping it against the palm of his hand. "I'm not good at these tricky sorts of things. You'll be there, of course?" He felt more comfortable when she was in the studio, especially when he could see her face and expression. Watching Emily was like being graded by a teacher, he thought. If things were going well and he was making his points, he got a gold star—her face was happy and animated. If he said something inconsistent or unclear, she'd give him a questioning look and tilt her head over to the right side to let him know he needed to rephrase his words. She seemed to have a sixth sense for media relations.

"Just keep in mind that you don't have to answer the question that's asked," Emily said. "Answer the one you've prepared for instead. Remember what the lizard said: Most viewers lose track anyway. They'll only remember the key points, the ones you repeat several times."

Smart. She was smart. Wesley smiled and arched his eyebrows. "The sound bites the lizard gave me?"

Emily nodded. "Right. Also," she added, "keep things simple. The audience will lose interest if issues get too complicated."

In his sleep that night Wesley sank deep into the soft mattress. The gray mist swirled around him once again. His mind's eye watched the liminal figures slowly emerge—bare outlines of people, some trees perhaps. A door slammed in the rectory, waking him abruptly.

For a moment he lay in darkness, disquieted, with a strange sense that things were somehow off balance. He strained to recall the dream, but it eluded him, receding as his mind cleared. Finally he reached to the light on the table next to his bed and, after fumbling for the switch, flicked it on. As he turned his head to look at the clock, his gaze fell on a small glass vase of unusual flowers that Miss H had placed upon the table. Wesley smiled at this thoughtful gesture. The flowers were the ones given him by the little girl at the cathedral almost a week ago, but even after all this time they looked fresh; the colors remained vivid.

As he lay in the half-world of dreams and reality, Wesley wondered what had happened to the little flower girl. Strange, how she hadn't shown up in any of the pictures taken that day by the news services. He switched off the light, turned over, and plumped the pillow under his head. As his lids grew heavy and began to close, the little girl's face rose in his mind. There was certainly something odd about those dark blue eyes, something timeless, almost mysterious.

CHAPTER SIX

The snap of the Roman whip explodes through the narrow streets of the ancient city, Jerusalem, breaking the spell. Hanna starts at the intrusion, and the prisoner releases her from his gaze. Once again the sounds of the drums, the jeering crowd, and groans from the prisoners and some of the spectators batter the little girl. As the soldiers of the emperor's prelate, Pontius Pilate, emerge and sharpen in Hanna's focus, her eyes settle on a thick trickle of blood seeping down the face of the man before her. The blood comes from a circlet of thorns on his forehead where the flesh is pierced. Her gaze takes in his features now—a strong nose, high heavy cheekbones, a short forked beard.

The prisoner's eyes leave her, slowly moving up past Hanna until his look stops upon her uncle's face. The girl twists, tilting her head to see that Uncle stares back at the man with a strange, stricken look, as if he knows him. His grim expression frightens her. Suddenly Uncle lifts his hands from her shoulders to yank the cowl of his cloak over his head, partially hiding his haggard face. She's bewildered to see tears fill his eyes while he stares at the prisoner. Pressed against his legs, the girl feels a shudder run through him.

Suddenly soldiers prod the prisoner, and the crowd surges, knocking against Hanna. Long legs wedge between Hanna and Uncle. Blinded by the forest of legs and thick cloaks, Hanna stumbles, groping for Uncle's hand, fighting against the jostling, shifting mass.

"Uncle!" she screams, but her words drown in the cacophony of the shouting, seething, shoving, angry crowd.

The crowd closes around her now, crushing her. Gasping, she fights to remain upright, struggling for air, straining to see as she pushes and shoves against the bodies that imprison her. For an instant the crowd parts and she spots Uncle, hunched as he moves away, keeping pace with the soldiers and the prisoner as if she's been forgotten. The crowd shifts again and Uncle disappears.

A cracking whip galvanizes everyone. Shouts grow louder now and bolder as the procession moves off down the road to the drumbeat. Hanna, unable still to move, can hear the cries of the prisoners and soldiers and the ominous roll of the drums slowly fading. One by one the men that pressed against her move away. Dust left behind fills the air. Hanna coughs, sways, and gulps deep draughts of air.

When everyone has gone, Hanna peers around, hugging herself to become small, invisible. She's alone, she realizes, except for a beggar squatting in the shadows of a narrow alley across the way. He slumps against a hulking wall of rectangular rough-cut stone, like the stones that pave the streets, and all around him are rotting palm branches and flowers and dried grass blown by the wind days ago into the corners of the buildings. Wrapped in his own misery, the beggar ignores Hanna. Wheeling to her left, far down the street she can see the last of the crowd squeezing through a high stone archway, following the grim procession. In a few seconds they've rounded the corner, and suddenly they're out of sight.

The realization that Uncle is really gone, that she is alone and lost, drops through Hanna's mind, stunning her. For a moment she's stilled by the thought. But raucous laughter from the direction of the Temple Mount sends a chill through her, and she comes to a decision. She'll follow Uncle; Mother said to stay close to him. He's just around that corner, she tells herself, breaking into a run.

Breathless, Hanna races down the street and ducks around the corner, but immediately she's forced to halt. The small group of stragglers still following the soldiers and prisoners blocks her way. Hanna scours the faces for Uncle in vain. The spectators in front of her have pressed against the walls of buildings along the street, forming a solid barrier.

Her heart beats wildly as she squares herself for an ordeal and begins squeezing through the crowd, working her way inch by inch toward the soldiers and prisoners ahead. Frantically she searches the faces, but still Uncle is nowhere to be found. At last her eyes stop on the prisoner—Uncle's friend—and her heart drops. He seems exhausted now, bleeding and bent under the wooden beam. Choking back tears, she trails down the main road and, after a moment of hesitation, out through the city gates.

Once outside the high walls that surround Jerusalem, Hanna looks back at the city. She's never been outside before. Much of it is hidden from her view, but the glistening white temple is still visible, and she finds the sight comforting. Even from this distance she can see the Antonia soldiers standing guard on the great porticoes, as they do every feast day. It's Passover, she remembers.

A shrill scream from one of the prisoners draws her attention, and she turns toward the ugly sound, watching as the soldiers force the three men along the dirt road. A rocky hill rises before them, brown from the deadening heat; but, despite the blazing sun, the area seems to absorb all light and life. Garbage from the city is scattered over the field, and at the bottom of the hill patches of dry grass grow in the hard dirt among rocks and thornbushes. A few trees, bare and delicate with branches creeping out from withered trunks like spindles, are scattered across the dull terrain. Beyond the road and hill and garbage, however, are lush green meadows. There trees seem to flourish. But not here; here the earth is barren, brown, and dead.

The air is still and the sun is high, but Hanna knows that evening brings the cold. She glances up with a worried look, wondering what time it is. Following the crowd, she sees gray clouds beginning to streak the white sky, dulling the light. Ahead the prisoners are herded off the road toward the hill. Someone in the crowd mutters the name, and Hanna recognizes it at once: *Golgotha.* She shudders. This is the place of the skulls. Overhead, great black birds slowly circle on the drift, cawing over the human invasion.

With a backward glance at the high city gates and the stretch of road behind her, she fights a prickle of fear as she turns to follow the prisoners and soldiers across the field, certain that Uncle will find her there.

CHAPTER SEVEN

Little Guy opened the door to the apartment and halted, rooted to the spot. He hadn't expected to see Father Leo this evening. It was Tuesday, and Father Leo almost never came for dinner on Tuesday. Something was wrong.

Father Leo looked up from a place on the couch next to Rebecca and smiled at him. He fingered the ring box in his pocket as he looked at Little Guy, his future son, thinking about the reservations he'd made for dinner on Saturday night at Twenty-One. The dinner would be expensive—almost a week's salary—but worth it. He'd resolved that Rebecca would never forget the night that he proposed their marriage.

"Where've you been, son?" Father Leo asked cheerfully.

Little Guy grew cold at the sight of Father Leo. Since the baseball game a few weeks ago, he'd tried to avoid the priest. Father Leo reminded him of Sam lying all alone in that box in the graveyard. Sam whom God had abandoned. Father Leo's God.

You said to let him go.

The words slithered through his mind, and he balled his fists. It was not his fault that Sam had died. *It wasn't.* The old fury rose, threatening to consume him; and he veiled his eyes, letting the anger settle on Father Leo while he focused on the fat roses splashed across the wallpaper behind the couch. He preferred to think of the roses. Sam had liked those roses. He used to trace them with his baby fingers. Sam again. All at once something snapped inside.

"Don't call me son," Little Guy heard himself say in a flat tone, keeping his eyes on the roses. "I'm not your son."

Leo felt a hot flush crawl up his neck as he gaped at Little Guy. The room rang with silence.

"All right, Little Guy," he finally said in a careful tone. His fingers grasped the ring box in his pocket as he turned the boy's words over in his mind, trying to understand them. "All right."

Leo felt Rebecca shift beside him, as if to distance herself. A shadow of fear, like a bad premonition, crossed Leo's face as he twisted inside. "I don't understand, Little Guy," Leo said, after a small hesitation. "What's wrong?"

Little Guy shrugged, determined to think of nothing but that wallpaper. Funny how he'd never before noticed the color *behind* the roses. The paper had once been white; now it looked old, yellowed—maybe from cigarette smoke. He wished Mother wouldn't smoke. And he'd always thought those roses were too big.

"Little Guy?" his mother said softly.

He glanced at her, then at Father Leo. "Oh, nothing's wrong," he said in a tone of resignation, fixing his eyes on the roses again. "What do you mean?"

Leo thought about that, then sucked in his breath. When he spoke, his words came out all at once in a worried stream. "I care about you, son . . . ah . . . Little Guy. Haven't seen much of you since the ball game. What's come over you? You're like my own blood, you know."

Liar!

A roar in Little Guy's ears, like a torrent of wind or water rushing downhill, smothered the rest of the words. The roses on the wallpaper wavered. Father Leo, his own real father, the judge. Father Leo's God who wasn't there. None of them cared about Sam or him. None of them knew how he felt. So what? He didn't need any of them. He turned his eyes to Father Leo, watching his mouth work, observing the flexing muscles around his lips as the priest talked. But a strange thing happened: he could not hear a thing over the roaring in his ears. Father Leo's face was growing red, he observed; and the priest began gesturing as he spoke, eyes riveted on Little Guy. As Little Guy watched, he was filled with new contempt.

Go away! He wanted to shout. *Leave us alone, Mother and me!* But he held the words inside and merely shifted his gaze back to the roses, and after a moment the roar subsided.

"I think I'm entitled to an answer. Speak to me, son!" Father Leo was saying. His voice was tight and strained; and Little Guy, sensing anguish in the words, suddenly felt a surprising surge of power and confidence. He almost smiled before he caught himself. *Good.* He glanced at the flat, stiff stick figure sitting beside his mother on the couch, staring up at him with an expression of disbelief.

"We should talk things over," Father Leo urged. He moved to rise, then seemed to think better of it, and spread his hands before his chest in a pleading gesture. "I'm not just a priest, you know." He gave Little Guy a tentative smile. "I care about you and your mother. Why don't you sit down, and let's talk about what's troubling you?" Rebecca, beside him, nodded.

Little Guy felt light and strong, weightless and in control. Father Leo's eyes were fixed on him, and so he allowed a small flicker of annoyance to cross his face, just long enough for the priest to glimpse it before it disappeared. "Sorry," he answered with a careless shrug. "But I don't really see the point." He moved into the room now, closing the front door behind him.

Leo felt Rebecca tense. His head hurt and he leaned forward, stroking his forehead absently, squeezing the flesh above his brows with his thumb and forefinger. "The point I'm trying to . . . ," he paused, looking up. The boy was only twelve years old, after all. He lowered his voice. "I'm trying to make *the point,* as you put it, that I'm here for you, to help you."

Little Guy heaved a loud sigh. The world was full of idiots, and one of them sat right before him in this room.

"Little Guy!" Rebecca rose and started toward her son. "Mind your manners!" She reached for him, but Little Guy spun away and disappeared through the door. Her arm dropped slowly to her side; then she turned back to Leo with a wooden smile.

"I'm terribly sorry, Leo," Rebecca said in a careful tone. She paused before continuing. "This must be an example of raging adolescent hormones. He's going through a rebellious stage." She averted her eyes and adopted a false smile, shaking her head. "He challenges everything these days. But I suppose it's better for him to examine things. He's extremely bright, you know." Leo's expression stopped her, forcing her to turn away.

Leo watched her slender back as she walked over to a small table underneath the window and rummaged in the drawer for a cigarette. Finding an old crushed pack, she pulled one out, lit it, and blew smoke at the ceiling as she stared out the window, giving Leo time to compose himself.

"This is just a stage he's going through," she murmured. "Perhaps you should leave it alone for awhile." But that was not the truth, she knew. Over the past few days she'd come to realize that for reasons that she didn't understand, Little Guy had developed a strong dislike for Leo. She'd hoped that it would pass, but a feeling of despair gripped Rebecca. She cared for Leo—might even love him, she admitted to herself—but it came to her now that Little Guy would never share her attention with anyone.

Rebecca hugged herself and stood very still, listening to each tick of the clock on the wall. *If I hold on to this minute,* she thought, *the future won't change. Leo will still be here with us.* It was so comfortable to have a kind and thoughtful man around. So she inhaled smoke, closed her eyes, and waited, telling herself to enjoy this second, and the next, and the next.

She heard Leo rise from the couch and walk toward her, changing things. She knew what he would say, and she knew what had to be. That much and more was owed to her son . . . after Sam.

"Rebecca."

She opened her eyes, and when she turned, he stood facing her. Leo took the cigarette from her hand and stubbed it out in an ashtray, then cradled her hands between his own. "I have a special feeling for you and Little Guy," he began. He hesitated and looked down at her. "I love you both. Do you understand? I have hoped that we . . . "

"No. Not now," she interrupted in a firm voice. She looked up at him, and in that instant she understood. They'd reached the end. Little Guy was all that she had left; he was to be her life.

She stepped back and freed her hands, clasped them together underneath her chin as she regarded Leo. The room was silent. Seconds passed as neither she nor Leo spoke. Finally, Rebecca took a deep breath and shook her head, banishing a fleeting feeling of self-pity. *Don't let him see,* she told herself. *He's a kind man. Don't make it harder than it has to be.*

"I must be honest with you, Leo," she began, looking past him and straining for a casual tone. "The problem is that you're a young priest beginning a long, demanding career," she shrugged, "and I . . . All my energy must be directed to Little Guy right now." She turned back to him and, when she saw the anguish in his eyes, dropped her own. "He hasn't been the same since Sam died."

Leo reached for her, but she stepped back, away from him. He dropped his arm and waited.

"I just don't think I can deal with another complication in my life." She glanced at the door Little Guy had slammed behind him. "Even if it were possible otherwise."

"It *is* possible otherwise," Leo urged in a low, intense voice. "Little Guy's just going through a phase. He'll snap out of it." He tried to ignore the growing sense of desperation as he reached out and touched the underside of her chin with the tips of his fingers. Her skin was silk. "Rebecca," he moaned. "We could be a family. The three of us—you and me and Little Guy."

Steeling herself, she pulled away, turning her back to Leo, and stared out the window at the street below. Ants in a crevice. She forced herself to observe the steady flow of people on the sidewalk, to control the emotion that threatened to overwhelm her by controlling her thoughts. *Where were all of those people going?* she wondered without caring. She rubbed her hands up and down her arms in a steady motion, feeling tired and fighting a sudden sense of futility. But Little Guy's face rose before her, and she lifted her chin. She'd make up for her failures—for letting his father desert them, for leaving the boys alone on that afternoon. Little Guy would have the best life, she resolved—the best of everything to make up for what he'd gone through when Sam died. Little Guy came first.

Leo stared at Rebecca's rigid back, at her lithe body silhouetted against the light in the frame of the window, and found he couldn't move. The thought that he might lose her made him tremble. She stood there before him, pulled up and out of her torso in that determined stance. And with all the force that he could muster, he willed her to wheel around and fall into his arms. *I can't lose her!* he thought.

She is so beautiful, he reflected, watching her. It wasn't the sort of beauty found in magazines or movies. Instead Rebecca radiated a deep intelligence, confidence, and inner strength. But something else was in her posture now; he'd seen it in her eyes—an iron will. He knew this was the same resolve that made her work day after day to the point of exhaustion to provide small comforts for Little Guy, to overcome obstacles, to do without, to sacrifice everything for her son.

His heart sank as she turned back to him and slowly shook her head. "It won't work. It doesn't really matter whether this is just a phase or not, you see. The reality is that my entire life is Little Guy. I owe that to him."

Leo opened his mouth to speak, and she held up the flat of her hand to silence him. "No. That's the way it is. That's the way I want it."

"I love you, Rebecca."

I love you, too, she thought. "That doesn't matter," she said out loud.

"The boy needs a father," Leo said. He hesitated, but she said nothing more. With a sinking, desolate feeling, he picked up his hat from the couch and held it, tapping it against his leg as he studied her. He worked to keep his voice even. "And what about you, Rebecca? You can't live life through your son."

"Why not?" She gave Leo a fierce look. "We're all each other has." Her voice, pitched high, was tight and strained. "You have your beliefs, Leo. But all I have is Little Guy. His father's gone. Sam's dead." She shrugged and reached for the cigarette Leo had ground out in the ashtray, held it between the tips of her fingers, and studied it as if it were lit. "He's a strong kid, very independent."

Leo's hat stilled. "He's full of rage, Rebecca," he said in a low voice. "Don't be fooled by that self-possession. He's younger than he acts, and anger can push a boy like him in the wrong direction."

"He's a young man."

"No." Leo shook his head. "He's a little boy looking for answers."

"Perhaps he feels entitled to answers," she said, suddenly fatigued at the turn of events. She wanted to be alone now. "I don't have answers for him. Do you?" She stared at Leo. "In all our hours of conversation, you've never once been able to explain how your God could let my baby die."

Leo moved toward her, but she stepped back and shook her head, conscious of her need for distance between them. She armored herself with anger. "Don't patronize me. I don't want comforting. Or pity. Give me a rational explanation for Sam's death, not a supernatural—religious—one." Her voice broke; her mouth twisted and she glanced away, hiding the pain. "Sam was so innocent, so young. Can you explain this evil?"

As she spoke, years of resentment bubbled to the surface. "Where is the justice for Sam and Little Guy and me?" she cried, turning back to face him. "Do you realize that monster, Jesse—the one that dropped my baby from the roof—he's already free?" She shivered and crossed her arms, hugging herself again. The words came before she could stop them. "I can't believe in anything but myself and Little Guy now. Not even you, Leo."

Leo turned pale. He hesitated, but Rebecca gave him a cold look.

She stared at his back as Leo started toward the door, longing to beg him to forget her words, to give her more time. But Little Guy's hatred for Leo had been clear and alarming. No, it wouldn't work. Little Guy came first. Her son was her future, her obligation, her hope. His happiness would be hers as well.

As his hand grasped the doorknob, Leo paused. This might be the last time he'd ever touch the cold, smooth steel of this doorknob, he thought with wonder. How had this happened? How had everything changed so fast?

"I'll be here for both of you if you change your mind," he said without turning around. For a moment he stood, frozen. Then he opened the door and walked through it, closing it quickly behind him so that he wouldn't stop and plead with Rebecca to reconsider.

I'm still young, he told himself as he hurried down the narrow hallway to the elevator. He clenched his jaw. My life will not be empty without Rebecca and Little Guy. I have the church and my music; that's enough for me. He punched the button on the wall and planted himself in front of the elevator door to wait as her name beat through his mind . . . *Rebecca, Rebecca!* He choked back a sob, and his thoughts whirled.

When the elevator finally arrived, he took one last look at the door to Rebecca's home before stepping inside. As the doors closed and Leo descended, he took a deep breath and recited to himself again and again the harsh wisdom of Ecclesiastes: “For everything there is a season. There is a time to seek, and a time to lose.”

Months later, from his spot across the street just down from the old grey stone apartment building in which Rebecca and Little Guy lived, Leo watched Rebecca emerge from a bus that had stopped at the corner. It was an obsession, he knew. He'd taken to calling it “The Watch” to himself.

She was late tonight, he observed. Rebecca was working long hours, as usual. She held onto the exit door handle as she climbed down the steps and, clasping her purse and a package in the other hand, landed on the curb with a heavy step. She looked tired, he reflected. Her shoulders were hunched as she shifted the weight in her arms and started toward home. Leo's spirit lifted a bit as he decided that Rebecca looked somewhat depressed. *Schudenfreude.* Perhaps she missed him.

Streetlights came on just then, and for an instant the light caught her hair in an amber halo effect. By the time she reached the stoop in front of her building, Rebecca's shoulders and back were straight and her chin was held high, as if she drew strength from the proximity of her home. Her step grew light as she climbed the stairs. She fumbled in her purse, pulled out a key, and after a moment disappeared through the front door.

Leo saw the door close, then slumped back against the wall, exhausted. For a moment his thoughts were muddled, then when the lights came on in the window on the tenth floor, he shook himself and continued the watch that he allowed himself once a week. Never more—that would seem obsessive. Never less—that would be torment. For an hour he stood waiting with his worn trench coat pulled tight around him. Finally, his shoulders bowed, and he buttoned the coat with one hand as he strolled away into the darkness.

Leo stuffed his hands into his pockets and stared at the ground as he walked. Rebecca had made plain that she would not marry him, and he'd found it impossible to be around her since that day, to act as though they were nothing more than friends. It crossed his mind that since that terrible day months ago, he'd not seen Little Guy. But then, he always began his watch in the evening when Rebecca came home from work, so perhaps that was not unusual. Little Guy was probably upstairs doing homework.

At the thought of Little Guy, Leo's stomach muscles tightened. Anger rose inside. But, as always, the image of Little Guy staring at his baby brother's body on the day that Sam died brought pity, and the pity subsumed the anger, leaving only a bleak and lonely void in its place. As usual after The Watch, Leo headed to his small church for solace.

Day by day Leo struggled, coping with the pain of Little Guy's inexplicable hatred and Rebecca's withdrawal. But even worse, as time distanced him from his dream, gradually Leo faced the futility of his lonely life—a new feeling that after everything is said and done, regardless of how we live, at the end the same fate awaits us all.

Faith is such an ephemeral thing to rely upon for comfort, he reflected. As a priest he knew that faith should sustain him through this time, should transcend his deepening despair. But at night when he could not rest for thinking of Rebecca, and during the day when he could not do his work, the questions roiled in his mind. Why had his dream been smashed? Why had Little Guy bludgeoned his dreams with hate?

CHAPTER EIGHT

The strong studio lights were placed behind Paul Johnson's chair and shone directly into Wesley's eyes. He tried to mask his irritation, but he noticed that Paul, standing to one side of the set, was smiling. The production assistant clipped a microphone onto the lapel of his jacket and pointed out the various cameras. He asked Wesley to count to ten for an audio check.

When the production assistant had finally bustled off, Wesley sat in the chair indicated and peered into the darkness behind the cameras and lights, looking for Emily. He was surprised to find that he was nervous. Paul Johnson was a snake, Emily had warned. His interview style was blunt, hard-hitting; he seemed to cultivate tension among his guests. One-liner preview ads for the show on the previous night had taken Wesley by surprise. They were hostile, called him a "liberal" in a tone clearly meant to be insulting.

He located Emily, and when she waved at him, Wesley smiled, thinking how sometimes she reminded him of his own mother. A low table was beside his chair, and he drummed his fingers on it, looking around and wishing that Mother were here to see him now. The thought of her sudden death three years ago still left him with a hollow sense that he was alone, that no one really understood him. He missed the reflection of pride in her eyes when she looked at him. Just then Paul walked over with an outstretched hand, and he banished the gloomy thoughts.

"Welcome to the show," Paul said in a voice like buttermilk. He took a chair on the other side of the table, angled so that even facing the camera he could observe Wesley. Beside him on the table he placed a small stack of papers, and he placed a book on top. "We have a few minutes before we begin," he said in a friendly tone. "Can we get you anything? A glass of water?"

"No thanks," Wesley said, leaning back and stretching his long legs out before him in a practiced sprawl. His face grew stiff as the music rose—the show's theme, he realized. When the camera moved forward, he relaxed and shifted slightly toward it.

"All right, ready in ten," someone called from the interior of the room behind the cameras. "Nine . . . eight . . . seven . . ."

At the signal Paul looked directly into the main camera and began his rapid trademark spiel. "Welcome to *Target Zero* . . . free fall, no holds barred." He grinned, "It's Friday, the end of a hectic week on Wall Street, the beginning of a beautiful weekend here in New York, and hopefully for the rest of you across the country as well. But if you were just settling down to relax, *think again* because our first guest tonight will probably elevate your blood pressure."

With a chuckle and a conspiratorial look: "He's generally successful in shaking things up. Tonight we have with us the man recently elected—" Paul swiveled to Wesley. "Is that the right word? *Elected?"* At a nod from Wesley, he went on without stopping for breath. "Okay, *elected* as the new and presiding archbishop of the Apostolic Church. And for those of you who've been asleep for the past few years, the Apostolic Church is now the largest Christian church in our nation."

A long shot of Paul and Wesley appeared on the monitor. Wesley, dressed as usual in khakis and a crewneck sweater with no shirt underneath, gave the camera his now-famous grin.

"Our guest is the Reverend Honorable Archbishop Wesley Bright. Whew!" Paul leaned forward, swiped his forehead dramatically, and gave the viewers a humorous look. "How's that for a moniker, my friends?" He turned to Wesley. "And we're glad to have you with us tonight, Archbishop."

Rat-a-tat, rat-a-tat. Paul Johnson's jackhammer voice annoyed Wesley. He rested his hands one on top of the other across his slumped—but still trim—midsection and thanked the host with an uneasy chuckle, wishing that he'd paid attention to Emily's suggestion that he watch the show ahead of time. But he'd been so busy lately.

"Now let's get started." Paul leaned back in his chair and tapped his chin with the side of his knuckle, as if deep in thought. "Archbishop Bright," he began, "you've been called the most rebellious and controversial clergyman to come out of a church since Martin Luther took on the Catholics four hundred years ago in the great Reformation." His voice held a hint of amusement. "In fact, I've seen you described as *outrageous,"* he raised his eyebrows at the word, "in what, some might call, the 'conservative' press. But in any event, you're credited with turning Christianity and Judaism in this country upside down and inside out."

He paused and gave the archbishop a challenging look. "Do you concur?"

"Well now," Wesley drawled with a boyish, mischievous look. "I suppose I am a bit of a rebel." He chuckled, crossed his ankles, and turned to the camera. "But let me speak boldly."

"Please do."

"Yes, I intend to." Thrown off by Paul's caustic tone, Wesley paused before continuing. "I'm sure you'll agree, Paul, that in this postmodern, Darwinian-Freudian world, with our new understanding of astrophysics and quantum physics, of gay and lesbian rights, not to mention the rights of women in the church . . ."

"Oh come now, Archbishop," Paul interrupted with a small, impatient toss of his head. "You're wasting our time."

Wesley stiffened, but Paul spread his hands and gave the camera a sideways look before turning back to Wesley. "Spare us, please. Those issues are straw men, sir. Let's go straight to the heart of the controversy. What you've called the Jesus myths." He tapped his fingers on the book beside him, frowning.

What's he going to do with that? Wesley wondered, glancing down. The book was one of his earlier publications.

"I prefer to call it the Jesus *experience,"* he said with a dry smile.

Paul nodded and held up the book to the camera. "And that brings us to the real question, the fundamental one." He read the title from the spine and opened it to a marked place. "Let me read for our audience something you wrote about four years ago, before you were called to lead the church." He ran his finger down the page and stopped near the bottom.

"The great fraud of Christianity," he read, "is the cross, and it must be removed from our churches. Nietzsche has said that God is dead. I'll go one better than that. God isn't dead. God, as understood in traditional religious terms, does not exist and never existed." Paul stopped reading and gave Wesley a quizzical look before continuing.

"The idea of a supernatural being that looks like us," he went on in a heavy voice, "a being that intervenes in our lives to reward and punish us, is childish nonsense." Paul paused, flattened his brows, glanced at the camera, and shook his head before continuing. "And the idea that this supernatural being would send a son to live among us and permit his crucifixion is even more ludicrous." He emphasized the last word before closing the cover.

Still holding the book, Paul frowned into the camera and turned to Wesley. "Now. I have no problem with speaking your mind. But, please explain to me, sir. How can a cleric—excuse me, an *archbishop*—make such a statement?" He shook his head as if dumbfounded by the idea. "Isn't that kind of like biting the hand that feeds you?"

He gave a short laugh and looked off. "Seems somewhat contradictory to me for a man of the cloth to deny the very existence of God, or to call the idea of a messiah *ludicrous.*" Turning his head to the viewers, he rubbed his chin and cocked his head. "I just don't *get it.*"

A rush of adrenaline shot through Wesley, and he bolted upright. Bracing his forearms on the table, he leaned forward to answer. "Paul, I'm certain the viewers understand the difference between *obsolete* religious theories and modern spirituality," he said, crinkling his eyes, aware that the camera had moved in for a close-up. He changed his expression to one of grave concern. When you're under attack, kill them with kindness, the lizard had said, but be firm.

"U'mmm." Paul dropped the book onto the table, folded his arms across his chest, and waited.

"The Christian church has been dragged into the twenty-first century!" Wesley hit the table with his fist just hard enough to be heard. "And this change has occurred in the nick of time. The institution was on its deathbed."

He locked eyes with the host. "I'd even go so far as to admit that my leadership role has stirred things up. But," he gave the camera an impish look, "this *is* a revolution. We're modernizing outdated religious teachings in order to make them relevant. It's time to redefine terms."

"Such as?" Paul leaned back, distancing himself from Wesley. "Give us an example."

Wesley's eyes drew together, and his face settled into a grave expression. "Well, since you've asked, in mature terms when we invoke the name of Jesus, we must distinguish between the *cultic* view of the man as the divine Christ—the myth created with the storyteller's license in the Gospels—and the true, historical sage." He smiled. "Of course, over the years scholars have learned to recognize the words of Jesus written in the New Testament as anecdotes supplied by the storytellers."

Noticing Paul's frown, Wesley smiled to himself. *You don't have the understanding or academic credentials to challenge me on this,* he thought. But nevertheless, Wesley decided to swing from this blunt approach to a more appealing—more spiritual—explanation for the viewers.

"True Christianity is merely introspection," he said. "It's centered on our *selves.* When we understand our own natures, we come to know God." His voice soared as he spoke, and he turned and looked into the camera. *"We, ourselves, are God."*

Leaning forward and tapping his chest over his heart, he added, "God is a name for the spirit within us; it's the wind that flows around and through us." With a satisfied smile, he sat back. "You see, for each one of us, God is an *experience."*

Paul tilted back in his chair, and his voice cracked through the airwaves. "Sounds like narcissistic psychobabble to me, if you'll pardon the expression." He gave the camera a wicked grin. Seeing Wesley's stunned expression, he threw up his hands in mock dismay.

"Sorry, but nothing's off limits here, Archbishop. No one has protected status on *this* show, not even the church."

Wesley smothered his rising anger. "We're all ruled by emotion and desire," he said, working to control his tone of voice. "Even you, Paul. It's human nature. Why not acknowledge that?" He gazed into the camera and modulated to the reasoned tone that his teachers at Yale had used in lectures.

"The old Christianity based on Jesus myths is dead," he said, looking grave. "Those stories have some metaphorical value, of course. But we can't be expected to take them literally." He cocked his head with a slight smile. "And we certainly can't accept them as a moral yardstick." The smile curled down at the corners of his mouth as he pressed his lips together and shook his head. "After all, we're intelligent, educated adults."

"So where do we look for moral guidance?" Paul asked.

It always comes to this, Wesley thought with an inner sigh. *The same old question—sheep, looking for the missing shepherd.* "Each of us is capable of determining right and wrong for ourselves, according to circumstances at the time," he replied with the answer that he always gave. "To put it plainly, Paul, we must make choices according to how we feel about a thing at the time without dabbling in supernatural concepts."

He shot Paul a sympathetic look. "It's simple. Human nature is to act from self-interest. There's nothing wrong with that; it's how we've survived for thousands of years."

"Ah," Paul nodded, "so our principles have to fit us, like old shoes?" His expression was blank as he pushed on, "Is that the new doctrine of the Apostolic Church, Archbishop Bright?"

"In a manner of speaking, yes," Wesley chuckled, amused at Paul's attempt to suppress his natural belligerence. "The thing to remember is this: what's right for you may be completely wrong for me."

He turned to the camera and smiled out at the viewers. "Paradise for one person may be black-eyed virgins in a garden; for another, it's just a good book, or fishing on a lake on Sunday morning. Every culture has a different view of what's good or bad, right or wrong. It's all in how you see it." He paused for breath and Paul cut him off.

"But there are those who argue that new evidence shows the old orthodox Christian teachings might not be far off base, after all," Paul said. He fingered Wesley's book as he spoke. "What if after all we find that the stories of Jesus and the resurrection are true? Where would that leave you and the church, sir?"

"Evidence!" Wesley exclaimed as his eyebrows jumped. "How does one prove supernatural claims that contradict everything we know about the universe?"

Paul squared the stack of papers on the table with an air of reflection, lining up the edges against the lengths of his fingers. "Wouldn't you agree that scientific discoveries today often seem to contradict things we thought we knew about the universe?" he asked.

"Like rising from the dead?" Wesley scoffed.

Paul lifted his eyes with a sly look. "Well, since you've mentioned it, Archbishop Bright, what about the Shroud of Turin? It's causing quite a commotion in this city right now."

Good Lord! Wesley slumped against the back of his chair. How had he managed to let the conversation take this turn? This show was supposed to be about him, not that relic.

Paul raised one eyebrow and gazed at the archbishop. "According to polls taken after the Shroud exhibition began last week, the number of people who say they would *like* to believe the Shroud of Turin is the actual burial cloth of Jesus after seeing it for the first time is growing. They cite 9/11, natural disasters, the Middle-East situation. And many think it's possible that the Shroud might be real. Tell us what you think of it."

"I *don't* think about it," Wesley snapped. "Looking for truth in the Shroud is like believing in the tooth fairy; it's wishful thinking. No rational person can accept that it's anything but a hoax." Conscious that his voice had grown shrill, Wesley paused for a deep breath. He remembered to train his eyes on the camera lens as the lizard had taught.

"The Shroud is nonsense, Paul." He spread his hands flat on the table before him and pushed back. "Look around and judge for yourself how out of touch traditional Christianity was before we changed it, with the old ideas of hell and heaven and life after death. Rewards and punishments!" He shook his head. "Today the church must *work* to prove its relevance in order to survive. We can't rely on miracles and Jesus artifacts."

"Well, sir," Paul replied, turning away with a little laugh. The camera swung to Wesley, and as it did, Paul raised a finger, signaling to someone without interrupting the flow of conversation. "As C. S. Lewis once noted, rare exceptions to natural law *are* possible." As he turned back to Wesley, on the monitor behind him a close-up of the facial image of the Shroud appeared.

Caught off guard, Wesley stared at the picture and congratulated himself. He'd scanned the newspaper article Emily gave to him and remembered the most important point as he gathered his thoughts. Paul Johnson was cornered now. When he spoke, his tone was crisp. "As I'm *sure you know,* in 1988 radiocarbon testing established that within a 95-percent probability the Shroud is a fake; the cloth was manufactured between the years 1260 and 1390."

Paul raised his eyebrows but remained silent.

"And, of course," Wesley went on with growing sarcasm, "since Jesus is believed to have died around AD 30–33," he paused, "that makes it difficult for the Shroud to have been his burial cloth. A seven-hundred-year gap is mighty hard to explain." With a dry smile he slid back into his languorous pose, slouching as he spread his elbows over the arms of the chair and folded his hands across his chest.

"Radiocarbon dating is notoriously inaccurate for ancient cloth," Paul said.

Wesley did not reply.

The Shroud disappeared from the screen, and Paul gave Wesley a long look. In the dark studio Emily studied the host's satisfied expression on the monitor. His insistent focus on the Shroud of Turin took her by surprise.

"Hmm, I have something here," Paul murmured, pushing aside Wesley's book and shuffling through the neat stack of papers on the table. He selected one sheet, glanced down at it, and looked up.

"Archbishop Bright," he began. "Are you aware that the radio-carbon dating of the Shroud is currently challenged on several fronts?"

Wesley was startled. It crossed his mind that he might have scanned that article of Emily's too quickly. "Of course," he said, masking his apprehension. Collecting himself, he formed a patient smile, waiting.

"For our viewers, then," Paul said, looking into the camera. "To begin with, scientists at the University of Texas have found natural contaminants on a sample taken from the Shroud."

"What's the relevance of this information?" Wesley interrupted, straining for a pleasant tone.

"The relevance is this, Archbishop." Wesley smothered his irritation as Paul began punctuating his words with his index finger. "Two professors at the University of Texas, Doctors Garza-Valdez and Stephen Mattingly, report that the Shroud is covered with a thin layer of bacteria and fungus, which, over many years formed a bioplastic coating on the linen."

He glanced at Wesley as he went on. "It's a film often found on cloth wrapping ancient mummies and would have skewed the radiocarbon date. The bioplastic coating would have been measured for carbon right along with the cloth, resulting in an artificially late date for the Shroud."

"I haven't seen a retraction from the laboratories that tested samples for the Vatican, have you?" Wesley asked, looking into the camera. Focus, focus, stay calm. No fidgeting; hold hands still when you're tense, as the lizard taught.

"But there's more," Paul said, smiling. "In addition, as it turns out, the official samples tested by the three laboratories chosen by the Vatican were apparently not even part of the original Shroud."

"That's ridiculous," Wesley blurted. "A Vatican Cardinal supervised the cutting of those samples." He glanced into the darkness of the studio, searching for Emily. This wasn't in the newspaper article—he was almost certain.

"Who knows? You may be right," Paul said in a cheerful tone. He raised his shoulders with a mocking air of resignation. Wesley watched expressionless as the host began shuffling once again through the stack of paper. "Here it is," he said with an apologetic glance toward the camera. He pulled out another sheet and, holding it up, scanned it.

"According to this recent announcement," Paul added, reading, "'The sample given to the three laboratories by the Vatican was cut from a rewoven piece added to the Shroud, probably when repairs were made and probably around the time of the Crusades in 1290 or 1291.'"

Taken aback, Wesley frowned. "Probably?" he repeated with a short laugh.

"You caught me," Paul laughed, snapping his fingers toward the camera. "Okay. Here goes." He drew his brows together, still grinning. "But I'm leaving out the math, folks. This stuff could give you a headache."

Heaving a sigh, Paul went on with a practiced air. He'd rehearsed this, Wesley realized.

"Several scientists working independently have recently confirmed that the radiocarbon-dated samples—taken from a single site on a corner of the Shroud—have a different composition from the main cloth," he read. "An almost invisible line of stitching at the edge separates the newer rewoven strip from the original cloth. The rewoven strip has completely different properties from the original, which also chemically tests older." He glanced up at the camera, looking into the eyes of his viewers for an instant before returning to the page.

"For instance," he continued in a new and sober tone. "Raymond Rogers, of the Los Alamos National Laboratory, University of California, tested fiber samples from all areas of the Shroud against threads taken from the area of the official radiocarbon sample that was distributed to the three laboratories. Rogers now reports that the radiocarbon samples contain cotton and a dye not found in the original cloth fibers."

He looked at Wesley and lifted his eyes from the page that he'd been reading. "After extensive testing, Rogers concluded that the radiocarbon samples were taken from the newer rewoven piece that had been dyed to match the original material."

"Assuming you're correct about the new strip being woven onto the Shroud with *invisible* stitching," Wesley said, raising his eyebrows, "how can you know when these repairs occurred?"

Paul leaned back, holding the page up to the side of his face as if swearing an oath. "The dye process used to match the sepia color of the original linen was first introduced in Europe around the end of the Crusades in 1291."

Without waiting for Wesley's response, Paul tossed the page onto the table before him. "So there you have it, folks. It appears that the rewoven patch on the Shroud was carbon-14 tested in 1988, not the original cloth." He turned to Wesley. "That seems to indicate that the date of the Shroud is still an open question." Standing beside the main camera, the producer made a rolling motion with his arms.

"Your turn, Archbishop," Paul said. "I'll give you the last word."

As the camera shifted to Wesley, he worked to hide his relief. Resolving to speak to Emily about screening the interviews from now on, he shook his head. "Sorry, Paul," he said. "I'll have to leave it to others to address the validity of those particular tests and conclusions, or their scientific relevance."

He paused for a sip of water and shot the camera a stern look, what Emily called his *archbishop* look. "I have my own opinions on the Shroud, of course, but at this point," he gave a little shrug, "it's just too bad we don't have more time tonight."

Paul's eyes glittered. "That's what I hoped you'd say, Archbishop Bright." He glanced into the camera, then slid his eyes back to Wesley. "Why don't you join us on the show again next week to finish this discussion? We've scheduled another guest for that night who you might find interesting."

Wesley flinched. He was trapped. Emily was right: Paul Johnson *was* a snake. He'd planned this ambush all along, and now what could he say? He searched the dark again for Emily, but the camera had moved close and she was hidden.

"Well, how about it, Archbishop?" Paul urged. "I can't recall anything that's generated such excitement in this city since 9/11. The Shroud of Turin's become big news. What do you say? Our guest won't bite."

Wesley glared, speechless. *Just what I needed,* he thought, *another week spent worrying about the Shroud of Turin.* Then he caught himself. Johnson drew a huge national audience. If he said no to the invitation, he'd seem petulant, afraid.

"I suppose it could be arranged," Wesley said, suppressing his irritation. He adopted a hearty tone. "There *are* one or two points that I'd like to make clear on this subject next week." He forced a smile and crinkled his eyes at the viewers.

"Wonderful. You'll have every opportunity," Paul said with a confident grin, swiveling to the camera. "It's a date then," he announced. "Archbishop Bright will join us at this time next week, and we'll also have Professor Jonathan Marley of Stanford University as our special guest. Dr. Marley, as some of you may know, is well-known for his work as a professor of botany at Stanford, but he's also a self-described amateur archeologist. And he's considered to be one of the world's foremost experts on the Shroud of Turin."

As the camera moved back for the closing shot, Paul added, "Many of you may also remember that Professor Marley is one of our true war heroes. He received the purple heart after service in Vietnam in the early seventies."

A war hero! Emily slumped against the back of her chair. She'd just recognized the name—Jonathan Marley was mentioned in the article she'd given the archbishop to read before this show. He'd be a tough opponent.

The theme music swelled, and Wesley maintained his smile for the camera. The minute he stepped into the empty elevator with Emily, however, he turned to her with a frown. "What's all this about the radiocarbon tests?" he demanded. His voice was low and angry.

"I don't know," she admitted. "But I'll find out. Since you're committed to return next week, we'll have to do some homework." She stared at the closed elevator door as she spoke.

Wesley closed his eyes with a sigh. "This interest in the Shroud is the sort of nonsense that must be handled quickly and decisively, or I'll look like a fool," he said. "I'll need some talking points."

"By next week you'll have an in-depth report that will be more than enough for a fifteen-minute television interview."

"Fine, Emily, fine." Wesley rubbed his eyes, feeling tired. "When am I scheduled for *Good Morning, America*?"

"Let's see." Emily searched her pockets and fished out a small leather notebook. She flipped through the pages until she came to the right date. "You're set for next Monday morning. They'll expect you in the studio at five a.m."

"Five o'clock in the morning?" he exclaimed. His eyes widened.

"Yes." Emily hid her smile. "Unfortunately, that's the time that's been scheduled."

"Well. Humph. I certainly hope they don't bring up the Shroud of Turin." Wesley gave Emily a mischievous look. "I'd never get things right at that time of day, you know."

Emily laughed with relief.

✣ ✣ ✣

"What's that you're reading?" Wesley asked. He stood in the door of Emily's office wearing a smile. She hadn't been around since the *Paul Johnson Show* two days ago, and, to his surprise, he found that he'd missed her.

Emily looked up.

"You were a million miles away, my girl," he said jovially. "Where've you been? What are you doing?"

"I've been working on your report."

"Report?" Wesley gave her a puzzled look.

"The briefing report I promised. On the Shroud. For your interview next week with Paul Johnson."

"Ah, yes. Talking points for Jonathan Marley and the *Shroud*. Well?"

"It's somewhat surprising," she said, conscious that the archbishop was not going to like her next words. "The issue's not as clear as we first thought." She'd spent two grueling days at home on her computer and at the library scanning newspapers—staring at small microfiche print—and journals and magazine articles on the Shroud.

But a photograph of the image on the cloth in an old magazine had caught her eye. She'd seen the photograph somewhere before, she thought, but hadn't paid attention at the time. Now she was intrigued. In the first picture only faint, blurred impressions of the image could be seen, but when she'd turned the page, suddenly she saw a clear and detailed picture of the front and back of a wounded, naked man. She'd checked out the magazine to show the picture to the archbishop.

"What's so interesting?" Wesley asked, dropping into a chair nearby. He curled up a corner of his lips as he waited.

She told him of the difference between the two pictures, explaining that the first was the image as seen by the naked eye, and the second, a photographic negative of the same piece of cloth.

"You mean to say it's a photograph?"

"No." She shook her head. "The actual image on the cloth—the positive image—is faded and difficult to see. It almost seems to be the *reverse* of a photograph; but, of course, if you accept the official radiocarbon date . . ." Wesley scowled at this, "photography wasn't known at that time."

She picked up her notebook and scanned it. "In 1898 an amateur photographer named Secondo Pia took the first known photograph of the Shroud." She looked up to see if he was listening, and he nodded. "And when the film began developing, he realized that the negative—unlike the faded original—showed a clear and detailed picture of an adult male who appears to have been crucified. The light values on the negative were reversed."

She dropped the notebook onto the desk, and her face grew hot as Wesley snorted. "Wait, you don't understand," she urged, leaning toward him. "The detail on the negative image is astonishing. Take a look." She shuffled through the books and magazines and journals on her desk for the article containing the two pictures.

"The photographer was obviously either incompetent or dishonest," Wesley said.

Emily shook her head. "That's what I thought at first. But the Shroud's held by the Vatican, you know, and in 1934 the same thing happened when a professional photographer, a man named Enrie, was allowed to photograph it again. The earlier discovery by Pia was validated."

She located the magazine and, folding it open to the pictures, handed it to Wesley. "Here, compare these," she said, pushing it across the desk. "Since the 1934 Enrie photograph, the positive-negative images have been confirmed by many other photographers. But the oddest thing is that the original image on the cloth is the indistinct one. It's so difficult to see."

Emily watched as he studied the pictures. The negative showed that the man on the Shroud had been brutally tortured. In addition to bloody, savage wounds on his hands, feet, chest, and forehead, across the dorsal image countless marks striped the back, as if he'd been struck repeatedly with a three-pronged whip. She'd dug out her old Bible and found that these wounds matched the description given of the crucifixion of Jesus in the New Testament Gospel stories. "There's no consensus on how the image was created," she added.

"It's a trick," Wesley said, tossing the magazine down on the desk in front of him. "If it wasn't done with photography, it's a clever painting."

"Take a look at those wounds, though." She nodded to the pictures lying faceup on the desk in front of the Archbishop. "That certainly looks like blood. It even shows anatomically correct blood flow—something that wasn't understood in the medieval period. Maybe it was actually a cloth wrapped around a crucified person."

"My dear," Wesley interrupted, "blood does not flow from a dead person."

Emily flushed. "I suppose not."

"What about the challenges to the radiocarbon testing that Paul Johnson mentioned?"

She veiled her eyes. Last night she'd located the new information Paul had described. She'd missed it. "It looks like the Vatican's considering new tests," she said. "The radiocarbon date could be wrong." As she spoke, Emily's heartbeat quickened, and a surprising question ran through her mind: What if the Shroud is genuine?

"Nonsense," the archbishop said in a brisk tone as he eased himself up from the chair. "It's difficult to believe that the Vatican and sophisticated laboratories in three different countries could make such a mistake. Anyway," he flipped his hand in the direction of the magazine on the desk, "as to the image, I'm sure you'll find that the thing is painted."

Emily stared at the wall in front of her desk after he'd gone. *He must be right,* she told herself. Still, it wasn't as clear as she'd first thought. She lowered her eyes and noticed that she'd written in her notebook the name of a local expert on the Shroud: Reverend Leo Ransom, former rector of St. Luke's church in Manhattan. He was quoted frequently in articles on the Shroud. She'd been surprised to find that he was a priest in the archbishop's diocese.

Maybe Leo Ransom could shed some light on things. She wondered if he was still around, and since he was a priest in the Apostolic Church right here in Manhattan, why she'd never heard his name before. St. Luke's must be very small, she decided, picking up the telephone on her desk.

"St. Luke's Apostolic Church?" she asked the information operator. No.

"How about Ransom. Leo Ransom?" She spelled the name for the operator and waited. Yes. He was listed.

She dialed the number, and the phone rang five or six times before an answering machine picked up. A man's voice identified himself as the Reverend Leo Ransom.

Emily tried to ignore a twinge of disloyalty as she left her name and phone number, explained that she was researching the Shroud of Turin for the archbishop, and asked Reverend Ransom to call.

When she hung up the phone, she sat quietly gazing at the pictures on her desk. Dad had said that religion was hypocrisy, but, on the other hand, what if the Shroud was real? A horn blared and brakes screeched on the street below, and suddenly she laughed. It was ridiculous to think of such things as a man rising from the dead thousands of years ago while sitting in the middle of Manhattan in the twenty-first century. Neither Dad nor the archbishop would hesitate to ridicule her interest in the Shroud of Turin.

They must be right, she told herself. *Who was she to question their judgment?*

CHAPTER NINE

As soldiers push the prisoners toward the hill called Golgotha, someone stumbles and falls. Hanna tenses and strains to see what is happening. Once again the scourges prod the prisoners forward. She can't tell who is being beaten.

Hanna halts as the little group continues across the rocky field to the hill, moving farther from the safety of the city. She searches for Uncle but can't pick him out of the small crowd. After a moment she trails behind. Moving closer, Hanna can see that three beams of wood are planted upright on top of the hill. The ground is dry, and small puffs of dust fly from the dirt beneath her sandals as she walks.

When the procession reaches the top of the hill, the soldiers suddenly turn and knock the beams from the prisoners' shoulders in quick succession. Hanna is taken by surprise and stops in her tracks.

The sun has emerged through the clouds, hot and high. She looks up and realizes that it's past time for the midday meal. Mother will be worried. Where is Uncle? Hanna looks to the top of the hill, shading her eyes from the glare with her hand as she searches for her uncle with a new sense of urgency. After a moment, she sighs, smooths her long tunic, tucks it under, and sinks to the ground to wait. A veil is not required for a child her age; and even though the sky is streaked now with thin gray clouds, the sun beats down on her bare head. An ominous pulse seems to ripple in the air around her—not a sound, rather, a change in the atmosphere. The air is heavy, oppressive. She keeps her eye on the group above, pulling her long braided hair over her shoulders, tugging on it in an absent manner.

The soldiers gather around the prisoners, forming a tight outer circle. There's something menacing about the maneuver, and abruptly she turns her head away. To her right, below, at the bottom of the hill, she spots a pack of dogs. They must be wild. Her eyes widen as the sight registers, and she starts to rise; then instinct stops her. She fights the temptation to run.

The mongrels are thin, hidebound, with skin hanging loose from their bones; and they crouch, huddled together on the road just outside the city gates, blocking her return. Her heart sinks. Mother has warned many times of the animals that roam lawless and hungry beyond the walls of Jerusalem. With growing desperation, Hanna glances around for Uncle, willing him to emerge from the crowd, to wind his way down and take her home.

The crowd that has followed the little procession from the city now presses in upon the soldiers, jostling them. Suddenly, at shouts from a centurion, they move back, muttering as they spread into a wide arc that blocks Hanna's view.

She shivers and draws her legs up close to her chest. Dark birds circle overhead. Conscious that the dogs slink closer, she cringes, watching them with a covert look until at last the pack hunkers down once again into a dry swale. Then at once everything is still. The sun is scorching. Flies buzz in the tall weeds. A veil of silence descends upon Golgotha.

Suddenly the ring of iron on iron shatters the stillness; and the sound is accompanied by a long, high-pitched scream, an inhuman shriek that slices through the air. Hanna catches her breath, almost feeling the cry, a razor of sound that seems to cut through her flesh. She jerks her knees closer to her chest, squeezing her eyes shut. When another scream follows the first one, her hands fly to her ears. Her palms press tight against her head while the agonizing sounds, mingled now with jeers and catcalls, continue the assault.

Once a woman's shrill cry causes Hanna to look up. Through the prisoners' anguish she can hear the pitch of the woman's voice rising to a long, keening wail. Hanna shuts her eyes again, squeezing them tight as she mutters silent prayers; but images of reality break through the barrier, and she fights them. Finally, the red, raw sounds blend and swirl around Hanna until every other sensation is submerged. These are cries of a sort that she has never heard before. In the shadows of the pain, she rocks back and forth, back and forth.

A bolt of fire splits the sky, followed immediately by a long, deep roll of thunder. The ground beneath her trembles, and Hanna looks up quickly, rubbing her eyes. Above, high on the hill three crosses stand in bright relief against a blackened canopy, and she shrinks back at the sight of the three prisoners hanging there, arms spread wide. The soldiers mill about nearby, and several women and some men are gathered beneath the middle cross. Everyone else has gone.

One of the women weeps, and a man embraces her. As Hanna stares, roiling clouds twist down from the sky—writhing first around the crosses, foaming and spreading over the hill and across the land beyond it like pestilent waves of evil loosed from hell—virulent furies of cruelty and hate, of jealousies, pain, confusion, longing, discord, and desire—black winds that roar, surging over the hills and into the city like a raging sea—dark chaos tossing, howling, swirling, dipping, rising—blasting everything before it.

Thunder crashes; lightning arcs across the sky. Hanna scrambles to her feet and looks wildly about. Golgotha is a wasteland. The earth seems to hiss and thrash in pain around her, and turning she sees that a gorge has opened on the flat plain behind her near the main road. The sun has disappeared and the sky is dark. Rain falls now, turning quickly to a torrent, an angry spray of needles. Hanna's heart pounds—where is Uncle? From the depth of the black clouds, whirlwinds plunge and lift in anarchy, driving the noisy rain before it as a scourge.

The dogs! Suddenly she remembers and wheels around. The pack still lurks between Hanna and the city gates, but they've grown bold and have moved close. She stares transfixed at a yellow cur, larger than the rest. His eyes fasten on her; and despite the wind and rain, he stares, nostrils distended, as if he's caught the scent of blood and death.

Gripped by the mongrel's fixed gaze, Hanna freezes for an instant before instinct forces her to move. Slowly she lifts one foot behind her and steps back. Without moving his eyes from the child, the dog crouches, hunching his shoulders as he slinks closer to Hanna, arching his neck and watching his prey. She stops and waits, not daring now to move.

At last the animal slinks down, resting on his haunches. Now, ever so slowly, she backs away from the pack, inching toward the soldiers at the top of the hill and the spectators still huddled below the crosses. Tears blur her vision. She's wet and cold, and the wind whips around her. Frantically she prays that Uncle will come.

He'll come! She tells herself, holding tight like Mother would do, like all women in Judea must do when danger lurks and no man is near. Uncle will take her hand in his large rough one, and together they'll stroll past the dogs, glancing down with a little laugh as they pass them. Uncle will shake his head and say how foolish she's been. Then back to the city they'll go, far away from this terrible place. Home. She sees Mother weaving on her loom near the warm stone oven at the hearth and feels the heat. The thought comforts Hanna. Ah, if only she could be there now, *any place but here.*

The yellow dog turns rigid as he seems to sense a change and shifts his attention to the top of the hill. Hanna turns her head, following his gaze to the prisoners, each stretched naked on his cross. Her eyes rest on the one in the middle. He's far away, and she can't see him clearly, yet somehow she knows that he's the one.

You have a destiny, child. A duty to fulfill.

No. She shakes her head slowly and sobs. He didn't really speak to her again, *or did he?* The words tumble through her mind again and again—a destiny, a duty—and they're all mixed up with the yellow dog, the cross, and Uncle. Suddenly a gust of wind whips around her, rushing, hissing, until it seems the universe itself is swirling and she's at the vortex, whirling. Threads of silver spiral through the darkness, circling Hanna as she sinks to the ground, and then the light fades and she can no longer see or feel or think in the spinning black. She's drifting, floating, falling through the chute of time as everything dissolves.

The rushing wind slows, and Hanna opens her eyes to a strange, pewter light. She blinks and rubs her eyes. She's standing in a city. At least, at first glance she decides that it's a city; but it's nothing like home, Jerusalem. Slowly people emerge around her from the light, and they are dressed in odd clothes, all crowding together on stone steps, shouting and chattering in languages she's never heard before. She turns her head to a large cart beside her full of pretty flowers. Feeling bolder, she looks around, too curious to be afraid. Now she can see impossible things—towers taller than any that she's seen or could imagine, and she tilts up her head, gazing at the gleaming shards of limestone and granite reaching into the sky.

Sudden movements to her right accompanied by loud noises like one hundred camels in distress startle Hanna. She wheels to see a wide but crowded road. Vehicles on wheels race by without oxen or horse to draw them. Lights, not fire-light, not torches or burning oil or candles, all shine and flash around her. Hanna stares, trembling at the glittering scene.

You have a destiny, child. The gentle voice fills her mind, caressing her and comforting. As if by command Hanna turns toward the wooden cart and lifts a small bouquet of flowers that is waiting there for her. Looking down at the flowers, she recognizes the rockroses, the chrysanthemums, and bean capers that grow at home; and with a little cry she buries her face in them. The familiar fragrance calms her.

When she looks up, a man wearing a long crimson robe is moving toward her. Hanna stares at his approach, struggling to ignore the frightening sounds of the strange city. As the man dressed in shining red bends down to Hanna, she thrusts the bouquet into his hand, understanding somehow that this is what she's here to do.

A duty to fulfill—the words hover in her mind as Hanna looks up into the hawk-like face before her. For an instant she thinks she knows him; then suddenly he's gone, and the darkness embraces her again. When at last she opens her eyes, the city bathed in pewter light, and the boulders reaching to the sky and all of it—the noise and the crowd and the man in red and the street and the flower cart—have disappeared.

In confusion Hanna presses her hand into the hard, wet earth of Judea, clawing the dirt with her fingers to see if at least this much is real. She strains to remember something, some memory that troubles her, that hovers at the edge of consciousness. What has happened? Nothing comes to mind. The thought eludes her; memory has slipped away.

Hanna pushes herself up to a sitting position and spots the mongrel dogs below. The gates of Jerusalem are behind them; the men on the crosses are on the hill above. Slowly she gazes about. The wind and rain have died; and clouds drift away, revealing the last light of day. At the horizon the sun gleams through rising mist. She watches it sink slowly while the sky streaks with lights of purple, pink, and gold. As quickly as the pandemonium began, the earth settles into silence. All is calm; the air is heavy and damp, and already it bears a slight edge of evening chill.

A furtive glance at the dogs tells her that now is the time; they've settled down in a huddle. Minutes pass as Hanna waits, on guard for any sign of movement. Over her shoulder she sees the soldiers on the hill above preparing to leave. Still Uncle is nowhere to be seen. At last only the women and two men are left, and she watches as they struggle with the middle cross, lowering it onto the ground with the human burden.

CHAPTER TEN

Little Guy sat in biology class watching a colony of bees at work in an experimental observation hive. The hive was suspended in a special room by threaded rods from a metal overhead bar, and the bees entered and left through a transparent entrance tunnel from outside. The students watched through glass walls. Little Guy was fascinated by the constant, busy movement.

"The queen rules the hive," Mr. Waldrop told the class.

"How does she do that?" Little Guy asked.

"Expert communication," Mr. Waldrop replied. "Bees are extremely sensitive to odors, even more so than dogs. The queen releases chemicals called pheromones that act as a signal to the workers, stimulating them into specific behavior. Somehow the bees transfer the information to one another very rapidly through the hive."

Little Guy's eyes followed the worker bees racing between the cones behind the glass wall.

"What you're looking at here is the inner machinery of a complex living system," Mr. Waldrop went on, lecturing. "Here we are in 1960, but even thousands of years ago Plato and Socrates, ancient Greek philosophers, recognized that all societies revolve around strong leaders, like bees in a hive revolve around the queen." Mr. Waldrop dug in his pockets for a pencil and touched it to the glass edge encasing the hive. "See here, the queen's right in the center. And here," he moved the pencil in a circle on the glass, "here are her followers, the workers and the drones."

Rebecca listened when Little Guy described the hive to her that night. It was dark outside, but the kitchen was bright and warm, filled with the smells of chicken and corn and green peas, his favorite dinner. They sat together, just the two of them, at a small square table in the middle of the room; and she smiled to herself as he wolfed down his food and related how the queen controlled the workers and the drones.

"You won't ever be a worker or a drone, Little Guy," she said when he finished his story. "Take a lesson from the queen." She put down her fork and dabbed the corners of her mouth with a napkin as she spoke. Propping her elbows on the table, she leaned forward and lifted her coffee cup to her lips, cupping it in both hands as she gave Little Guy a hard look over the rim. "Listen to me, son. This is important."

"What's so important about bees?" he asked with surprise.

She sipped the coffee and put down the cup. "I'm talking about your future, about how power and leadership work in the world."

He gazed at her, still chewing on his food. "I don't get it."

"I don't want you to have to live in a place like this all your life." She looked around as she spoke. The furniture was secondhand and worn, the wall paint was chipped, the icebox rattled in the corner. "You have to make choices in life," she said, looking back at him. "You can be a leader, like that queen. Or you can be a drone. It's up to you."

His gaze trailed hers around the room, lighting on one shabby thing after the other. Little Guy put down his fork and nodded. Rebecca was pleased; she could see that she'd caught his attention. *He's so intelligent!* she thought.

"I want the best for you, Son." She rested on her arms, leaning toward him as she spoke. "You can have the things that really matter if you want them enough: money, influence, an easy life, success." *Not like me,* she reflected, fixing her eyes on her son. "We have one chance, you and I. It's all up to us."

Little Guy watched her. He was silent, listening. "Question everything," she went on. "Don't take anything for granted. Learn how other people think. Speak their language and communicate."

"Like the queen bee," Little Guy said, smiling. She nodded.

"Everyone has a currency, something they want. If you're smart, you'll learn to figure that out when you meet them."

"I can do that," Little Guy said, reaching over to smooth the skin on top of her hand. She saw the light that entered his eyes as he drew back and stood. "Wait right here," he said in an excited tone.

He disappeared and she could hear a drawer open and close in his bedroom. When he returned, flushed, he held out his hand and uncurled his fingers. There in the palm of his hand, loosely wrapped in old tissue paper, was a silver dollar shining up at her.

"I'm going to make us rich," he said in a low fierce tone, handing her the coin.

A thrill ran through Rebecca as she heard the resolve in his voice. She examined the silver dollar, wondering where he'd gotten it. "You're going to go far," she said, handing the coin back to him. "I feel it.

"And by the way," she tilted her head to the side and gave him a thoughtful look. "You're growing up. No more nick-names; no more *Little Guy* for you, Wesley Bright."

He'd stopped The Watch after about three months when he'd realized that the pain of seeing Rebecca without being a part of her life outweighed the pleasure of watching her. Leo's fleeting dream of marriage and a family seemed distant and illusory now. He had no siblings; his mother and father were both gone, and he was alone.

On the day he made the decision to cease The Watch, to let it go, he went into his church and sat in the front pew before the altar in silence, looking up at the cross. The year was not yet over, and for an hour he sat there wondering how many more mind-numbing years he had left to endure alone on this earth. Priesthood was a lonely, thankless profession.

Why did you let this happen? he demanded, staring at the cross. With the thought his chest constricted, and blood rushed to his head all at once, leaving him with a disembodied, disoriented feeling. At last he dropped his head and took a deep breath as his hands balled into fists on his thighs.

I have sacrificed for you, served you, put all of my energy and hope into walking the righteous path for you, and what have I gained? He glanced up at the cross. *Not a thing. I've lost my dream. I'll live a solitary life with no one beside me; no wife, no child, no one on earth who cares for me. I'll live in a rented apartment that looks like a cheap hotel room instead of a home. I gave up my job teaching at Julliard—a profession I loved—to preach in this miserable church to a small, disgruntled congregation, stupid people consumed by the effort it takes just to survive in this cold, hard city. I don't even know their names. And they don't know mine; they just drop in from time to time.*

Are you there? Are you listening?

He pounded his fist on his thigh. *Give me a sign, it's the least you can do. Are you really there?*

The empty church was silent.

Leo exhaled, slumping against the back of the pew. He gazed down at his hands with a sense of total isolation, listening to the muffled sounds of life outside continuing without regard for his grief.

A sigh broke the silence. It seemed to echo around him, startling Leo before he realized that it was his. He sat upright at this and glanced around the little church. There were the pictures he'd purchased for the walls; there was the table he'd found in a secondhand store in the Village, perfect to hold the prayer books and the hymnals by the door. There was the old lady's sweater, folded where he'd placed it on the back pew. She'd left it there last week. He twisted back toward the altar. There above the altar was the cross; and now, gazing at the cross, he felt the tension begin to ease from his muscles one by one, felt the anger dissolving, loosing him from its grip.

I made a vow. The thought as it came was painful. It seemed to crash through his mind. But it was a holy vow.

Seconds passed. At last Leo threw up his hands. Looking up at the cross, he announced in a faltering tone, "Well? Here I am Lord." The silence mocked him. A small stab of fear gripped his bowels. Forcing himself to ignore it, he raised his voice. "Here I am," he said again in a firm and steady tone.

But still, something had changed inside.

Wesley was outspoken, and as he grew older, he found he enjoyed challenging his teachers. He liked to surprise them, asking out-rageous, unexpected questions that made his class-mates laugh. At night he regaled his mother with stories of his exploits.

"You're a ball of fire, Wesley," Mother said, mirroring his exhilaration while she listened. "It's good to be unpredictable. You're special. A challenge. Anyone can be predictable."

His teachers gradually realized that the boy was a force to conciliate. It was easier to have him with them than against them.

So in gym class the coach usually appointed Wesley as captain of a team. Each day as the other boys perspired in the bleachers, waiting to be chosen and terrified of not being picked, Wesley took his time deciding who would play. Once Wesley was angry at Henry Clarke, and that week Henry found himself sitting on the sidelines day after day, waiting in vain from Monday through Thursday to be one of the boys. Fear was a powerful weapon, Wesley learned, and retribution was an exquisite perquisite of power.

At lunchtime on Friday of that week right before gym class, Wesley strutted into the cafeteria and found Henry waiting there for him. He frowned, but Henry motioned him over, smiling as he moved aside so that Wesley could take his place in the long lunch line. That afternoon Wesley chose him in the fourth slot for his team. Both negative and positive reinforcement were tools of power, Wesley realized when Henry beamed.

At noon on the following Monday, Wesley watched as Henry sat down beside him and pulled a hamburger from his lunchbox. Wesley's mother had fixed his lunch that day as well. Casually, Wesley suggested a trade, the hamburger for some healthy raw carrots that Mother had packed. Without hesitation Henry slid the hamburger across the table to Wesley and took the carrots. That afternoon Henry was the first boy chosen for Wesley's team.

The instant Wesley sat down for lunch the next day, Tuesday, Henry offered to trade his sandwich for vegetables again. Wesley took the sandwich without a word and watched Henry's eyes follow his first bite. Wesley thought about this while he chewed, and after a minute, he handed half of the sandwich back to Henry without a word. Henry's eyes shone as he thanked Wesley, and from that day on Henry referred to Wesley as his closest friend. *Noblesse oblige* engenders gratitude, another building block of power. It was currency, Mother might have said.

At the age of fifteen, Wesley joined the debate club and quickly learned how to take either side of an argument on just about any subject. He already knew there are no clear answers to most questions and that an answer depends on who's asking and how that person sees things. But now in the debate club he learned something new. It wasn't what you said that really mattered. People don't listen to the words anyway. Mother was right, as usual—he was a born leader. What mattered was charisma, making people like you.

Yes, he realized over time, charisma was the key. If he was confident and passionate on a subject, if he empathized with peoples' problems and cranked up the band to celebrate their little triumphs, then they liked him and listened to what he had to say. It occurred to him once that some might call him manipulative, but Wesley thought of it as communication. He was no brilliant scholar, but he studied hard and made good grades. Even in subjects that were cut-and-dried, like mathematics, he was so affable and self-assured that his teachers acquiesced.

On a day in February in Wesley's last year of high school, Rebecca heard the front door slam and knew that he was finally home. She smoothed her apron and patted her hair as she sat on the stool waiting for him to come into the kitchen where he would see the letter propped up on the counter facing the doorway. The embossed return address of Yale

University on the upper left-hand corner of the envelope told her this was the response to his application.

He strolled in, slapping his books on the counter, and leaned down to brush her forehead with a kiss as he swung past. "Hello, little mother," he said, opening the refrigerator door and reaching in.

She turned her face to hide the smile. "Hello, son," she said in a voice trembling with excitement. The envelope was a thick one. She was sure it was an acceptance.

As Wesley spun around with a carton of milk in his hand, he spotted the letter. His eyes lingered on it before he put the milk down on the counter, walked over, and picked it up. Tapping the envelope several times against the palm of his hand, he glanced at Rebecca. She drew a deep breath and nodded, watching as Wesley pressed his lips together in a grim smile, the way he used to do when he was forced to take vaccination shots in elementary school. Her fingers twisted together in her lap as he slit open the envelope and pulled out the wad of papers inside, unfolded them, and began to read.

When he looked up, his eyes shone. "Done," he announced, this time giving her a genuine smile. *"I'm in."*

With a joyous shout, Rebecca jumped to her feet, wrapped her arms around her son, and wept for the first time since the trial of Sam's murderers. She wept on his shoulder for all the years of hard work that provided Wesley with the right clothes, the good schools and tutors when he needed them, and museum privileges and club memberships—even when she'd had to do without—and the overtime and second jobs for money that she'd put into his college fund, so that he'd have the things he would have had if he'd had a father.

She shook with relief and joy as Wesley held her. The sacrifices were all worth it, and she'd long ago forgotten Leo Ransom.

Wesley gazed at a small red bird perched on a branch just outside the library window. Spring already! Hard to believe his second year at Yale was almost over. It seemed just yesterday that he'd arrived, a naive young freshman. He turned back to the book he'd been reading for the past four hours and rubbed his eyes with his thumb and forefinger. His head hurt when he thought of telling Mother what he'd decided to do with the rest of his life. It was Jesse, Sam's killer, that had given him the idea.

Over the years, occasionally Wesley had run into Jesse. The first time this occurred, a few years after the encounter in the park, Wesley was leaving the market on the corner two blocks down from his apartment, when he spotted Jesse. He was sitting on a stoop across the street, engrossed in a conversation with three other thugs with greased hair, dirty skin, and worn, tight fitting shirts and jeans.

Peering over the top of the grocery bag that he held, Wesley saw Jesse glance over at him with no sign of recognition. With a racing heart, Wesley shifted the bag to his other arm to obscure his face and hurried away down the block. But after a few more encounters, Wesley realized that he was safe; Sam's killer no longer recognized him. Wesley was taller now. He'd filled out some, he knew—looked different.

But still the old fear of Jesse lingered. As the years went by, Wesley made it a point to keep track of his whereabouts. Knowledge is protection, he knew. Once in a while there were rumors in the neighborhood mentioning Jesse in connection with a theft or vandalism or some petty extortion, but nothing ever seemed to stick for long. Jesse was a survivor, like a cockroach scurrying in and out of alleyways and dark buildings, through the urban sprawl of neighborhood stores, pawnshops, and bars, and the hotel across the street that Mother referred to as "the dump." At Yale, however, Wesley wasn't much worried. Jesse wasn't likely to leave the city; in fact, he doubted that Jesse'd ever left Manhattan.

About a year ago, when Wesley was home from his freshman year in college, he'd once again found himself walking down the street toward Jesse. This time the hard eyes coming toward him had seemed to register a flicker of recognition. Jesse had halted, staring at Wesley with a puzzled look. Before Wesley could move, Jesse reached out and grabbed his arm. But Jesse's grip was weak, and Wesley jerked his arm away with an unconscious flick of his hand at the place on his jacket that Jesse had touched. Jesse staggered and caught himself, and Wesley looked at him with surprise.

"How 'bout a couple dollars, man?" Jesse's voice was a low growl, abrasive, but he dropped his eyes and took a step back as he spoke.

Wesley felt a smile steal across his face, and for some reason he'd thought of the silver dollar his father had given him so many years ago.

"Hey." Jesse fiddled with the hem of his shirt, avoiding Wesley's eyes. "A couple bucks, I said."

At once a sense of power infused Wesley, surging through him from head to toe as he looked back with contempt at the man he'd feared for so long. He jammed his hand into his pocket and dug out a crumpled five dollar bill. "Sure," Wesley said, flipping the money onto the sidewalk at Jesse's feet as he turned and walked away with the confident stride that he'd perfected at Yale. It felt good to throw that five-dollar bill at Jesse's feet and walk away.

That same night he'd sat in the living room of his mother's apartment after she'd gone to her bed. The room was dark, lit only by a neon sign outside the hotel across the street that flashed on and off all night. What if Jesse had remembered him? What if he told someone about Sam . . . and him? *You said to let him go,* the words roiled his mind, and the muscles in the back of his neck grew tight. If Jesse told, his chances for success would be lost; all the years of Mother's work, and his, would be wasted.

But as he'd sat there in the darkness, he recalled the way Jesse scrambled for the money he'd thrown on the ground. Suddenly Wesley realized that Jesse would never be a problem. Mother was right, as usual. All you have to do is look for the right currency. Jesse's was obvious if it ever came to that.

But thinking of Jesse brought Leo Ransom to mind. What about Leo Ransom? He rubbed the muscles on the back of his neck, squeezing them between his fingers, trying to loosen the vise. He hadn't seen Leo in years, but he'd been at Sam's trial and had heard everything. What if Leo, like the judge, believed that Wesley was somehow responsible for his little brother's death?

The thought froze him. Who knew what Leo's currency would be? Leo was judgmental, as he recalled—to him things were black-and-white. What if Leo told someone that he'd helped to kill his little brother? He remembered Jesse's words as if the thug had spoken them just yesterday: "Did you say to let him go?" What if Leo told?

So what? He told himself. *It was not my fault!*

But still. Leo was a problem. Now, sitting in the Yale library, Wesley's eyes dropped to the book open before him on the heavy wooden table, the book on the work of Friedrich Nietzsche that had changed his life forever. The old hatred for Leo had surfaced as he'd read and realized how the problem could be solved.

The black letters on the stark white paper of the book seemed to rise from the page, reassuring him. Nothing's right or wrong, true or false, the philosopher said. Moral phenomena do not exist, only moral interpretation. People who teach otherwise, and institutions—like Leo's church—are dishonest. Get rid of them. Replace them.

He looked off through the window, past the tree and the bird, into the distance. It was so clear, so simple, really. Leo and Leo's God who wasn't there and the institution that sustained them both, Leo's church, and all the Leos of the world—the people who live through lies, the judge, his father—all of these must be destroyed. He'd show them all.

This is wrong, a small voice nagged inside.

He shook the thought away. The ideas were his and Nietzsche's, Nietzsche's and his. They'd always existed in some subliminal part of his mind, he supposed. And now, sitting in the library at Yale in the springtime, as he'd read the words of the philosopher, he'd finally understood. The words explained everything, freed him—allowed him to understand the hatred he'd nurtured through the years. As Nietzsche said, sometimes it's necessary to destroy in order to rebuild.

Wesley relaxed and let himself drift in the miasma of this astounding idea. The man who exposed the righteous liars of the world would be remembered forever; he would be revered for his courage, famous, maybe even rich. And the institution of Leo's church was the perfect vehicle for this. A cold breeze gusted through the window just then, reminding him that spring had only just begun, and he smiled at the irony of the thought.

As he'd expected, Mother wasn't pleased with his decision. "Philosophy?" she exclaimed when he told her. He hadn't mentioned Father Leo's church. "Why not law, or politics, or something useful?" The pitch of her voice ascended the scale as she spoke.

They'd just finished dinner, and Wesley looked across the table at his mother. "Philosophy's only a tool," he said in a consoling tone. He toyed with his fork, willing her to understand. "But the guy that *thinks,* the one that knows how to use *ideas,* he's the one with power. He sets the goals, and it seems to me that everyone else just carries his ideas out."

At her incredulous look he hurried on. "Think about it, Mother," he urged. "Generals, economists, judges, politicians, diplomats, priests, rabbis, mullahs. They're all just following the philosopher's road maps."

"Ah. And do you have a particular *idea* in mind?"

He heard the sarcasm and veiled his eyes. "I'll figure that out when the time is right. Ideas aren't written in stone. They have to fit the circumstances."

His mother closed her eyes, shook her head, rose, and began clearing the table. "You might want to think this over a bit, Son," she said, turning away from him. She set the dishes down on the counter with a loud clank. "People take a dislike to philosopher-kings. It's a thankless job. I think it was Socrates who said they'll stick your head on a pole. No one likes being told how to think."

At least not directly, Wesley thought. But he remained silent. Leo's face formed before him once again, then Sam's, and angrily he forced the images away. He knew that he was right—realized now exactly what it was that he must do.

God! he demanded. *Where were you on the day that Sam died?*

Where? Well, Nietzsche has declared that God is dead.

She'd tried to understand Wesley's decision to go into the church after he'd graduated from Yale and then dragged himself through that seminary. The Apostolic Church, of all things! Leo Ransom's church. Of course, on the other hand, it had kept him out of Vietnam.

But, honestly, there was no sense in it, no money in being a priest. A priest! What an archaic word that was. Rebecca sighed with exasperation and pressed the doorbell. It had taken forever to get a taxi, and the driver who barely spoke English had blamed it on the gas shortage, and she was tired and cold and hungry. When Wesley opened the door, she snapped, "This country's in a mess, Son. Here we are in 1973, and I can't even find a taxi. They're all waiting in lines for gasoline. If you'd gone into politics like I told you, instead of seminary, you could fix it."

He laughed, kissed her on the cheek, and pulled her inside.

"And for God's sake, Wesley," Rebecca said, thumping a book she clutched in one hand. "What are you trying to do, *end* your career?" She tossed the book onto a small wooden table in the hallway as she slid out of her coat. Wesley, dressed in blue jeans topped by a black shirt with a stiff clerical collar around his neck, took the coat and hung it on a hook near the door with a sigh.

He glanced at the book, then said mildly, "I expect it will be a success, Mother."

"Humph." She walked past him into the kitchen where she opened drawers, pulling out spoons, coffee, filters, sugar. "Where's the cream?" She spun around, looking for the refrigerator. Wesley had moved into this apartment just yesterday.

"A wife would certainly be a help," she muttered as she yanked open the door to an almost empty refrigerator. Picking up the small carton of cream, she closed the door and turned to her son. "What in the world do you live on, anyway? There's not a thing to eat in that refrigerator."

Wesley stood in the doorway and rolled his eyes. He took the coffee and filter from her hand and steered her to the table where he pulled out a chair and gently pushed her into it.

"I don't need a wife, Mother." His tone was low and soothing, and Rebecca slumped, settling into the chair.

"And I won't let you be my maid." He glanced at her as he turned back to the counter, poured water into a glass coffeepot, and switched on the machine. Then he turned around to face her and leaned back on his elbows, waiting for the coffee to perk.

"And as for the book, well," he studied the ceiling, "I have to speak up, come what may. I've never shrunk from a battle on principle yet." When he looked back at Rebecca, he lifted his chin just a bit.

"You're very brave. But I worry that you're reckless," his mother sighed, removing her hat. She placed it on the table beside her and folded her hands in her lap.

"As a modern philosopher, I think that it's my duty to redirect Christianity, to bring it into the new age." The coffeepot gave a burp, and he turned to inspect it as he spoke, inhaling the fragrance with half-closed eyes. Columbian. Only the best.

"I *want* to challenge authority and hypocrisy and give candid answers to questions about the old fundamentalist teachings," he went on. "That's the *sine qua non* of my work, if you like."

Rebecca pursed her lips and frowned. "What does the bishop say?"

"About my book?" Wesley pulled some cups out of the cupboard overhead and set them down near the coffeepot. "Just what you'd expect from a bureaucrat. After all, I'm an upstart challenging the source of his power." He gave his mother an amused look.

Rebecca narrowed her eyes and grimaced. Perhaps Wesley was self-destructive.

"Don't worry," he added, seeing her expression. "There's not much the bishop can do. I'm entitled to my own opinion, and I'm not alone. It's the correct intellectual position. The debate over Christian thought started over a hundred years ago with the German skeptics. *Most* thinking people today understand that Bible stories such as Jesus rising from the dead are childish."

He poured the cups to the brim and brought them to the table. Placing one beside Rebecca and his on the other side, he sat down facing her. "Besides, the media likes me. Controversy stirs things up." He chuckled.

He was right, of course. Rebecca studied her son from beneath her lids as she sipped the coffee. Although she admired his courage—she had taught him to stand up for himself, to question everything—his constant David-and-Goliath battles still made her edgy.

She shifted her gaze to a serene picture on the wall behind him of a wide beach with sand dunes and a white picket fence standing sentry against a ruffle of bright green sea grass. A gentle surf rolled in, and far out the smooth water gleamed in the sunlight. Suddenly she was almost overcome with fatigue. There were no people in the picture. That was good. A week at the Jersey shore would be nice. She could almost smell the salt air. Maybe she'd do that in a few months, now that Wesley was established and it was no longer necessary for her to work so hard.

Yes. A week at the beach might be just the thing. The thought warmed her, and she began to feel better.

"When the reporter asked him for a statement," Wesley was saying, "the bishop hemmed and hawed. His only response was that such things are matters of individual faith. *Faith!"* He made a wry face. "That's what Leo Ransom told me when I was a kid, and last I heard he was poor as a church mouse."

Rebecca started and the Jersey shore disappeared. Leo Ransom, again. "Well," she said after a moment as she stirred her coffee, "that's what makes you different, Son. You're a leader, not a follower."

Wesley nodded. "Just think of the suffering that could have been avoided if Christianity, or most religions for that matter, dealt with reality instead of mythical lotteries, or hell and brimstone." He meditated on this idea for a moment, raising the cup to his lips, enjoying the aroma and warmth of the coffee as it slid down his throat, then shook his head. "This isn't an abstract problem, you know. Think of the horrors of the Inquisition, the Crusades. Can you even *count* the number of people who've been tortured, maimed, and killed in the name of God?"

Not to mention *in spite* of God, like Sam.

His mother arched her eyebrows. "This little book is going to touch some nerves, Son. You've challenged every core belief of the church—the creed, the divinity of Jesus, even the authority of the clergy." She inhaled, then smiled at Wesley, thinking how smart, how *brave* he was, but wishing that just once in a while things could be a little easier.

She picked up her cup, took a few sips of coffee, and set it down again. "Well, I certainly hope the Holy Spirit's in a good mood when he reads it," she added in a dry tone.

"U'mmm," Wesley drawled. "I refuse to worry about ghosts until someone answers the big question: why does evil exist in the first place? In fact," he added without thinking, "I'd like to know why that old Spirit wasn't around when Sam fell from the roof." The instant the words slipped through his lips, he regretted them.

His mother's eyes grew wide. She stared at her son.

"Sorry," he muttered as he rose and picked up the coffee cups. "I don't know what made me say that." He set the cups in the sink with a clatter, then glanced at her over his shoulder. Her back was stiff and straight, and she didn't turn to him with her usual smile.

He bent and whispered into her ear. "You mustn't worry, Mother. I know what I'm doing." When he straightened, his voice was firm, full of determination. Mother admired strong convictions.

"In my mind it's a question of integrity," he said, resting his hand on her shoulder and looking down at her. For the first time he noticed strands of gray in her auburn hair. "Christian doctrine has passed the *sell-by* date," he went on when she was silent. "It's stale and irrelevant. Clergymen like Leo Ransom have used promises and fear to subdue the credulous long enough."

"You *are* the clergy, Son!"

He lifted his hand, walked around the table to his chair, and sat facing her. "It's a new day. I intend to replace the old myths—no, *lies,*" he corrected, thinking of Sam. "I intend to replace them with a compassionate viewpoint that honors *all* human needs and desires." His eyes glittered and he looked away. "But first the old order has to go."

Rebecca's throat grew thick. "That all sounds fine," she murmured. "But what happens then?" Wesley had always been self-confident, certain that he was right about things, but this confrontation with the bishop seemed a bit over the top. She tried to ignore a tingle of apprehension. This was the extreme side of Wesley that she'd always chosen to ignore.

"I'll rebuild." Wesley grinned and crinkled his eyes. "It takes courage to stand or fall on convictions, Mother. You've taught me that."

Rebecca sighed again. She was beginning to hate these kinds of conversations.

The book was a howling success. It hit best-seller lists within the first few weeks of publication. On talk shows Wesley, the flamboyant and outrageous priest, was witty, charming, smart, sometimes funny, and viewers liked him. With his casual demeanor and nonchalant grin, he was easy to like. He seemed to understand a guy's, or a gal's, problems in their day-to-day battles with the establishment.

Theological hold outs who believed in the old conservative Christian teachings were taken aback by his glib answers and warm personality when they were booked as guests on the same television and radio shows. By contrast to the young rebel priest, traditional biblical scholars came across on camera as condescending, intolerant, and boring. They all agreed that Wesley Bright was a formidable opponent.

He was so, well, so *likable.*

CHAPTER ELEVEN

Less than a week was left before the archbishop had to return to *Target Zero,* Paul Johnson's show, to discuss the Shroud of Turin with Jonathan Marley. Emily frowned as she reread her unfinished report on the computer monitor screen. She'd spent hours trying to get in touch with Leo Ransom, who had yet to return her call. Frustrated, she hit the print button and whirled her chair toward the window, waiting for the first draft to slide out of the desktop printer.

She mulled over the information she'd collected. Even if the Shroud was a fraud, Emily mused, it was a good one. She gazed at taxis, trucks, and cars dodging pedestrians crossing the street below. Wind whipped the colorful flags just across Fifth Avenue at Rockefeller Center. A tired-looking woman herded a small group of children into the plaza. Probably an exhausted teacher.

She jumped as the printer clicked off the last page, turned, picked up the report, and slapped it down on the desk as she came to a decision. She would take a look at the Shroud.

The exhibition had been sold out for weeks, but the archbishop's office was provided with several complimentary tickets. After obtaining one of these from the archbishop's secretary, Margaret Brown, Emily hurried out the front doors and down the cathedral stairs, turning left when she reached the sidewalk. She glanced at her watch. It was already almost one o'clock as she started off, walking down Fifth Avenue.

The day was beautiful, sunny and brisk, but not yet cold. Emily enjoyed the bustle of noon traffic as she hurried along, conscious that it had been a long time since she'd allowed herself the luxury of walking anywhere for pleasure. Time. Time was always the problem. When she came to Central Park, she crossed the avenue and headed down the tree-shaded sidewalk toward the art museum.

As she approached the massive stone building, Emily slowed her stride when she saw that a line of people waiting to get in wound down the street from the entrance. On the sidewalk to her left, artists displayed their work on easels and folding tables—pictures and figurines and toys in bright, cheerful colors. A whimsical watercolor caught her eye, and she stopped to examine it. When finally the line to enter the museum grew shorter, she took a place at the end. Still, it was almost twenty minutes before Emily reached the cavernous entrance hall.

Once inside, a clerk at the information counter directed her to a uniformed attendant standing near a large group gathered for the start of the afternoon viewing of the exhibition. The young man glanced at the archdiocese seal on

Emily's pass and motioned her to follow him past them and up the stairs to the second floor.

"Take your time," he whispered when they reached the door of the dimly lit exhibit rooms. "This is a private viewing. You have about forty-five minutes before the afternoon exhibition begins."

"Thanks," Emily said with a twinge of guilt as she looked at the mass of people patiently waiting below. They'd probably had tickets for months. The attendant steered her through a large dark room filled with people who appeared to be praying or meditating. Preparing themselves for the visit to the Shroud perhaps?

"Do you want to stop here first?" the attendant asked.

Emily shook her head, and she was ushered forward into a second room. Here various large photographs of the ancient cloth were displayed throughout. To her left another shorter line moved slowly toward an inner chamber where she supposed the Shroud was displayed. Emily could see the farther room was even darker than the one through which she'd just passed.

Before joining the line, Emily turned to her right and stopped to read a sign near the door. Special lighting was necessary to protect the ancient cloth from further deterioration, she read. That explained the dim lighting in the next room. Although the Shroud was usually stored in a vacuum-sealed container to protect it from oxidation, light and time and the environment had already taken a toll, and there was concern that in a few years the cloth would disintegrate.

Emily walked slowly past the series of photographs until she came to one that caught her attention. The image of a man's fat, distorted face was spread across the width of a large sheet of paper. An explanation was printed below the picture.

The image on the Shroud could not have been formed by an ordinary contact process, she read. The face is three-dimensional, the same view one has when looking in a mirror. Emily looked up at the photographs illustrating the effect of draping a cloth over a face and pressing it around the side to the hairline and against blood marks. The image on the cloth resulting from this contact mechanism was distorted, grotesque; broad, flat, and spread out.

Now Emily studied the photographic negative of the Shroud. The contrast was dramatic. The image was proportionate, like a reflection in a mirror, and not at all distorted.

"If it's a forgery, it's certainly clever. Simply wrapping the cloth around the face and pressing doesn't work. And yet there it is."

Emily turned her head to the speaker who stood beside her. His look caught hers and held it for a split second before he smiled, as if surprised. He looked about thirty-five years old, Emily guessed. His light brown hair was neatly parted, brushed back on the sides. When he smiled down at her, she saw that the smile began in his eyes.

"I suppose the image was painted," she said.

He shook his head. "Extensive research has proved that's not the case." With a nod, he moved to the back of the line waiting to enter the room that held the Shroud. Emily glanced back at the picture, then followed. He stepped aside, motioning her in front of him.

"Thanks," she said. He was a handsome man. Her head reached to his chin as she stood beside him. He wore tennis shoes and blue jeans, with a cotton shirt and a tweed jacket that looked slightly worn. She registered the fact that his clothes were well cut, made of good fabric.

"Martin Allen," he said, extending his hand.

"Emily Scott." They shook hands, and he held onto hers for an instant before releasing it.

The line began to move forward, and Emily stepped through a door into the hushed, quiet inner chamber. At the far side of the room hanging about fifteen feet above a raised platform was a glass case containing the Shroud of Turin. It was illuminated by spotlights mounted on the walls but seemed almost to glow, as if lit from within. On each side of the glass case, the detailed negative image of the Shroud was projected in blue light upon the wall.

"The glass is bulletproof. The Shroud was in a fire a few years ago, and the firemen had a hard time getting it out because of that," Martin whispered. "I understand that arson was suspected."

From across the room while still at the end of the slow moving line, Emily peered at the Shroud. She could see that the worn cloth, faded to a dull, straw-colored yellow, was stitched to a white lining. The whole thing was draped length-wise over a purple backdrop. "It certainly looks fragile."

"It is. We're lucky to see it," Martin said as they moved closer to the display. "It's usually kept hidden away from human eyes at the Turin Cathedral in Italy. There've only been a few exhibitions since its discovery in medieval times."

"Discovery?" Emily asked, as they inched forward. "Do you mean to say, manufacture?"

"No," he hesitated, adding, "but that's another story."

She had reached the glass case now and stopped, staring at the shining cloth with a sudden, unexpected feeling of awe. The Shroud display was stark against the darkness of the room. She moved closer, leaning slightly over the velvet inner rope marker to stare at the faded, but now familiar, image. The image seen by the naked eye was fainter than she'd expected, difficult to make out. But, while it wasn't nearly as clear as the photographic negative, by standing back against the outer rope, she could begin to make out the form of a naked man bearing marks that might be blood on the face and circling his forehead, on his wrists and feet, and his right side. She breathed in a long shallow breath and held it as she stared, shifting her gaze between the original cloth and the detailed negative. The Shroud had the aura of a living thing in the hushed, dark place.

"How in the world was this image created?" she whispered after a moment.

"Don't know. That's the big question," Martin said. "It's not painted. It's like something out of a time capsule, isn't it?"

Emily nodded, transfixed.

Feet shuffled impatiently behind them. Emily started, then turned away.

Martin paused to wait for Emily just outside the exhibition room. She composed herself, then gave him a sideways look. "Do you believe the Shroud is real?" she asked.

"Oh yes," he said. "I believe it's real, all right."

She remained silent while they worked their way downstairs through the crowd to the front exit doors of the museum, then Martin put his hand under her elbow as they started down the steps toward the sidewalk. The glare of reflected sunlight blinded her after the darkness inside, and she found herself squinting.

"Can I buy you a cup of coffee?" Martin asked, gesturing toward the Stanhope Hotel across the street. The Stanhope's sidewalk café, shaded by a green-and-white-striped canopy, seemed to be doing brisk business in the lovely weather.

"Sure," Emily said. "If you'll tell me what's convinced you that the Shroud of Turin isn't a medieval forgery."

"It's a deal."

They waited for the light to change, then crossed to the Stanhope. A waiter led them to a table in the corner of the patio closest to the museum and took orders for coffee. Outdoor heaters warmed the café, and Emily shrugged out of her coat. Martin reached over and arranged it across the back of the chair, then leaned back with a sigh. "It feels good to sit down," he said.

Glasses clinked and voices hummed around them while they waited for the waiter to return. They chatted about the weather and the traffic and two small white puppies that romped past with an elderly matron pulling back on their leads. Once Emily's eyes met Martin's briefly, and before she glanced away, Emily saw that in the outdoor light his were an extraordinary color, as bright green as new grass in Central Park in the springtime.

When the waiter arrived with a small silver tray holding two cups of coffee, they stopped talking while he whisked a crisp white cloth across the table and set the tray carefully down before them. Emily added cream and sugar to her coffee, but Martin tipped his hand over the cup and shook his head.

"Black's fine for me," he said. His eyes caught hers again, and this time it was a moment before she shifted her gaze away from him.

Emily stirred her coffee, then picked it up and took a sip, watching people entering and leaving the art museum across the street. This man, Martin, was intriguing, she thought, conscious of his eyes on her. "How is it that you know so much about the shroud?" she finally asked.

"It's a fascinating relic from a scientific standpoint," he answered. "I've kept up with it for years." He picked up his own cup and took a sip. "Just a quirky hobby, I suppose," he added.

"What is it that you do?" Emily asked.

"I'm a physicist," he said. "I teach at Boston University. Came in for the day especially for this exhibition."

Emily set her coffee down and stared. "A physicist!" she exclaimed. "That's surprising. I'd have never guessed."

"Why's that?" he asked with a mild look.

She blinked and shook her head. "It surprises me that a scientist, of all people, could believe the Shroud is anything but a fake. It contradicts everything we know about the physical world. If the thing isn't a forgery, then what is it?" She smiled to take the sting out of her words. "A miracle?"

Martin laughed. "I hate to disillusion you, Emily. But we scientists accept as fact things that we don't understand all the time—human consciousness, quantum particles, black holes, cold dark matter, the opposite sex." He wiggled his eyebrows and Emily laughed.

"Seriously," he added. "It's protocol to reason from the unknown. Just look at mathematics. Most interesting calculations are based on unproven hypotheses."

"Still," Emily objected, "we have to base conclusions on *something* other than speculation."

"I agree with you," he said, taking a gulp of the coffee as his eyes followed the traffic on the avenue. "But I believe the evidence that's available today suggests this is a cloth that was actually wrapped around a real, crucified man; and since the radiocarbon tests are questionable, it's possible that this occurred as early as the first century."

The archbishop's scowl rose in her mind. "But what good is evidence that leads to a supernatural conclusion?" Emily asked.

Martin glanced at her with amusement. "Are you suggesting that we hide our eyes and refuse to examine information because it leads to conclusions that we don't understand? Do you realize that no one, *no one,"* he emphasized, leaning forward, "understands how human consciousness works, not even the simple things like memories triggered by the fragrance of a rose, or love, or mathematical intuition?"

He shook his head. "But we can't ignore these things. You know the old saying: don't throw the baby out with the bathwater."

"I understand that," Emily said, brushing off his words with a little shrug. "But if the image on the Shroud wasn't created by a contact process, and—as you seem to believe—wasn't painted, then something *very* strange occurred." She drummed her fingers on the table for a moment, then ran her forefinger around the delicate edge of the porcelain cup and added, "Dead people don't usually leave lifelike images on their burial clothes. And they don't generally rise from the dead either."

Martin's eyes twinkled. "Perhaps science will come up with an explanation for the Shroud someday." He seemed to enjoy sparring. "But sensory perception can't be our standard. Science doesn't limit exploration only to things that can be seen, or heard, or touched. I've taught physics for over fifteen years, and I've yet to actually *see* a neutrino, but I know that they exist."

Emily gave him a blank look.

"It's a quantum particle so *infinitesimally* small that it can't be directly detected, even under the strongest equipment and best conditions," Martin explained. "They're like ghosts—detected once in a while by sparks of light given off in collisions with other particles in underground accelerators." He lounged back and fiddled with a silver spoon beside his coffee cup, tapping it lightly on the table as he spoke.

"And yet," he went on, "there's probably not a physicist in the world who would argue that the neutrino doesn't exist. In fact," he paused, studying Emily, "recent studies in Japan have confirmed not only that the neutrino is a form of matter—that it actually has mass—but also that it can zip through a trillion miles of lead without displacing a single atom."

"How is that possible?" Emily asked in a skeptical tone, wondering where a trillion miles of lead might be found.

"We don't yet understand it." Martin shrugged and looked away. He picked up the spoon, rubbing the smooth silver with his thumb in an absentminded manner as he gave her a sideways look. "But I'd say that makes the resurrection and the Shroud sound pretty tame."

"Yes, but . . ."

"If anything," he said, replacing the spoon, "scientific knowledge today raises all sorts of unanswered questions, things that we can't explain." With a half smile for Emily, he added, "At least not yet. And maybe never."

He held her eyes for a beat, and then she frowned, turning her attention to an inspection of the dregs of coffee in the bottom of her cup. "The question I'm most interested in is how the image was formed on the cloth." She watched him under lowered lashes. "Why do you think that it wasn't painted?"

"I have a friend that can give you a more informed answer to that one," he replied. He fished a pen from his jacket pocket, pulled a paper napkin from across the table and began to write. "Her name is Amy Roper and here's her phone number." When he'd finished writing, he handed the napkin to Emily. "She's an artist. Sort of a nut, actually," he said with a grin. "But you'll like her. I think she's actually tried to recreate the Shroud image herself but found it impossible to replicate."

"Great. Thanks." Emily took the napkin from him and, with a glance at the name, folded it into small squares, thinking of the unfinished report and the archbishop's rapidly approaching interview. "I wonder if she'd see me tomorrow," she said, tucking the address into an inside pocket of her purse. "Could you give her a call to mention my name? I'd appreciate your help."

"Sure," Martin said. He reached into his pocket, pulled out a five-dollar bill, and set it down on the table, anchoring it with the small cream pitcher. Pushing back his chair, he stood waiting.

Emily drank the last of the coffee and set the cup down on the table as she rose. Martin helped her with her coat and steered her back through the noisy, crowded tables, past the waiter leaning against a post at the entrance, out onto the sidewalk. "I'm curious," he said as she halted, fumbling with the buttons on the coat. "What's your interest in the Shroud if you're convinced it's a fake?"

Emily told him about her job and the research she was doing for the archbishop.

Martin nodded. "I read one of his books a few years ago. Didn't agree with it, I have to say, but he's certainly popular."

Emily was surprised. She seldom met anyone that wasn't impressed with the archbishop. "He's a busy man," she said, giving the buttons all of her attention. The sun was going down, and away from the heaters on the terrace, she felt cold. "The research is for an appearance next week on the Paul Johnson show. The archbishop had no intention of becoming involved with a discussion of the Shroud. But he's committed now."

When she came to the top coat button, Emily paused and glanced up. "Public interest is overwhelming; people are arriving from all over the country to see the exhibition." She shrugged, smiling. "Which, of course, is precisely what the Vatican wanted."

"Why do you say that?" he asked. Reaching over, he fastened the remaining button, fingered the collar, and dropped his hands.

"Thanks," she said, disconcerted. She stepped back, struggling to remember what it was she'd been ready to say. Oh yes, the Vatican. "I suspect they hope the exhibition will boost morale."

"You might be right," Martin said, turning to scan traffic as he spoke. "From what I've read, it would take a crisis to convince the Vatican to exhibit the Shroud outside of Turin." He glanced at his watch before looking back at Emily with a wan smile. "I wish I could stay longer," he murmured, "but I need to find a taxi to LaGuardia. Come with me, and we'll drop you off."

Emily shook her head. "I'll walk," she said. "It's not far."

He stuck his hands in his jeans and jangled some coins. "I'd really like to see you again," he said.

Her heart skipped a beat. "I'd like that too." She hesitated, thinking of Wesley's schedule, "But, time is a problem just now." She smiled at him with regret. "Archbishop Bright's interview with Paul Johnson is important, and we need to prepare for it. My schedule doesn't leave much room for a social life until that's over."

He seemed to weigh her answer. "Okay," he said, after an instant. "Then let me walk with you."

"Won't you miss your plane?"

"It's a shuttle. I'll get the next one."

Twilight stole across the city as they strolled down the busy avenue. Street lamps flickered on, and the air grew colder when the sun disappeared at last behind the buildings. It was easy to talk to Martin, she reflected. They both loved dogs—he had one, a yellow Labrador—and traveling, and music, especially light jazz. She told him about her mother's piano, how she used to play and wanted to take up lessons again.

"Just go for it," he said.

"I will. But I don't have time right now." She caught his look and laughed, feeling a little flustered. "It's just a temporary problem," she said, surprising herself with the words.

"I bet you've been saying that for years."

When she shifted her purse onto her other shoulder, Martin caught her hand and held it. His was warm and large and covered hers. There was strength in his touch. Emily gave him a covert look, but he caught her eyes and with a smile, pulled her arm through his.

Martin glanced again at his watch when they reached the Pierre Hotel and stopped under the awning near the front entrance. Down the street the cathedral bells chimed the hour—six o'clock. Across the avenue near the bubbling fountain in the Grand Army Plaza, carriage horses stamped their feet in the cold air, feeling frisky as they waited for evening tourists.

"I suppose I should go, Emily." He turned to her, releasing her arm. "It's easier to catch a cab at a hotel this time of day."

"Yes." Emily said, suddenly feeling the cold again, wishing that he could stay. His eyes held hers.

"It's rush hour, so . . ."

"Yes."

"I'm glad we met this way. Maybe it's a miracle." He gave her a mischievous look and she laughed.

"I'd really like to see you again," he said. "Soon." His eyebrows rose, and he mugged a funny face. "You have to eat, don't you? Take a short break, and I'll come into town one night next week. What about dinner on Wednesday?"

Don't think. Don't analyze. No time. "Can't do it," she said before she could change her mind. "I'll be working Wednesday night getting ready for . . ." She stopped herself and looked up at him, conscious that she wanted him to understand. "I don't have any choice," she said in a low voice. "Just let me get the archbishop past this show. It's a big one—a nationwide audience."

A flicker of something, maybe disappointment, crossed his face before he looked past her, gesturing to the Pierre doorman. "I'll make a point to watch it," he said.

She nodded, wishing he'd asked about Friday night instead. "It's on the World News channel."

While the doorman stepped into the street with his whistle, signaling a taxicab, Martin wrote his home number on the back of a business card, and Emily did the same. She handed her card to him, wondering if she'd ever hear from him again. Why didn't he ask about Friday night?

"I'll call," he said, as a yellow cab swerved out of the traffic and stopped alongside them. He trailed his fingers across her cheek, tipped up her chin, gave her a long look, and turned. With a tip for the doorman, he slid into the back seat of the cab.

Emily waved and walked on, trying to ignore the vague depression that seeped through her, willing herself not to turn around. She stepped down from the curb and crossed the street, gazing at the backs of a young couple ambling along in the evening stream of pedestrians. Their heads bent close together as they talked and laughed, and a lonely feeling engulfed her. She turned and looked back, but if Martin's taxi was still there, traffic made it impossible to see from where she stood.

Wesley stared unseeing at the briefing report he held in his hand. He'd picked it up from Emily's desk. This appeared to be only a working draft, but he was bored and took it back to his office to pass the time. There was a quaint little bistro down the street, and he'd decided to treat Emily to dinner. He'd even had his secretary make reservations for two, ignoring her curious look. But when he'd walked down the hall to Emily's office to surprise her, he found she wasn't there. He shuffled the pages of the report irritably at the thought. Margaret had told him she'd gone to see the exhibition at the Met when he'd come back to his office out of sorts. That was hours ago.

She went to see the Shroud, of all things!

He felt a stir at the thought of Emily, and this took him by surprise. For a moment the usual street noise faded, and the report dissolved as he let himself picture the two of them sitting together in a booth at the bistro. Soft music plays in the background. Candles flicker on the table. Then he forced his eyes back to the pages of the report.

It was certainly too late for dinner now. Anyway, he reminded himself with a resigned feeling, the second interview with Paul Johnson was coming up, and he needed to organize his thoughts. But as his eyes scanned the report, the archbishop sighed at the detailed discussion of such things as the radiocarbon dating. Emily confirmed that the samples tested by the three laboratories for the Vatican in 1988 were cut from a single site on the bottom left-hand corner of the shroud, believed to have been rewoven in the medieval period. She'd included results of numerous tests with long names to support this conclusion—such things as pyrolgsis-mass spectrometry results and microscopic and microchemical observations—he was sure she'd thrown these details in just to annoy him. The report concluded that this sampled area had been dyed to match the older, original cloth, and that unlike the original it contained cotton fibers.

In addition, she added, results of chemical analysis of samples from the original cloth compared to the Dead Sea Scrolls linen and other ancient linens around that date, indicating that the Shroud was much older than the medieval period. His blood pressure rose when he read the next sentence. "Stay away from this issue on the Paul Johnson show," she wrote. "The radiocarbon test results have probably been discredited."

What nonsense! He sniffed, tossing the papers on the desk before him.

Wesley rested his forehead in the palm of his hand for a moment. What a long day this had been. Emily. Now why was he thinking of her again! He hoped she wasn't getting *off track*—his protégé, no, she was more.

He lifted his head and grunted, thinking about that. Recently Emily had been distracted by the nonsense over the Shroud. He resolved to talk to her about this. He sometimes worried that she seemed to have no social life, but then it was true that he needed her full attention. Of course, Emily had things in perspective and understood the importance of his work. And he had to admit he was becoming quite dependent on her.

Emily wants what I want, he thought with satisfaction. It was gratifying to suddenly be recognized everywhere he went, to have people listen with all their attention when he uttered a word to them, to go home in a limousine, to have someone like Miss H to anticipate his every need, to be able to buy almost anything he wanted, when he wanted it. And most important, to know that when he was gone, he'd be remembered—probably revered, if he was to be honest with himself.

I'm on the brink of phenomenal success, he reflected, dropping the report onto the desk, *on the verge of fame, wealth, and power.* At last count the church had eighty million members in the United States who accepted everything taught by their leaders, especially himself, almost without question. He smiled and the thought slipped in: *Machievelli didn't have a thing on the church.*

Maybe one day he'd share all of this with Emily. This idea brought a warm glow. It had been a long time since he'd cared for anyone—on a personal level, that is—not since Mother died. For all the years since, he'd been alone. He'd never gotten used to the fact that she was gone, that Rebecca lay in a box beneath the ground like Sam, that he'd never see her again, never bask in her approval, never have her there to listen to his plans.

But now, maybe now there would be Emily. He'd have someone once again to care for him, perhaps even to love him. He was surprised at how pleasant this idea was when it came to him. Wesley leaned back in the chair and clasped his hands behind his head, imagining Emily sitting across the breakfast table in the morning, lying beside him in bed at night. And why not? *We may have a finite number of years on this earth,* he mused, *but I'm going to make the most of them. Why not?* he asked himself again. *What else is there?*

After a moment he shook off the reverie and picked up the draft report on the Shroud. Enough daydreaming! He'd save those thoughts for later on, after the Paul Johnson show was behind him.

As he began to read again, his irritation returned. Snatching a piece of paper from his desk, he scribbled a note to Emily that she was missing the point. "You seem to be fixated on details supporting the validity of the Shroud," he wrote. "But all the scientific mumbo jumbo in the world isn't going to transform this fraud—the Shroud of Turin—into a thing worthy of serious debate. It's nonsense, a forgery."

He paused and tapped the pen against his lower lip. Everything the Shroud stood for was anathema to him—the silly story of the resurrection, the woolly headed dependence people developed on literal interpretations of the New Testament—on all Scripture for that matter. He'd really been taken by surprise at the recent interest this exhibition had generated. A sliver of ice slipped through his bowels at the thought and twisted.

Could he hold his own against the Shroud? His people—he thought of them that way, the members of the Apostolic

Church—had the natural human desire to believe in a personal God who intervened in their lives, changed history, an extrinsic being familiar with each one of them, every little sparrow, and so on.

He snorted, then turned sober. Religion, philosophy, fear—whatever you wanted to call it—the childish narcissism that we will all be rewarded with eternal life and happiness if we adhere to certain moral guidelines—this was the weakness exploited by religion for thousands of years, exploited by the Apostolic Church, Leo Ransom's church.

Wesley dropped his head into his hands again. His head hurt, and a drum beat away inside, muffled but relentless—distant but inevitable. His neck muscles tightened as he waited for the dull, inner pounding to grow, as it had since he was a small boy. Suddenly he felt a chill, recalling his ordination as a bishop years ago, that point in the service where he'd had to acknowledge out loud the apostolic succession of the clergy—the idea that each priest or pastor descends in spirit from the fisherman of Galilee, Peter, the apostle Jesus called his "rock." Wesley winced as pain shot up the back of his neck. That was the first time he'd realized that the throbbing sounded just like drums.

The church had been so silent when it happened! The choir was mute; nothing broke the quiet. Not one child cried. No one coughed or snuffled or shuffled prayer books or hymnals, almost as if someone had planned it that way. Horns and sirens outside had seemed to disappear in the strange silence.

Then, the anointing bishop had asked the ancient question taken from the Gospel of John. The bishop's voice rang out through the great cathedral, tolling like bells as he repeated the words of Jesus: *"Simon Peter, lovest thou me?"*

With an inexplicable feeling of dread, he'd raised his head to answer. It was then he'd recognized the beating drums, faint but insistent and familiar somehow as if they called to him. The cadence, a mere pulse that stirred the air, had seemed to throb all around him, or was the sound inside of him instead? He'd grown cold and glanced around from beneath his lowered lids, but no one else had seemed to hear the drums or feel the sudden chill.

After an instant he'd turned his face back to the cross, and he'd bowed his head before it, the same cross he'd later removed from the altar when he was made archbishop. He smiled now, thinking of it. But then he'd given the answer just as required, as he'd rehearsed and sworn to do.

He shook off the recollection and tried to ignore the pounding, throbbing headache. The cathedral bells tolled and he looked up. Six o'clock. Emily must not be coming back tonight. Wesley finished writing his note, then picked it up, determined to drop it on her desk on his way home. He'd rest for the remainder of the evening, put this whole thing about the Shroud of Turin out of his mind.

As he rose to leave, he glanced down at Emily's report once again and grimaced. Facts! Whatever happened to such things as self-examination, personal satisfaction, spiritual experiences—things that make a difference in our lives?

CHAPTER TWELVE

His eyes sweep the walls of Jerusalem, then to the top of the hill where only two men and three women remain with the crucified prisoners. Dead. The word is heavy in his mind. He holds back, hidden as he waits; he knows these people well. Although he worries they'll spot him, he remains where he is, watching. He's seeking a sign of life, a signal that the prisoner has defeated death, as he had promised.

Suddenly a quick, small movement to the right and below him on the hill catches his eye. He turns his head just in time to see Hanna rising from behind a small brown bush. Hanna! He'd forgotten the child. He sucks in his breath and follows her gaze. She's staring at a pack of dogs that he'd not noticed before. She backs slowly away from them, then suddenly bolts toward the top of the hill, running. He starts forward, then seeing that the dogs have not moved, checks himself, realizing that he'll be seen.

He cannot be seen.

Hanna has almost reached the women when she halts and drops down behind a bank of rocks and bushes once again. She's hiding, too, he realizes. One of the women standing at the foot of the cross turns in his direction, searching the fields below. Even from this distance he can see her face shining in the fading light, and he shrinks back. His heart races while he waits. When at last she turns away, he releases his breath with a sigh of relief.

The sky has cleared, and the rain and strange winds have finally died. He glances up. For the first time he notices that the sky is growing dark. It's late. *Joanna will kill me,* he thinks. Suddenly he frowns, annoyed at Hanna and this new responsibility. He's hungry, wet and cold from the storm, and his muscles have grown tight and stiff as he hunches, shivering, watching.

Two men at the top of the hill are lifting the prisoner's body between them, almost sinking under the weight, while the women stand back. Yeshua was not a small man. The women follow as they slowly begin making their way down the hill toward the city walls, stumbling as they traverse the rocky terrain. When they veer off to the left, he realizes that they're avoiding the gates. Where can they be going?

The child's head pops up behind the rock. After a moment she stands. A glance back at the dogs sends her scurrying after the sad procession, keeping close. He waits until she is well down the hill before following. As he rounds the other side, he sees the mourners below, followed by Hanna.

Hanging back, Hanna fixes her eyes on the little group of men and women descending with the prisoner's body, refusing to look at the two still hanging on the crosses at the top of the hill. She wards off images of what she would see if she should look, of the dogs, of what the men carrying the prisoner might do if they spot her; focusing her attention on the immediate danger of being left behind. At last they reach the bottom of the hill where she is relieved to find that the hard earth and rock give way to a grassy field. Here it's easier to walk, and she scampers around a few small boulders and low flowering bushes.

Pretty wildflowers illuminated by the fading light catch her eye. They seem almost to glow as if from within. She halts, staring at the sight, then quickly ducks here and there along the way to pick a few, plucking randomly as she passes through the field. She knows the names of some of them, the white chrysanthemum, rockroses, the little bean caper, and others, familiar but unnamed. The flowers remind her of something, a memory that hovers on the verge of consciousness, a flash of light on the periphery of vision startles her, a crimson cloak. Uncle? Something strange. Then it shimmers into nothing.

Bunching the flowers into a tight bouquet, Hanna trails behind the unknowing guides. They're headed toward a copse of trees. A flood of relief rushes through her at the sight of the city walls rising just behind the trees to the right of a cliff, but it vanishes when she realizes that the gates they came through in the morning are far away. The thought hurries her on, and she runs to catch up with the prisoner's friends.

When the men with their burden and the women enter the small forest, Hanna hesitates, frightened by the darkness beyond the line of trees. In the distance a mongrel howls, and the sound echoes across Golgotha. The howling drives her forward. Taking a deep breath, Hanna pushes aside the low branches that bar her way.

As he watches Hanna and the little group of mourners disappear into the trees, suddenly he's overcome with the shameful memories. His eyes close with the full realization of what he has done. *Betrayal.* Then angrily he shakes his head. Think of the good times instead, the early days.

He holds himself very still for a moment. There. Yellow sunshine washes over the images he's conjured. He smiles to himself and feels the tension melt, remembering. A small band of men, and the teacher, Yeshua, straight backed like a king and expectant, walking through fields of grass, brushing the small wildflowers that tremble in the breeze under his fingertips. A blue sky is streaked with thin white clouds, like wisps of gauze. The day is warm, and he can almost feel the sunlight on his skin. The fragrance of dry grass and flowers and the salt sea air mingle. In the distance flashes of gold and silver reflect off the still, azure water, and farther out fishermen from the village cast their nets from small boats. Forever and forever he once believed. Yeshua had trusted him then. *You are my rock,* he'd said. *I will build my church on you.* Puzzling words.

And now. The pleasant pictures drop away; his neck and shoulders twitch and grow taut as the hard muscles tighten, sending small silver darts of pain up the side of his head. Unconsciously he rubs the painful area, remembering. Unwanted images form, pushing aside the happy ones:

Yeshua's body being pried from the cross. Thank God he was dead during those long minutes. Cold sweat had poured down his face as he'd watched the ordeal from his hiding place on the hill, far away, hidden by the shrubs and rocks.

Yeshua is dead.

The memories bludgeon him: Yeshua stumbling through the streets of Jerusalem, bent and sweating, suffering like any man. The whip tearing his flesh as he carries the crossbeam . . . *like any other man.* Betrayed as all men are ultimately betrayed by life. The crucifixion that he forced himself to watch as penance, coward that he is.

A groan escapes from deep inside his chest as he doubles from the grief and shame, his hands clenched before his face. He groans again, this time falling to his knees from the impact of his cowardice and the sudden, urgent thought . . .

No one must ever know that he was here.

Messiah?

Only last night he had reclined at the long, wooden table with Yeshua and the others. The room was lit by candles that flickered in the dark as they ate, talking among themselves in low voices. Yeshua had seemed subdued. They'd just finished the Passover feast when suddenly the Teacher spoke up, a warning of betrayal. The murmuring stopped, and the room grew silent at the words.

One of you will betray me.

At first he'd been confused, then frightened. His thoughts had spun as his eyes sifted the group of friends around the table, one by one. Andrew, Matthew, Judas—all of them had looked stricken at the accusation.

Not me, Lord, surely? He'd finally said.

Yeshua had answered. "Someone who has dipped his hand into the dish with me."

And now Yeshua is dead. Like any other man.

Abruptly remembering his promise to Yeshua that he would go to Galilee after Passover, his eyes spring open. Hanna must be found quickly, when it's dark and he can slip through the city. He stands, peers down the hill, hesitating only a moment before starting toward the trees. *Joanna will kill me,* he thinks again. At the edge of the forest, he pushes the underbrush away with an angry sweep. Ahead he hears voices, soft murmurs that are absorbed by the twisted trees and bushes and loam before the words can reach him.

The forest is dark and silent, but he realizes they can't be far ahead. The last light of day filters through the branches overhead. Stooping to push through the trees and brush, he comes to a small garden in a clearing just below a natural, rocky cliff. Dry branches spring from crevices in the cliff, and several tombs, caves with large rolling stones that cover the openings, are carved from the bedrock. As he moves to the edge of the wooded area, he can see that a large stone has been rolled from the entrance to one of the tombs. Light flickers from the interior. Unsure what he has seen, he peers again through the foliage.

There, another flicker that soon steadies to a yellow glow, and he realizes that it probably comes from a torch inside the tomb.

"Uncle!"

Startled, he pulls back into the shadows and, losing his balance, braces against the trunk of a tree. His heart beats wildly as he waits. He must not be discovered cowering here in the forest.

"Uncle, is it you?" The childish voice comes again, whispering, but each word rises with hope and urgency. His eyes shift to a spot at the edge of the garden. Hanna is huddled under a tree between two large roots that shove through the ground.

"Hush, child," he commands. "It's me. Be still." He catches her eyes now and gestures, touching his finger to his lips. She falls silent.

His eyes fix on the entrance to the tomb as the light inside glows and dims, dancing and shifting, as if someone moves between the fire and the entrance. But no one emerges. Still he waits.

"Uncle!" she whispers again.

His eyes slide to the child, and he sighs, then hisses once more to silence her. Keeping watch on the entrance to the tomb, he slips between the line of trees, inching through shadows toward the little girl.

"Here. I am here," he whispers when he reaches her, hunkering down. She throws her arms around his neck, pulling him to the ground, nestling into him. His heart softens as he embraces his niece. With the sudden release from prolonged terror, Hanna begins to sob; and he hugs her to his chest to smother the sound. When finally she looks up, he brushes the tears from her cheeks and smiles down. Hanna, comforted, shudders and grows calm.

"I was so frightened," she whispers after a moment, leaning against him. His wool cloak is soft and warm, and she grasps a fold of the cloth in her fist, holding onto him. "Did you see the dogs?"

"Yes. But keep your voice down, child. I can't be seen."

"Why?" she demands.

He ignores this question, pulling her back with him into the darkness of the trees. "Who is there?" he asks.

"Two men, and the prisoner."

"Only two?"

She nods.

"Where are the women?" he whispers.

"They've gone." The child points, and the man, following her gaze, spots a trail winding past the clearing and through the trees. It seems to wind around the side of the hill from which the tombs are carved.

He turns his eyes back to the cave. For a long time the man watches the entrance until the child, leaning against him, falls asleep.

A dog howls in the distance. Soon it's joined by others, and the grim noise multiplies and grows. The man grimaces, wondering whether they've found a feast. He glances down at Hanna. Her eyes are closed, her breathing is even, and gently he moves her aside, settling her upon the ground nearby. Then he returns to the vigil.

CHAPTER THIRTEEN

The music soared as his hands pounded the keyboard with more force than necessary even for Rachmaninoff's Concerto Number Two. Leo loved the minor key, the deep emotion of the first movement—as if all human sorrow flowed from his fingers while he played. Like water, music has no boundaries, no limitations; and so, as he played, the harmony flowed free, cooling the fire inside. Leo let it carry him along—crashing chords that swooped, soaring up, up through the hot starry spheres.

At last his hands rested on the keys, and he let the notes fade, resonating through the room. Then, Leo Ransom bowed his head and wept for all the years gone by, for Rebecca, for Little Guy—little Wesley Bright and the archbishop that Wesley had become, the terrible parody of spiritual leadership that he embodied.

Finally he raised his head. Here, after so many years, three messages on his answering machine had informed him that some woman from the archbishop's office wanted to talk to him. Emily something-or-other. She was very persistent. A few hours ago he'd returned her call, and now he was stuck with seeing her tomorrow. She wanted to know about the Shroud of Turin! Of all things, why was she interested in the ancient cloth that represented everything the archbishop she worked for had destroyed? And what could she possibly want from him?

Leo wished that Emily hadn't called; it brought back the wretched memories. Once again the old tableau rose before him—himself, Wesley, and the dead body of little Sam, the three of them still wheeling together through time like related keys in a circle of fifths. He saw himself, a naive young priest talking to the policeman. He saw the courtroom washed in yellow haze, burnished by mocking sunshine that streamed into the dim room through a row of windows on the side. Rebecca . . . *oh, Rebecca* . . . he refused to think of her again—smart, scintillating Rebecca and his dreams, lost to him forever. The growing love he'd sensed between them had been buried under Little Guy's avalanche of hatred, the unending hatred that Leo had never really understood.

So why was this assistant coming now to ask about the Shroud? He recalled Wesley's last book, the archbishop's sneering critique of everything the Shroud meant to Leo.

"It is incomprehensible that any intelligent person could believe that in the first century in Judea a felonious rebel was hung from the cross—crucified—and then died, 'rose' again, and ascended into heaven. Even the basics don't add up. Ascended! UP? I ask you now, up to where? I look for the place every time I fly. But of course up and down are relative terms,

depending on where you're standing in the universe at the time."

Leo scowled. The smug words weren't even original, he knew. Wesley had borrowed the prattle over *up* and *down* from Friedrich Nietzsche. Without attribution, of course. Leo had made it a point to keep track of the boy through the years—Rebecca's boy. He'd majored in philosophy at Yale before seminary, Leo recalled.

Wesley's recent words on a television interview came back to him now, and he shivered: "The man called Jesus was nothing more than a salesman who traveled from door to door, town to town, hawking a philosophy, fermenting the seeds of rebellion." What sort of thing was that for a religious leader to teach? And Wesley's view had gained credence when, not long after, many well-known religious scholars . . . *religious scholars!* . . . from the best universities across the country had supported him.

Sitting at the piano in his small apartment in New York, Leo couldn't help shaking his head. This was something that had always baffled him, why many of these prominent scholars, professors of comparative religion, and their followers, Wesley in particular, seemed so determined to *proselytize* their skepticism, to transform Christianity into their own secular vision, bit by sneering bit.

Why can't they leave it alone? he wondered. These celebrity scholars already had plenty of money, success, all the trappings. What more did they want? With their academic credentials and easy messages, they were darlings of the media; and slowly, slowly they were succeeding in their mission—confusing things, infusing new meanings into the old words and symbols of the church. They were using the traditions of the church to destroy it, Leo knew.

Wesley liked to tell reporters that he kneaded the old ideas of Christianity, like clay, into new shapes. "Just toss out the word *religion,*" he laughed. "The old order is gone, it's *kaput.* Theology has evolved. We're in a post-Christian world. Think freestyle. Think personal spirituality that's practical in every aspect of our lives, from losing weight to personal finance to prosperity. No one way is right or wrong; everything is relative. Spirituality is a progressive journey. It's not where we're going that matters; it's how we experience the journey that counts."

One thing Leo knew for certain. He had failed Wesley when he was a boy, when he was just Little Guy. The boy had asked for answers, had searched for something real to sustain that ephemeral, illusive faith that allowed the lucky few to believe in things not seen, not observed—things mysterious, the spirit that is holy and divine. And Leo had given the boy nothing to grasp, not even a wisp of hope.

"How do you know God's taking care of Sam?" Little Guy had asked.

"We just have to have faith," he'd told the boy.

"And what is faith?" Little Guy had asked.

Nothing more than trust, he'd replied. The words ruptured the surface of Leo's mind once again—the boy's disappointment reaching up with the memory through the muck and mire of Leo Ransom's life like a twisted root, choking him, reminding him that he had failed Little Guy. He'd offered nothing more than platitudes.

With this, Leo dragged his fingers up the piano keys, *arpeggio,* scattering his thoughts.

He'd spent over forty years attempting to rectify this first and worst mistake of his ecclesiastical career. He'd focused like a laser on the question of faith after losing Rebecca and, he admitted to himself, had probably neglected his other pastoral duties as a result. With dogged determination he'd searched out the available facts today to support rational belief in the resurrection, to be ready to answer the question the next time it was asked: *"How do you know that it's true?"*

Sitting upright before the piano, Leo closed his eyes, thinking of the first time he'd seen the Shroud of Turin, and even now he smiled at the recollection. It was in 1978 when the Shroud was exhibited in Turin. He'd spent his savings traveling to Italy to see it. In the cathedral his eyes had slid from the faded image on the cloth to the photographic negative, and his heart had almost stopped beating. His breath had grown shallow as Leo realized that at last he'd found the answer he sought.

He'd followed the Shroud since that day, devoured new research as it was published, attended seminars, conventions, and lectures across the globe on the Shroud. At first he was merely an observer. But after a few years, when the experts came to know him, Leo put his energy to work getting the information out to those who needed it the most—the doubting Thomas, the lost sheep, anyone with the questions that Little Guy had asked. For some of them, and for Leo, the image on the Shroud was a picture of the moment of the resurrection.

His music and the Shroud sustained Leo through the bleak years after Wesley was installed, first, as a bishop, then only a few years ago—unbelievably—as presiding archbishop of the church in the United States. Music had lifted him then, let him soar above his failure; and the Shroud had grounded his faith.

And now Archbishop Wesley Bright's skepticism was the new foundation of the Apostolic Church, of his church, Leo's church that was no more. Now it was Wesley's church. Wesley was the new Martin Luther, the philosopher king, the ubiquitous talk-show guest. And he'd recently sent out a mandate ordering the depressing cross removed at once from all churches across the country. Leo smiled bitterly at the recollection and wondered if the archbishop might have considered substituting a mirror in place of the cross.

He bent toward the piano, spreading his hands across the keyboard. Music dark and angry rose, soaring around him once again. Leo had watched with wonder as Wesley worked his magic. He'd sent a letter to the archdiocese once, raging against the removal of the cross from church altars. He worked for days before settling on the words. "The crucifixion and resurrection are fundamental Christian beliefs," he wrote, bearing down on the pen, leaving heavy, angry lines of script slashing across the paper. "Without Christ and the cross, Christianity is nothing more than a feel-good philosophy."

The letter had generated a storm of warnings from the arch-diocese. Each missive, signed by the dean of the cathedral on behalf of the archbishop, arrived at Leo's small church in the part of Manhattan known as Chelsea on heavy, embossed stationary; and each one said the same thing: complaints had been lodged. Leo was too conservative, outdated, intimidating. Orders were issued: the cross must be removed from the altar. Leo was to cease all reference to stories of a resurrection of Jesus of Nazareth in the first century.

For a while Leo ignored these demands. But each Sunday he'd looked out over the congregation to find attendance dwindling. Finally, when only a few steady worshippers remained and the archbishop's office could no longer be ignored, Leo closed the rotted wooden doors of his little church and retired.

And now, here comes Emily, the assistant. Maybe he'd have another chance. Against reason, for a split second Leo allowed himself to hope. Perhaps it was fate and Wesley's assistant was coming here to give him one more chance to answer Little Guy's old question. Perhaps the archbishop was sincere. The thought was accompanied by a burst of energy. He would lead Emily through the evidence he'd found and make her *see!*

Suddenly he lifted his hands and slumped over the keyboard. The music died. *I'm too old for this,* he told himself. Too old and tired. What is faith? Little Guy had asked in that ballpark years ago. In the silence Leo realized that, once again, he would likely fail.

CHAPTER FOURTEEN

Emily glanced at her watch and picked up her pace. She was late for an appointment with Amy Roper, Martin's artist friend. She tried to ignore a vague sense of depression at the thought that Martin hadn't yet phoned.

As she approached the corner of Fifty-first and Lexington, she saw TeeBo leaning against the stone building, reading a book. "Hi, TeeBo," she called.

He looked up, and his face lit with a smile. "How ya doin', Emily?" He laid the book he was reading facedown on the concrete pavement and patted the sidewalk next to him. "Come sit a while."

She thought of the wheelchair. *I've put it off again,* she admonished herself. A wave of guilt dropped her down beside TeeBo to sit on her heels so that her eyes were level with his. "Can't. I'd say I'm late, but every time I see you, I seem to say that. And I'd say I don't have time to stop, but you'll just remind me time's the only thing I *do* have."

"You're correct about that, Lady." He gave her a wry look. "Well then, stay for a bit while you work out the reason you can't."

She laughed, then shook her head. "Nope. I'm off to an appointment."

"You have a problem?"

"No. I'm just doing some research, trying to make sense of bits and pieces of strange information. I work for a church."

TeeBo cocked an eyebrow. "Oh, you're one of those church ladies?"

"Not really," Emily laughed and dropped her purse to the sidewalk, anchoring her hand upon it for support. She struggled for a way to describe her job. "I'm trying to solve a mystery."

TeeBo nodded, leaned back against the wall, and lifted his face to the sun with a smile. "A mystery, hmm? Well, as my mama used to say, just walk back the cat."

"What? Walk back the cat?" Emily smiled at the rhythm of the words.

"Yeah. You know, if you want to get to the root of a thing and really understand what's happening, go back to the beginning, trace events all the way back to the first one, the thing that started it all. Ever watch a cat find its way home?" He opened his eyes, raised his brows, and regarded her. "First thing you know, you'll find the reason. Everything happens for a reason."

"Your mother sounds like quite a philosopher."

"She is . . . was, in her own way. Not much education, but smart." He tapped his head. "Naturally smart. She's the one got me interested in books." He patted the book beside him.

Emily nodded and glanced at it. "What's that you're reading?"

"Confederacy of Dunces," TeeBo said sleepily, closing his eyes. "It's the funniest thing I ever read. Written by a kid down home. Makes me laugh out loud."

"I can't remember when I last read a story like that, for fun."

"No time?" TeeBo asked in a dry tone without opening his eyes.

"I guess," Emily said as she pushed herself up. "But that's just a temporary situation."

One eye opened, and TeeBo looked at her. "Right," he drawled.

"Later." She laughed and waved her fingers at him.

TeeBo watched her hurry away, then shook his head. "Girl needs to learn how to relax," he muttered. When she was out of sight, he picked up his book, shifted himself into a comfortable position and began to read, chuckling quietly.

Emily came to the address given her by Amy, climbed the worn concrete steps to a row of doorbells, and pressed the one with "A. Roper" printed just underneath. After a moment a buzzer rang, and she pushed open the door, then stepped into a small, musty hallway. The air inside was cool and damp, and she shivered.

"Up here!"

She looked up to see a young woman leaning over the railing and waving from the second floor. The wooden stairs spiraled to the visible roof, about five stories high. The face that looked down at her was smiling and friendly. "Come on up. I'm afraid you'll have to walk up the stairs though. There're no elevators."

"No problem," Emily said with a little wave. The face disappeared and she began to climb the stairs. The clatter from her shoes echoed through the building.

When she reached the second floor landing, she saw that a door to her right had been left open. The paint on the outside wall and door was peeling. Soft classical music drifted from the room. Chopin perhaps. She hesitated, then crossed the landing and entered a large bright space devoid of ordinary furniture but filled with canvas, pictures, an easel, and the pungent odor of turpentine and paint. The woman she'd seen now sat on a small round stool before the easel. Light streamed in from a row of windows behind her.

She looked up, put down her paintbrush, setting it on a table near her elbow, straightened, and stood. "Hi," she said in a friendly tone. "You must be Emily." She scrutinized Emily while she spoke, wiping her hands on a long apron that hung over jeans and a loose white T-shirt. Paint smears appeared on the apron. "You're Martin's friend?"

Emily nodded. "Yes. And you must be Amy. Thanks for letting me come by on such short notice."

"Well," Amy said, "any friend of Martin is a friend of mine." She stretched her arms overhead, lowering them to brush her long brown hair away from her face. A faint blush on her cheeks highlighted fine bones when she smiled.

Emily stood in the doorway while Amy crossed the room to meet her, holding out her hand and pulling it back at the instant she reached Emily. "Sorry," she said, laughing. "Better not. I'll get paint on you."

Emily smiled and glanced around the room as she shrugged out of her coat. Colorful pictures were stacked everywhere. "Looks like you're busy," she exclaimed, gazing at the canvases.

Amy nodded and gestured to a coatrack near the door. "Hang your things right there," she said, "and come sit with me while I finish." She dragged a small wooden chair across the floor, placing it just to one side of the easel.

Emily hung her coat as directed. "Are these all yours?" She swept her hand to encompass the canvases scattered in every direction.

Amy looked about. "Yes. The ones in the corner are quite old, but I've kept them anyway. These," she indicated some pictures propped in a row against a far wall, "are ready for a show next month."

Emily walked over and studied them. The style was representational, realistic, and the colors were deep and rich. While they reminded her of the Old Masters, the subjects—mostly people—were altogether modern. The brushstrokes were light and fluid. "I love them," she told Amy. "You really have a gift."

"Thanks." Amy said. She patted the chair she'd placed near the easel. "Make yourself comfortable, and we can talk while I work. How about something to drink, some tea or a cola?"

"Great," Emily said. "Whatever you have is good." She completed her tour of the room and sat down while Amy went to a small refrigerator in the corner and took out two soft drinks. Handing one can to Emily, she snapped the other open and set it on the small table that held her extra paints and brushes.

When Amy was settled before the easel again, she picked up the paintbrush, dabbed it into a swirl of paint on a small pallet, and began brushing small strokes across the canvas, talking while she worked. "Martin tells me you're interested in the Shroud," she said, biting her lower lip as she leaned back for a moment to inspect the picture with one eye half closed. Satisfied, she resumed painting.

"Yes. I'm assistant to Archbishop Bright." Emily reached down and pulled her notebook and a pen from her purse as she spoke.

"Who's he?"

"He's head of the Apostolic Church. We're doing some research." Emily told her about the television interview on the Shroud scheduled in a few days, and Amy raised her eyebrows.

"Paul Johnson! I'm impressed. I suppose I'll know who your archbishop is soon enough."

She's right about that, Emily thought. This talk show was the most popular in the country. And from the archbishop's point of view, the show wasn't about the Shroud. It was about him.

"Johnson is tough," Emily said, taking a sip of her drink. "The archbishop has to be up to speed for that discussion. I'm hoping you can tell me something about how the image on the Shroud was created."

She watched as Amy's hand moved across the canvas. A shaft of sunlight from the windows illuminated the colors in the picture. Dust motes drifting in the light seemed to dance to the music coming from the CD player.

"I'm just a painter, you know." Amy glanced up with a self-deprecating grimace. "But I *have* tried to figure out how the image got on that cloth. At first I was convinced it was painted, but," she shrugged, turning back to the picture, "I've concluded that's just impossible. It isn't a painting or drawing of any sort."

"How do you know that? I thought . . . just a minute." Emily reached down into her bag for her notebook, opened it, and flipped through the pages, nodding. "Yes. Didn't a scientist from Chicago, a microanalyst named Walter McCrone, maintain that he found paint on the Shroud."

Amy nodded. "He was given slide samples taken from the cloth by STURP. Are you familiar with that term, STURP?" she asked, with a quick glance at Emily. Emily shook her head.

"STURP is the Shroud of Turin Research Project, a team of about thirty American scientists the Vatican permitted access to the Shroud in 1978. For five days they were allowed to subject the cloth to the most advanced, sophisticated tests at the time and to take away sticky-tape samples containing all types of microscopic debris for further study."

"And McCrone was one of the scientists?"

Amy shook her head. "No. He was loaned the samples to test afterwards. STURP had already concluded there was no evidence that the Shroud was painted. McCrone, however, claimed to have found particles of iron oxide, which is a natural artist's pigment." She dabbed the brush into another swirl of paint and bent forward, touching it to a spot on the canvas.

"Second opinions were obtained on McCrone's findings because of the discrepancy," she went on. "John Heller, a professor of medicine and medical physics at Yale, and Alan Adler, a professor of chemistry at Western Connecticut State University, followed up."

Emily scribbled in her notebook as she listened. Since her visit to the Met, she'd found several articles about McCrone's conclusions and had thought they were persuasive.

"Heller and Adler found that the iron oxide identified by McCrone was insufficient to account for the visible image," Amy went on, glancing between the canvas and Emily as she spoke. "Except for the area of the bloodstains, iron particles are found only in trace amounts on the Shroud, and it's randomly distributed so it can't account for the image."

Check bloodstains, Emily wrote. "And STURP agreed?"

Amy nodded. "They're certain that the image wasn't painted, and Heller and Adler's work has since been verified. Also," she added, "paint is opaque and would register on an X-Ray." She lifted the brush from the canvas and shrugged in Emily's direction. "But it didn't when tested. So, if the image was created by a pigment, its atomic weight would have to be extremely low, too low to register."

The paintbrush paused, hovering midair between Amy and the canvas. "But even aside from that, it's virtually impossible for anyone to have painted it."

Emily arched her eyebrows. "Why's that?" she asked.

"For one thing, it's three-dimensional. For another, there aren't any brushstrokes on the image," Amy replied. "And to paint it, the artist would have to have understood the concept of photography and reversing shadows and light."

Emily looked off, suddenly remembering something she'd once read. "What about Leonardo DaVinci?" she asked. "Didn't he write about a *camera obscura?"* she asked.

"Yes, but DaVinci was born in 1452," Amy said, leaning back to inspect her work again. "The Shroud was displayed to the public almost one hundred years earlier in Lirey, France. It was exhibited beginning around 1360." She frowned at her picture as she spoke and rubbed an area on the canvas with the edge of her thumb. "And there's no evidence at all that DaVinci ever used the technique," she added.

"What if an earlier artist also knew of the *camera obscura*? Maybe it was a photograph."

"Photography wasn't invented until the 1800s," Amy said. "Before that the *camera obscura* was only an aid for an artist to visualize scenes." She set the paintbrush down and looked at Emily. "There are all kinds of problems with the idea of using a *camera obscura* in the medieval period, not the least of which is that there is no evidence of such sophisticated shading, much less of anyone producing a photograph."

Amy spread her fingers and ticked off the problems: "To create a photographic image, the artist would have had to find the necessary silver compounds and understand the chemistry of photography centuries earlier than the recorded date of invention, acquire enough crucified cadavers to experiment with the new process before they rotted; or create an anatomically correct, medically accurate, detailed sculpture of a crucified man; and maintain the secret for all these hundreds of years." She paused and heaved a sigh.

"Is there any evidence of silver compounds on the Shroud?" Emily asked.

"Nope."

Amy rose from her chair and motioned to Emily. "Come with me," she said, walking over to a curtain hanging on the wall behind her that Emily hadn't noticed. Emily dropped her notebook onto the floor by her chair, rose, and followed.

The tan-colored curtain, hung on a rod set about a foot below the ceiling, was long, trailing about ten feet to just above the floor. As Emily stood before it, Amy pulled the curtain aside to reveal two life-size photographs of the Shroud of Turin showing the frontal and dorsal images. This was the original image, not the negative one, she realized, squinting at the photograph. She hadn't noticed before how abstract it was, how difficult it was to see.

Amy laughed. "It's hard to make out, isn't it?"

Emily nodded. "I saw it at the Met, but it looked clearer there."

"Now step back, away from it." Amy gestured toward the windows. "Move over there and look at it."

Emily backed toward the windows, watching the image emerge into focus as she moved away. "That's amazing," she said, staring at the image as she reached the far side of the room.

"There are no edges to the thing," Amy explained. "The closer you stand, the more difficult it is to see. It just melts away as you approach it." Emily moved close again, eyes fixed on the image.

"You were standing away from it at the exhibition," Amy went on. She walked to Emily's side, and together they regarded the large photograph. "My point is that even if you accept the medieval radiocarbon date, and even if you make the assumption that some mysterious person from that period whose work has never come to light was able to create a reverse image with shadow and light, this characteristic—the way the image almost disappears at a close distance—would make it almost impossible for an artist to have created it."

She laughed, touching Emily's shoulder as she turned and walked back to her easel. "It makes quality control a problem, that's for certain. There's no outline, no frame of reference for an artist."

"But the negative image is so precise," Emily said, astounded at what she'd just seen. She lowered herself into the chair beside Amy and picked up her notebook once again.

"Right." Amy dabbed the brush in paint and turned back to the canvas. "It's a real mystery." She paused, gazing at the photograph across the room facing them, and said, "It almost looks like a scorchmark. It's yellow brown on one side of the flax weave, but the color doesn't show up on the underneath side at all. Whatever caused it penetrated only the top fibers."

Emily gave her a sharp look. "Maybe it *is* a scorch mark!"

"It's not." Amy shrugged and began to paint. "If the linen was scorched, it would fluoresce under ultraviolet light, and it doesn't."

"And that still wouldn't explain the detailed negative image," Emily said, picking up the soft drink beside her on the floor. She took a sip and thought about the puzzling relic. "What if the detailed reverse image was created first, then somehow transferred to the cloth, like a brass rubbing?"

Amy smiled, keeping her eyes on the canvas. "A few years ago a couple of scholars at the University of Tennessee claimed to have created an image like the one on the Shroud by a transfer process. They used a burnishing technique with a dry powder carbon dust, like medical illustrators use today. But they only pictured a face, showing none of the fine features or details of the shroud." She shook her head. "They claimed that it was three-dimensional, but it doesn't appear to be."

Emily looked at her. This was interesting. "How did they do it?" she asked.

"The initial drawing was of the detailed negative image, made on paper using the carbon dust," Amy replied. "Then it was transferred to cloth by the burnishing process and set with heat to produce the reverse picture. But," she warned, seeing Emily's expression, "again, there's no evidence that the method was ever used or even known in the middle ages."

"Why'd they use carbon dust?"

"They were trying to produce a three-dimensional effect, like the Shroud. Depth in the initial picture, before the transfer, was created by a buildup of dust." Amy pursed her lips and tilted her head, looking off. "The technique might work for a picture with limited variations in depth, or elevation, an inch here, a half-inch there, the ramping of the nose, perhaps; but the results don't come close to the properties of the Shroud."

She paused, glancing at Emily. "For example, the knees of the man on the Shroud are foreshortened, bent in *rigor mortis* to indicate a distance of eight and one-half to nine and one-half inches between the cloth underneath the body and the back of the knees." She spread her hands to describe the span and smiled. "That's a lot of dust."

Emily laughed but wondered privately just how important the three-dimensional aspect of the image really was. Surely the same effect could be accomplished with skillful artistic shading. She resolved to look further into the question.

Amy interrupted her thought. "Also, no one has yet found any evidence that the dry powder the researchers required is present on the Shroud."

"Is there any known technique during the Middle Ages comparable to that process?" Emily asked.

"No," Amy replied. She turned away, peering at the figure on her canvas and after an instant dabbed it with paint. "The closest thing to it is pastel painting beginning about two hundred years ago, using fine, loose, dry pigment which tends to smudge and dust off over time."

"But the pigments weren't available earlier?"

"They were hand ground in the medieval period, too coarse, so they wouldn't have resulted in the fine quality of the shroud image, especially after being transferred to coarse linen."

"Hmm." Emily looked down at the notebook and wrote. "How do you know the three-dimensional effect wasn't created by conventional artistic techniques like shading—just shadows and light?" she asked.

"Art from that period doesn't evidence that level of technique. But it's more complicated than mere shading." Amy shrugged. "I'm no scientist, but if you're interested, I think there've been some in-depth studies on the three-dimensional properties of the Shroud image. Before you leave, I'll see if I can find a source."

"Thanks." Emily made a note to follow up, then glanced at Amy, frowning. "So if we eliminate painting, photography, scorching, and maybe burnishing . . ." She hesitated, reluctant to dismiss this last process so quickly. "Did Heller and Adler have opinions on what *did* create the image?"

Amy nodded. "They finally concluded that the image was not created by anything *added* to the linen, such as paint. Instead, they thought it was created by *taking something away* from the fibers. In other words, it was probably created by a chemical change in the fibers."

"Like aging in a yellowed newspaper?"

"Yes. Good example—although *this* image was created all at once, not over time. Otherwise the body would have begun to decompose before it was completed." Amy set her paintbrush carefully in a narrow wooden tray attached to the bottom of the easel and turned to Emily. "High magnification photographs of the image fibers support Adler and Heller's theory. The fibers do appear to have been degraded by some sort of chemical change."

"Something like a blast of radiation?" Emily gave her a quick look. "Like the shadows imprinted on walls in Hiroshima from the nuclear explosion?"

"Perhaps. But so far no one's been able to explain what occurred." She dropped her hands into her lap and gave Emily a thoughtful look. "And, however the image was created, it couldn't have been by simple contact, as you probably know."

Emily nodded, remembering the distorted, spread-out picture shown at the exhibition of the effect of pressing a cloth to the face.

"What about the bloodstains around the wounds?" Emily asked. She rose and wandered over to the photographs of the Shroud, standing before them with her hands locked behind her back.

"They're real blood," Amy said. "That's been established beyond doubt."

A strange thrill ran through Emily at the words, raising the hair on her arms. What if it was all true? "Real blood?" she exclaimed, turning in time to catch Amy glancing at her watch.

"I'm afraid I can't help you with the blood analysis," Amy said. "But I can give you a name." She scooted her chair back from the easel and rose.

Time to go, Emily realized. "I'd appreciate that," she said, hurrying back to her chair where she scooped up her notebook, pen, and purse. She crossed to the door to retrieve her coat while Amy went to a table in the corner of the room.

"His name is Leo Ransom," Amy said over her shoulder as she pulled a tattered address book from a drawer on the side. "He used to be a priest—still is, I suppose."

"I know of him," Emily said, surprised. "I have his phone number."

"Good," Amy said. "Even if he doesn't have all the answers, he might be able to direct you to others who will.

These Shroudies all know one another." She looked down at the address book, flipping through the pages. "And here's the source I mentioned for the three-dimensional properties of the image." She wrote something on a piece of paper and walked back to Emily, waiting at the door.

"This man's a photographer with STURP," she said, handing the paper to Emily. "He maintains a Web site on the Shroud."

CHAPTER FIFTEEN

He looks down at Hanna while she sleeps and notices the flowers. Her little hand clutches the small bouquet to her chest. The night air has grown cold, and he slips off his cloak, shivering as he tucks it gently around the child, careful not to wake her. In her sleep she tightens her grip on the flowers.

Hanna resembles my sister, he thinks. She has the same delicate nose, wide-set eyes, dark hair. As he looks down, studying his niece, her mouth twitches in her sleep. The expression on her face softens, and now a smile plays around the corners of her mouth. He strokes her hair, wishing he'd visited Joanna before this week, wishing that he had known Hanna before today. He sighs with regret, conscious that he'd bullied his younger sister this morning, taking Hanna away with him like that. But what else could he have done? Everyone in the city was searching for the Teacher's friends.

After a moment he raises his eyes once again to the lighted tomb.

Suddenly a man's silhouette, backlit by the glow from within, appears in the entrance to the cave carved from the bedrock of the cliff. He stands there, still and listening, as if something has caught his attention. Hanna's uncle sucks in his breath and holds it, edging back into the darkness of the trees, out of sight. But the child still sleeps and lies partially exposed in the moonlight.

The man's eyes slowly scan the garden, skimming over the little girl, unseeing. Finally, glancing at the sky, the silhouette shrugs and turns away, disappearing into the darkness of the tomb. Hanna's uncle resumes breathing.

He starts toward Hanna, but muffled voices from the interior of the tomb halt him. Thinking of Yeshua lying dead inside, his heart pounds, seeming to swell in his chest. He pushes farther back into the darkness of the trees until neither the child nor the entrance to the tomb is visible, then slides down to the cold, wet ground once again. Leaning back against the trunk of a tree, his breath catches, and he struggles to fill his lungs with air. Gasping, attempting to calm himself, finally he draws a long, slow breath.

He can't be seen. They mustn't see him now.

Grasping his knees, suddenly his head drops in despair. *What have I done?* he cries to himself. A tear spills from the corner of his eye, and angrily he wipes it away. *Yeshua!* At last he slumps, waiting for he knows not what, immobilized by his thoughts: Hanna, Yeshua, his friends . . . gone now. The air is thick and malignant, murky, odorous with sorrow and the sort of contrition that is borne of self-inflicted wounds.

⁂

The moon rises and soft white light bathes the garden, slanting under the tree where Hanna sleeps. The child stirs and her eyes fly open. Overhead, silver stars wink and shine in the black sky. Below, around her, the pale light is striped by shadowed trunks of trees. Confused and sleepy, she turns her head, searching for Mother, for the comforting walls of her little house, and it is then she realizes that the light comes from the moon and stars above, that strange shadows dance around her. At once she's fully awake.

Hanna pushes upright, remembering, and glances wildly about for Uncle. Her eyes sweep the garden once, then twice, peering into the darkness beyond the clearing. Seconds pass and she grows still. There's no sign of Uncle now; he has gone. Swallowing, she turns to the entrance to the tomb. Fixing her eyes on the flickering light, Hanna waits. Perhaps Uncle is inside?

Yes, she decides. That must be where Uncle has gone.

The thought settles Hanna, gives her courage. Grasping the bouquet of flowers in one hand, she pushes to her knees, stands, and looks around. Now the entire garden is visible at once. It's small, she realizes, but quite beautiful—surrounded by the forest and filled with large, chiseled stones gleaming in the moonlight, low bushes, and flowers growing wild, like the ones in her hand. Still, she'll feel better with Uncle.

Hanna lifts her chin and moves closer to the open tomb. Walking on tiptoe, she inches toward the entrance. When she reaches the opening, Hanna pauses. Gathering her courage, she rests her hand on the large rock nearby, feeling the smooth cool surface of the stone while she waits and listens. Except for a breeze that rustles through the trees, the garden and the city behind the walls are silent. At last, with a deep breath, she squares her shoulders and steps forward.

Inside the air is cold and she's aware of a dank, musty odor, the smell of old wet stones mixed with the fragrance of spices and the hot smell of the burning torch. The tomb is dark except for a circle of light thrown from the torch that is jammed into a crevice. The stone wall behind the torch glistens in the firelight.

Hanna blinks, blinded by the light, and lowers her eyes. Bright pinwheels glow behind her lids for an instant, then vanish. As Hanna lifts her head, she sees the men, still unaware of her presence and kneeling beside a body stretched lengthwise over a ledge, a long, raised stone slab. She turns her head, searching for Uncle. He isn't in the tomb.

Trembling as the realization strikes that Uncle's really gone, she gazes first at the body on the slab, then at the two men. But in that instant the men recede behind a gauzy scrim, and it is only the body that grips her in a spell. She recognizes the dead man at once, even though now his face is peaceful and his eyes are closed, as if in sleep. He no longer wears the crown, the woven thorns and thistles. But she has no doubt. This is the prisoner that fell to his knees before her.

As she looks at the man stretched out on the stone, his voice comes to Hanna. *You have a destiny, child; a duty to fulfill.* The voice seems to fill her with something soft and warm and bright and, suddenly, she's no longer afraid.

An exclamation echoes through the tomb as one of the mourners, the elder, catches sight of Hanna. Abruptly he moves, but the other man touches his arm, and he sinks slowly back to the ground, staring at the child with shining eyes who stands before Yeshua.

Before what once was Yeshua.

Hanna stands motionless, eyes fixed on the prisoner. The two men glance from the girl to Yeshua, but he's still and dead, and the tomb is silent. They watch as the child drops her eyes to the flowers she holds. Then clutching the little bouquet with both hands, her lips curve into a smile; and she moves toward Yeshua with the little bouquet, gliding, as if an invisible cord links the two of them together.

Feeling the pull, Hanna gazes at the marred flesh of the prisoner's face, flesh that is streaked with thick, caked blood.

Unclean, a small voice warns inside. The ancient law is clear, even to small children. She'll be isolated if she touches the body; rituals must be observed. *Days and days alone for cleansing if you touch the dead.*

The prisoner in the center of the circle of light takes on a sharp, crystalline form as she moves close. He lies on a long white cloth that trails the ground, ready to be pulled over his head for burial. In this moment only the cloth, the prisoner, and the light are visible to Hanna.

The two men glance at each other. This is meant to be, their eyes say. Let us wait and see.

The tomb is still, silent as the deep part of the ocean, timeless as the ocean's waves. It is eternity. No time exists in here, no boundaries, no limitations. Hanna stands just beside the prisoner and looks down into the face that strangely she loves. Although his lids are closed, still his eyes seem to see her. She hears his voice again, gentle, like a stream of music for only Hanna's ears as if it comes at once from inside, near her heart, and from some other place and time. The voice tells Hanna what she must do.

Hanna nods, understanding. Leaning over the prisoner, pausing only for an instant, the child lifts her hand and tenderly places the spring flowers upon his breast—scattering them there where, illuminated by the glowing light, they will rest for two thousand years or more.

CHAPTER SIXTEEN

A knock at the door startled him. At the sound Leo's stomach muscles tightened. Memories flooded back, and he fought against the sense of failure, told himself that this was another chance to answer Little Guy's old questions about faith. Maybe the Shroud could convince the archbishop's assistant, Emily, where he, Leo, had failed the little boy. As the knocking grew insistent, he rose slowly because he was stiff from age and walked to the door.

Emily's hand was in midair as the door opened, catching her by surprise. The elderly man who stared back at her was gaunt and looked fatigued. His face, rimmed with a batch of fine white hair, rose from the round collar worn by priests of the old order, stiff black linen with a pristine rim of white around the edge. Not many of these were left—only the old school wore them now, priests living in times gone by.

"Leo Ransom? Excuse me," she stammered, remembering the old protocol, "I mean, *Father* Ransom?"

He nodded, distracted as he studied her, then took her hand. "Emily?"

"Emily Scott," she said with relief. "From the office of the . . ."

"Yes, I know," he interrupted, releasing her. "Come in." Leo stepped aside and ushered Emily into the room he called his music room.

Emily waited as Leo removed several stacks of tattered sepia-colored music books from an old couch near a window next to the piano. In front of it was a low, round table already set with cups and saucers, sugar, a plate of lemon slices, two napkins and two spoons, and a small blue china teapot with a chipped spout.

"I apologize for the mess," Leo said, turning to her. "Come sit over here and we'll have refreshments while we talk. Don't often have visitors these days."

"I heard you playing from the street when I arrived," Emily told him with a glance at the piano as she settled herself on the couch. Leo pulled a small wooden chair across the room, placed it on the opposite side of the tea table, and sat down. "You're very talented," she said.

"Thank you," Leo replied, wondering if she knew of his prior relationship with her archbishop. He hoped not; that would make it more difficult to convince her, to make her an advocate for the Shroud with Wesley. "Music is my life since I left the church." He gave Emily a sharp look but observed no reaction to his words. Slowly he began to relax.

"Usually I play only for myself," he added, picking up the teapot. He poured a cup of tea for Emily but left his own cup empty. He'd wait to see if Emily wanted a second one before pouring the last of the tea for himself.

"I'd love to hear some more."

"Perhaps another time," Leo said in a noncommittal tone. He watched Emily while she settled back and pulled a small notebook and a pen from her purse.

"So you're interested in the Shroud of Turin," he said, stretching his arms lengthwise down the arms of the chair and tapping his fingers against the wooden knobs on the ends.

Emily nodded. "I'm doing research for Archbishop Bright." She looked up and saw the old priest's eyes narrow. "Do you know him?"

He shifted his weight and dropped his hands onto his knees, avoiding the question. "I must say, it's surprising to find Archbishop Bright's office interested in the Shroud. Isn't the relic the antithesis of everything he stands for, he and his church?" He emphasized the word *his.*

His tone was cryptic, and Emily gave him a quick look. "The report will prepare him for a discussion on television—the Paul Johnson Show, *Target Zero.*"

Leo raised his brows.

"I'll admit that he's quite skeptical," Emily went on. "Perhaps it's more accurate to say that I'm here on my own behalf."

"Well, then, what can I do for you, Miss . . ."

"Emily."

"Emily. What is it you'd like to know?"

Emily opened her notebook and looked at Leo. His eyes reflected curiosity, but the hard look she had glimpsed was gone. She leaned back on the couch, crossed her legs, and propped the notebook on her lap. She thought she might like the old gentleman if he'd only loosen up a bit.

"I've read one of your recent articles and take it you believe the Shroud is authentic, that the date assigned by the radiocarbon tests was not dispositive?"

Leo nodded. "Yes. I was convinced even before the latest news about the rewoven sample tested by the laboratories."

Emily nodded as she added sugar and lemon to her tea and stirred it. "But even if the medieval date is wrong, that doesn't prove that the Shroud is Jesus' burial cloth." She glanced up at him as she stirred the tea. "I'm interested in learning what you know about the bloodstains on the Shroud." Her voice trailed off, uncertainly.

Leo studied Emily. He saw a pretty young woman wearing a pleasant expression, watching him as she waited to hear a string of facts. She sat comfortably on the couch, poised for his answer. But he thought, perhaps, that he saw a glimmer of real interest in her eyes. The room was silent. Occasional muffled sounds from the world outside intruded; they seemed disconnected somehow, unreal.

"I did a little research before going to the exhibition," she said to him. "Dr. McCrone concluded that there is no blood on the Shroud." She glanced down at the notes she'd taken from her own research and at Amy Roper's studio. "He thinks the so-called bloodstains are paint." She watched Leo as she added, "I know that his findings on the image are . . . controversial. But weren't there significant particles of pigment found in the area of the bloodstains to suggest paint?"

"Rubbish," Leo said flatly. He looked at Emily, but he saw Little Guy.

"Why is that?" she asked, conscious that her voice had taken on a note of defiance. "According to my notes Dr. McCrone was well regarded; he had the credentials to be taken seriously. And he was generally unimpressed with the Shroud."

Leo gave her a cold smile. "McCrone did find particles of iron oxide in the area of the bloodstains. But blood contains iron," Leo said. "And water contains trace elements of iron. The flax would have been soaked in water during the process of manufacturing the cloth."

Water. Emily nodded, half-listening as she tried to remember what Martin had said about water and the shroud.

"Iron oxide, of course, is also a component of pigment, or paint," Leo went on, with a little shrug. "But in pigment it's generally contaminated, and the particles found by McCrone were exceptionally pure."

Emily pushed the tip of her pen against her bottom lip, recalling that Martin had mentioned a recent fire. "Wasn't the Shroud also doused with water in several fires?" she asked.

"That's right. STURP scientists found watermarks on the cloth from a fire in the fifteenth century." Leo gave her a polite smile. "Are you familiar with the work of Doctors Alder and Heller?"

"Yes." She glanced at her notebook again. "They were asked to give second opinions after McCrone."

Leo smiled to himself. She'd done some homework. This could make his job easier. "Heller and Adler, and several other scientists after them, realized that the water used to douse the fifteenth-century fire could also have contributed to the presence of iron oxide particles on the Shroud."

He paused and lifted the teapot, offering it again to Emily. She shook her head, and Leo poured tea into the empty cup before him on the table, then added a spoonful of sugar and stirred it slowly.

"So you see," Leo went on, "McCrone's finding of iron oxide doesn't support his theory that the bloodstains were painted. In fact, plain old dirt contains iron. And," he added as an aside, "there's dirt on the Shroud, especially around the foot of the image. Material in that area is believed to originate in the Jerusalem area."

"That can't be right," Emily interjected. "There's no record of the Shroud being located in Jerusalem, is there? As I understand it," she looked down at her notes again, "the written record only places the Shroud in France and Italy."

Leo shoved back his chair, rose, walked to the window, and stood before it, folding his hands behind his back. The slant of the sun highlighted a layer of dust and grime on the glass in front of the old man as he stood staring out.

"That's why the dirt around the feet that I mentioned is important," Leo said, gazing out at the street. "Scientists at the University of Chicago, Fermi Institute, and the Hercules Aerospace Center in Utah recently examined samples of it under a high-resolution microprobe." He turned back to her. "They found that the substance around the feet was almost identical to the aragonite limestone found in ancient tombs in Israel."

"Meaning?"

Leo walked back to his chair, sat, and leaned forward. "Think about it Emily," he said in a low, intense voice. He gestured for emphasis. "You have to consider all the bits and pieces of information together—cumulatively, as you will." He fixed his eyes on her. "A finding of aragonite in the dirt might not sound important on its own, but it's a tangible link to the region around Jerusalem that hasn't been taken into account in the medieval recorded history."

"I understand."

"Okay." He studied her. "In any case," he went on, "to go back to your question, after high magnification studies both Heller and Alder concluded that neither the image on the Shroud nor the bloodstains could have possibly been painted in any conventional matter."

Emily remembered Amy's words. "I've been told that they concluded the image was created by *subtraction* of a substance from the fibers, not by the addition of something, like paint," she said.

"Right," Leo said. "It's still a complete mystery."

"So we're back where we started?" Emily was conscious that her voice held a note of disappointment.

An imperceptible smile played on Leo's lips. "Not quite."

Emily looked up and waited.

"When Heller and Alder performed their work looking for iron oxide, they used the most sophisticated new testing methods on the samples, including analyzing wavelength spectra on special computers. With these they determined unequivocally that the blood spots on the shroud are hemoglobin, very old blood."

Emily suppressed a flutter of excitement. Don't overreact, she told herself. He's leading up to an impossible conclusion.

"Those findings were subsequently confirmed by independent laboratories around the world," Leo said, smiling at Emily's intent look. She was listening. "The consensus is that the stains on the Shroud are human blood, type AB negative. They test positive for bile pigments and proteins. And under ultraviolet photography a halo effect occurs around the edges of the bloodstains."

"What does that mean?"

"It's serum. It shows that the blood was exuded from clots that formed on the wounds after death."

"So that explains it," Emily murmured, remembering the archbishop's comment not long ago.

"Explains what?"

"A dead person doesn't bleed."

Leo nodded. "More important," he added, "tests show that the blood clots protected the underlying fibers from the image-forming process. In other words, no part of the image lies underneath the blood."

"So the image was created *after* the blood came into contact with the cloth?"

"Right. It's the timing that matters." He gave her a sly look. "The placement of the bloodstains and the wounds and the flow of blood are medically correct judging by today's knowledge. So if the blood was there first, a forger centuries ago would have to have been extremely sophisticated to be able to match the wounds shown on the image to each and every pre-existing blood clot."

Emily stared past Leo as she thought about his words. Even if a forger had the artistic ability to accomplish such a feat, he or she would not have had the medical knowledge required to understand all of this hundreds or thousands of years ago.

"The bloodstains also indicate the presence of the X- and Y-chromosomes," Leo went on. "This confirms that the individual of the Shroud was of the male sex." Emily fixed her eyes on him with a skeptical look.

"Oh yes," he said, nodding, "it's been confirmed by several reputable laboratories." He paused, then said, "And finally, think of this—human DNA has also been identified."

"What!"

"Yes, the code of life." Leo cocked his head and watched her. "But that's not so surprising when you think of it. You probably know that archeologists often find DNA in blood and tissue in artifacts from thousands of years ago."

My God. She shook her head, thinking of the possibilities. "Could the samples possibly be used for cloning?"

"No. That would be terrible," Leo said. Emily felt a strange sense of relief as she heard his words. "Luckily, that's impossible. Only seven hundred base pairs have been isolated from the Shroud samples. The human genome, by comparison, requires billons."

As they talked, the shadows of buildings slowly blocked the light of the afternoon sun, and the room grew dark. Finally, reluctantly, Emily closed her notebook and moved, preparing to leave. Just then Leo leaned toward her, bracing his elbows on his thighs. He folded his hands together before him as if in prayer.

"Emily." She looked up and his eyes held hers. "I must ask a favor."

"Of course," she said uncertainly, sinking back onto the couch once again. She rested the notebook on her knees and waited.

This might be his last chance, Leo realized. He hesitated before speaking. When he did, his voice was low and strained. "You—must—not—let—the—archbishop—destroy—the—Shroud, my dear."

Destroy? She was stunned by his words.

The palms of his hands, pressing tight together, turned damp. He rested his chin on the tips of his fingers to steady them, willing Emily to hear him. She *must* listen, so that Wesley would also listen!

"The Shroud is much more than an old relic," he said. "It represents hope for millions. If it's real, it's a picture of the moment of the resurrection. It's proof that the story of the resurrection is true; that something endures, surpasses our mortality; that physical death is not the end of things."

He paused and gave her a hard look. "It gives people with fragile faith some hope," he said.

"Why are you telling me this?"

He looked past her now. "Do you remember the Old Testament passage from Ezekiel—his vision in the valley of the dry bones?" he asked.

Emily shook her head.

"Read it sometime. It's beautiful poetry," he said, looking back at her. "The bones in that valley were dead, lifeless; they were the bones of people left without hope." Thinking of Rebecca, of Little Guy, Leo fought to control a wave of despair sweeping over him. "I imagine you don't know what it is to have faith and lose it," he said, almost whispering.

He's rambling, Emily thought. *He's old and rambling.*

Leo was tired, but he took a deep breath. "We're all caught in that valley today, Emily. Wesley Bright brought the church to this."

Emily flushed at his words, snapped her notebook shut, picked up her purse, and stood. Was this retired priest trying to turn her against the archbishop, her Wesley, who'd removed the cross from every church to rid it of exactly this sort of superstition? Feeling as though she'd just emerged from a fugue state, Emily banished all thought of the Shroud of Turin and bloodstains and crucifixions.

"You don't know Wesley, . . . the archbishop," she stammered. "He's changed everything." She glared down at Leo and heard her father's voice, *"Hypocrites, all of them."* The archbishop's face rose before her, courageous, bold, as he'd been when he'd confronted Paul Johnson. Her breath grew rapid as words formed over the years by her father and Wesley rushed out: "Why, before Archbishop Bright came along, Christianity was a cruel fraud."

Leo watched her, wondering what had caused such a reaction.

"Think of all the rules, the self-righteousness that Christians today have replaced with honest spirituality." Dad's face rose again. *Hypocrites all of them, all of 'em.* "No mythical messiah . . ."

"Christians!" Leo spat. She'd been around Wesley too long, had no idea what the word really meant. He closed his eyes for an instant with a sense of doom.

". . . can dictate what's right and wrong," Emily continued, raising her voice over his. "That's simply absurd. The archbishop teaches us to act according to our own needs, from our own perspectives."

"You're describing a new-age philosophy, not Christianity," Leo said when she'd finished. He leaned back, feeling every muscle in his body tense. "Christianity is based on two facts," he said. "The crucifixion and resurrection of Jesus as they're described in the New Testament. Don't you see?"

His hands balled into fists at his sides as he worked to keep his voice even. "There's no scientific explanation for the image on the Shroud," he went on, eyes fixed on her, barely breathing. "But I believe that it's the image of Jesus, that it was created in a burst of energy at the moment he rose from the dead."

He took a deep breath and exhaled the next words. "That's why I care so much. It stands for something absolutely good—for *absolute truth* that exists beyond our emotions, beyond our physical, mortal world."

Emily stared at Leo. Nonsense, the archbishop would have said. But once again that small voice whispered, *What if it is true?* The Shroud *was* a tantalizing mystery. She shook away the unwanted thought. It contradicted every principle that Wesley taught, his entire system of belief.

Leo propped his hands on his knees and slowly, as if in pain, pushed himself up so that he stood close to her. He recognized the stubborn expression on Emily's face, but he cared too much not to try one last time. "Just imagine for one moment, Emily, the impact the Shroud could have on the world if it's determined to be the burial cloth of Jesus."

"If?" Emily asked, stepping back. Father Leo had invaded her personal space. He was too intense. Walls closed around her. "That's a big 'if,'" she said with a short laugh.

"Emily!" Leo cried. His throat constricted. "Think, Child! Think! It's amazing that the Shroud even exists. It's just an old piece of cloth, but it has survived centuries of war, weather, fires, earthquakes, all kinds of disasters." He waved his hand in an arc, as if each of these passed before him as he spoke.

"Think of the coincidence that now, just when the world is in such turmoil, everything comes together and suddenly archeological discoveries, historical records, medicine, DNA testing, physics all advance our knowledge and converge to a point that allows us to comprehend what happened back there in the first century."

Emily stood before him, torn between loyalty to Wesley and fascination.

Suddenly Leo swayed and put out his hand, grasping the back of the chair. Emily grasped his arm to steady him. After a moment he straightened, rubbing his eyes, and gave her a sorrowful smile. "Sorry," he said in a low voice, turning away.

The old priest's emotion touched a chord in Emily. His face was pale. She recognized the plea in his eyes, and it came to her that despite Wesley's contempt, despite her father, she *wanted* Leo Ransom's words to be true; she longed to believe that the Shroud was real.

Releasing Leo's arm, she hitched her purse over her shoulder and, holding onto the notebook, she walked across the room with him. "Don't worry, Father Ranson," she said, taking his hand when they reached the door. She spoke in a careful tone, conscious that for reasons she didn't understand, her opinion was important to him. "I appreciate your help, and the information you've given to me will be in my report to the archbishop." Leo nodded without speaking.

"If anything," she continued, watching him and wondering if he'd even heard what she's just said, "this visit with you at least makes clear that the question is open, and I think he'll agree. The Shroud will get a fair hearing on the show, and afterwards . . ." she hesitated, "well, viewers can decide for themselves." Emily ignored a flicker of doubt as she thought of Wesley. "The archbishop is fair. You wouldn't worry if you knew him."

All night Leo pounded on the piano trying to forget Emily's visit, but for once music couldn't wash away the bitter thoughts. His hands raced across the keys, and his body shifted and swayed with the music until dawn crept through the city.

Finally, Leo stopped playing and slumped, resting his forehead on the cool polished wood of the old piano. The Shroud offered a message of hope, but Wesley Bright could bury it with the authority of the church. How would he use that power? Would he destroy the Shroud and the hope it represented to millions as he'd destroyed the church?

Archbishop Wesley Bright was angry. He pressed his lips into a rigid line and from time to time shook his head as he read Emily's final report on the Shroud. Halfway through he lay it down upon the desk before him, smoothing the edges of the paper with his fingertips as he gazed unseeing at the wall.

What can she have been thinking? he wondered. Emily was supposed to have come up with some pithy talking points, not more facts. She'd been closeted in her office for days preparing this report. Wesley glanced down at it and quickly away. After a moment he rose from his desk with a sigh and picked it up again.

Emily heard the scuffle of his shoes coming down the hall before he appeared in the doorway. She straightened in the chair and squared her shoulders as she composed a smile, but she was unprepared for the glowering expression that he wore.

"Have you gone mad?" he demanded as he stalked into her office, ignoring the chair in front of her desk. He stood tall, looming over her and frowning.

Emily raised her brows, looked down at the report in his hand, and swallowed. "I think it's fairly balanced, all in all," she managed to say. "What is it that bothers you?"

Wesley rolled the papers into a cone and slapped it against the palm of his hand in an absent manner while he glared down at her. After a moment he pulled out the chair and sat. "My dear," he said with exaggerated politeness. "I thought we'd already had this discussion. It's not that I *object* to anything."

He tossed the report onto the top of her desk and shook his head. "Of course you're free to express your own views at any time. But the Shroud of Turin has been radiocarbon dated to the medieval period by three prestigious laboratories chosen by the Vatican. Frankly," he gave her a cold smile,

"I'm surprised that you've accepted the idea that the Vatican could make such a mistake."

Emily stiffened. She'd heard the archbishop use this tone of voice only once before when a delegation from a small church in West Virginia met with him last year, requesting permission to retain the crucifix over their altar. Of course he'd refused. "Idiots!" he'd muttered after they'd left his office.

She took a deep breath. "I was surprised as well," she admitted. "But there *are* valid questions about those radiocarbon test results. The rewoven sample is only one of them."

Wesley waved her words aside. "Arguments by fanatics," he said dismissively. "What I need from you is a rational response to *support* the date, not disprove it."

She clasped her hands tight before her on the desk, forcing herself to hold his gaze, not to look away. "There's not much left to dispute," she said, surprised to hear that her voice was steady. "The date of the Shroud is unknown, as it stands." She repeated to him now what she'd included in the report about the various tests invalidating the radiocarbon dating, of the discovery of type AB negative human blood in the area of the bloodstains, of the DNA, and, most important, the mystery of the creation of the image on the cloth.

Wesley gazed at her while she spoke, but instead of Emily, he saw himself standing at the top of the cathedral stairs dressed in the formal vestments of his office, scarlet silk embroidered with glittering gold thread. Miss H had videotaped each and every one of his television interviews. He often replayed them at night when he was alone.

Now Emily's voice receded as he saw himself gazing through the camera in those videotapes, eyes kindled with passion. He'd certainly practiced that look enough, reaching out across America with the gift that would free everyone from those old chains of religious superstition, ideas that made life difficult—the old fabrications about a messiah, especially the ones about the man rising from the dead and the so-called absolute truths set forth in the New Testament, the words of the sage called Jesus.

We're on our own, he'd told his constituents again and again. He always softened his words with a smile, though—*we're in this together, you and I,* his look would say. *It's time to grow up and face facts, to make the most of what we have, right here, right now.* He worked to hide his smile from Emily as he thought of how his words could change their lives, those viewers. Life can be easy and fun, he'd always add with a grin, just at the end of a show.

Emily's voice intruded—something about bile pigments and proteins—and he looked at her with a heightened focus, startled. The muscles around his eyes and mouth tightened. If the Shroud was authentic . . . which it wasn't, which it couldn't be . . . but invisibly he shook himself, forcing himself to face the unthinkable. Nevertheless, if it were somehow accepted as the real thing by the credulous moms and pops across the country, his new power base, he'd look like a fool. Worse, they'd hate him as a heretic.

Emily watched a strange expression flit across Wesley's face. For a split second she recognized the look as fear. Then suddenly his face lit with the smile that warmed her and reminded her of Dad, in the old days, the way Dad used to be—confident, articulate, and usually right.

"Ah, well," she said, rousing herself. She sat upright, flattening her hands on the top of the desk in front of her with an air of resolve. "Perhaps I've gone overboard. I'll revise the report."

Wesley nodded, but still he watched her. "The interview's day after tomorrow. Don't forget."

"It won't take long," Emily assured him, conscious of the strain in her voice. "You'll have a new draft by tomorrow," she told him.

"Fine." Wesley slapped his knees as he rose. His voice was toneless. "I'll be interested in what you find, Emily. Just leave it on my desk if I'm not there."

Emily swallowed hard as he stalked out of her office. She dropped her head and pressed her fingertips against the ridges over her eyes. The archbishop was annoyed, angry. *Was the Shroud of Turin worth all of this?* she wondered. She'd never confronted him before, never questioned anything he'd said.

She swiveled to her computer. She'd set aside the issue of dating the Shroud for now. And the blood, the DNA, perhaps those were nothing more than a medieval practical joke. Emily grimaced at the implications of this thought. Her fingers rested lightly on the keyboard without pressing down the keys as she considered the options. It was the creation of the negative, three-dimensional image that presented the most difficult problem.

Staring blindly over the monitor, she sifted through the theories that she'd discussed with Amy. The only process that

Amy had mentioned claiming to account for both a positive and negative image and a slightly three-dimensional image was the burnishing technique, the one that medical illustrators use with carbon dust. But she'd warned that while the resulting transferred carbon dust image did reflect some depth—as with artistic shading—she didn't think that it was really three-dimensional.

But, Emily mused, perhaps the three-dimensional aspect of the Shroud image was overrated, actually nothing more than artistic shading after all. Her spirits lifted at the thought. If that were true, if the three-dimensional properties of the Shroud were exaggerated, then the burnishing technique might offer Wesley an opportunity to clear up the mystery on Johnson's show.

She gazed at the wall behind the computer monitor and pursed her lips with exasperation. *I'm missing something,* she thought. What did it mean to say the Shroud was "three-dimensional" anyway? Suddenly she remembered the STURP photographer that Amy had recommended. Reaching across the desk, she picked up her notebook and found the Web site address. She entered the address on the search engine and, when it came up, scanned the home page quickly. Clicking on the "Contact Us" link, she typed in the questions that ran through her mind: "What evidence exists to prove that the image on the Shroud is three-dimensional, and why is that significant?"

When she'd finished the e-mail and proofread it, she clicked "send" and leaned back in her chair once again, hoping she'd get a response. The show was only a few days away.

She had to find something to help the archbishop, some ammunition for the show that would diminish the intrigue created by the Shroud. He expected that.

Something tugged at her thoughts—the light in Leo Ransom's face when he'd talked of the Shroud. Her chest tightened with the sense that she was failing him. Looking off, a wistful feeling came over Emily as the question rose again: *What if it is true?*

Voices in the hallway roused her. Turning away from the computer, she closed the notebook and set it aside. If she expected to keep her job, she had to let go of that fantasy. Emily suddenly realized how much she's missed seeing the gleam of approval in Wesley's face when he'd looked at her earlier from across the desk. A vision rose of Dad smiling down at her when she was young, a look that he'd drowned in the bottle years ago, that she'd discovered once again with Wesley.

Wesley. Yes, she would think of him as Wesley from now on.

As she left the cathedral and headed home to revise the report, Emily was disappointed to find TeeBo's corner already empty. She wondered where he lived and how he got into and out of buildings on his own, where he ate—the things she took for granted every day—then marveled at the inner strength of the man. TeeBo's strong character was probably courtesy of his mother, she reflected, remembering the soft look on his face when he'd talked of her.

Suddenly she recalled her resolution to help him and clucked her tongue with exasperation. Time. Time was always the problem.

How much time could a simple wheelchair take?

CHAPTER SEVENTEEN

Wesley faced Jonathan Marley across a table, with Paul Johnson sitting between them. Emily sat in the dark area of the studio behind the cameras and cables, studying the professor on a monitor. He was physically less imposing than she'd expected, nondescript. His hair was gray, and he was several inches shorter than Wesley, but he carried himself with military bearing and a touch of arrogance. She hoped the archbishop didn't underestimate Dr. Marley. She screwed her mouth into a grimace. At least Marley wasn't wearing his medals.

Wesley wore a jovial smile while Dr. Marley rested his hands on the table and gazed around the studio. When the opening music signaled that the show was beginning and credits rolled across the monitor, the archbishop lifted his eyes to the camera.

"Good evening," she heard Paul Johnson say in a hearty tone. "Here we are again at *Target Zero* with two guests and a subject I think you'll all find interesting." He leaned close and leered into the camera. "They're lined up and in our sights, folks, so stay right with us and see what happens!"

The theme music reached a crescendo, and Emily suppressed a wave of anxiety. She hadn't heard back from the STURP photographer yet about the three-dimensional element of the image on the Shroud. She'd hoped to have a definitive answer on the burnishing technique by now for Wesley, something that might explain how the image was created and put an end to the frenzy of curiosity over the relic. The archbishop had been constantly irritated over the past few days.

Paul introduced the guests, then shuffled papers, and, after some preliminary announcements to his audience in a conversational tone, turned to Dr. Marley.

"Well, Dr. Marley." He smiled at the professor and cocked his head. "First, I'd like to thank you for taking the time to appear with us this evening. We're honored to have a national hero as our guest."

"Delighted to be here, Paul," Dr. Marley said. His voice was deep and resonated throughout the room. Emily glanced at the archbishop and saw that his smile was tight.

"Have you had an opportunity to visit the Shroud of Turin at the Metropolitan Museum of Art since you arrived?" Paul asked.

"Yes indeed," Dr. Marley replied, with his first sign of real enthusiasm. "I've seen it before in Italy and arrived early yesterday especially for the exhibition. It's quite dramatic."

Paul nodded. "I'd like to ask a question, then, if I may."

"That's what we're here for," Dr. Marley said.

Paul grinned, steepled his hands beneath his chin and gave the professor a hard look. "We understand that the radiocarbon dating of the Shroud in 1988 is being challenged right now. What's your feeling about this?"

Wesley's face was expressionless. Emily's revised report had provided him with some talking points this time around, but she'd stuck to her position that the radiocarbon date was inaccurate.

"I think it's compelling enough that the Vatican will consider new tests," Dr. Marley said. "In fact, not only have the official findings been disproved, but alternate methods of determining the age of the cloth indicate that the Shroud is much older than the radiocarbon date."

"Such as?" Paul asked.

"The deep sepia color of the linen compares with ancient museum samples from the early centuries. And chemical analysis on the fibers measuring radiation absorption, and the rate of loss of vanillin from lignin at growth nodes on the flax, compares to that of the Dead Sea Scrolls." He paused. "I'm not sure we have time to go into the details, but I'll be happy to . . ."

"That's quite all right," Paul said, throwing up his hands and laughing. "I think we get the point." He turned to Wesley. "That's all pretty impressive. What do you say about that, Archbishop? It sounds like we have to deal with the idea that the Shroud might be much older than the radiocarbon date. Doesn't that change everything?"

Emily watched the monitor with a heightened focus. Wesley's face flashed on the screen; he looked serene.

"Not necessarily," Wesley drawled, composing a grave smile as he prepared to deliver the answer he'd thought of last night. *Why hadn't Emily come up with this?* he wondered with a fragment of his mind.

He turned to Jonathan Marley with a pleasant look. "Regardless of when the cloth was manufactured, the image could have easily been created on it centuries later when advanced techniques were available." Wesley flipped his hand toward Jonathan Marley in a dismissive manner. "You can't tell the age of a painting by the age of the canvas, can you?"

He shook his head to illustrate the point. "Artists use old canvas all the time. It's the same for the Shroud; whether the image was created by means of photography, or burnishing," Emily had mentioned this talking point—something about burnishing—but warned him not to use it, "or paint or some other trick, the age of the cloth itself is similarly irrelevant. The image could have been created in the 1800s for all we know."

"Well, Professor?" Paul said, turning to Dr. Marley. "Archbishop Bright has a point, doesn't he?"

Emily cringed, knowing what was coming. Wesley obviously hadn't finished reading her report.

Marley's tone was brisk. "If it were that simple, we wouldn't be here today." He tilted his head back and looked down his nose at Wesley. "Have you forgotten that a written historical record exists for the Shroud image at least since the medieval period?"

The archbishop flushed, realizing his mistake.

Marley smiled. "The Shroud was publicly exhibited in Lirey, France, around 1355," he said in a lecturing tone. "The exhibition was mentioned in a written memorandum dated 1389, and one of the souvenir medallions from the festivities is preserved in the Cluny Museum in Paris. And going further back in time, earlier artwork duplicates the image."

He turned to Paul with a spark of malice, Wesley thought. "Have you heard of the Image of Edessa?"

Paul nodded. "I believe Gibbon mentioned it in his tome on the Roman Empire."

"That's right." Dr. Marley slid his glance to Wesley. "The image of Edessa is believed by most experts to be the Shroud, and it's on record as early as the fourth century. The cloth was brought to Edessa, Turkey, today known as Urfa, probably sometime in the second century to protect the city from Persian invaders. It was kept folded there; only the imprint of the face was displayed over the city gates."

"How do you know the image of Edessa was the Shroud?" Paul asked.

Marley, at ease, folded his hands on the table before him. "The Edessa cloth was folded in fours at unique angles, and the Shroud evidences creases from those folds," Marley said. "But early artworks of the Edessa cloth also contain the features of the Shroud image—the short, forked beard, the nose, the swollen eye, the brows—they're all the same."

Paul lifted his finger in the air to punctuate his words. "Let me get this straight," he said to Marley. "You are contending that long before the official radiocarbon date, the image of Edessa was generally believed to be the cloth provided by Joseph of Arimathea for the burial of Jesus, and you think that's the same cloth we know today as the Shroud?"

"Right." Marley smiled, looking pleased.

So much for the neutral moderator, Wesley thought sourly. "A resemblance between the two facial images is not much to go on," he said, shrugging. "It's a shaky foundation for a supernatural claim." With a sideways look at the viewers and a short laugh, he added, "Kind of like building a house on sand, wouldn't you say?"

In the darkness behind the cameras and lights surrounding the set, Emily was alarmed by the argumentative tone in Wesley's voice. As the presiding leader of the Apostolic Church, he should at least try to appear neutral on the subject. The thought slipped in unbidden: *Why must he work at appearing objective? Wasn't the goal to discover the truth, as Leo Ransom had urged?*

"It's more than that," Marley said with an indulgent look. "Some of the early artwork depicting the Edessa cloth show the full-length image, displaying identical body placement as the Shroud, positioning of the arms, the wounds, the unique weave of the cloth."

"Unique?" Paul interjected. "How so?"

"The herringbone pattern of the Shroud is distinct, rare for the period," Marley said.

On the monitor Wesley appeared ruffled. Emily watched as he reached for the glass of water placed on the table beside him, spilling it as he raised it to his lips. She flinched.

"And for another thing," Marley went on, ignoring the quick flicking movements of Wesley's hands as he attempted to brush the water from the front of his sweater, "early descriptions of the Edessa cloth also describe the full-length Shroud image. A sermon on the Edessa cloth in the ninth century from Constantinople, for example, mentions the bloody wound in the side." He paused. "None of this is conclusive, of course. But it's certainly helpful."

Wesley sank in his chair and lapsed into silence, listening to Paul and Marley with a fragment of his mind as they droned on about the history of the Shroud, the bloodstains and DNA. Of course they had to mention DNA. Thank God they hadn't gotten to the question of the image yet. Emily had thrown too many obstacles on that issue into her report—pictures melting away when you moved close, bloodstains underneath the image instead of on top of the thing, three-dimensional something or others, no paint, no brushstrokes or outlines. His eyes roamed past the cameras searching for Emily, lighting upon one spot and another in the darkness. She'd failed him after all.

"Well, what about it, Archbishop Bright?" Paul's voice penetrated his gloom, and Wesley sat upright, flustered. "Doesn't all of this information raise questions in your mind?" He gave the camera a mischievous grin. "If the carbon-14 tests are discounted, then it's not out of the realm of possibility," Paul pronounced each word with precision in an ascending tonal arc, *realm of possibility,* "that this could actually be the burial Shroud of Jesus.

"Or," he paused as the archbishop began shaking his head, "at least it's not completely clear that the Shroud is a *fraud.*"

Emily hated the way he drew out that word—fraud—almost as if it referred to the archbishop instead of the Shroud of Turin.

Wesley lowered his chin and contrived a smile to mask his growing irritation. Resting his elbows on the arms of the chair, he drew his hands together, creating an arc bridged by the tips of his fingers. "Nothing I've heard tonight changes my mind about the Shroud. It's preliminary to discount the radiocarbon tests," he replied in a deliberate and steady voice. "The laboratories chosen by the Vatican were known to be excellent. And the Edessa cloth?" He drew his brows together and turned to Jonathan Marley with a suggestion of pity.

"As much as we'd like to think otherwise, what you've described is a fairly contrived connection between the two. There's just no way to tell after all these years whether the Edessa cloth and the Shroud were the same or whether the idea's just a figment of someone's imagination."

He paused and gazed into the camera. Just keep repeating the key points, the lizard had said. That's all the viewers will remember, only the sound bites. "But let's be clear about this," Wesley went on, spreading his hands before him. "There's no real evidence that the Shroud has ever been located anywhere but in France, where it was first exhibited in 1355 according to Dr. Marley, and later Italy. That much is known. Everything else is speculation."

From the corners of his eyes he could see Marley already lurching forward, ready with his reply, openmouthed like a beached fish gasping for oxygen. Behind the professor on the wall was a well-lit clock, ticking toward his own reprieve. There were only four minutes left in the show.

"If we have time, Paul," Dr. Marley broke in, lifting his hand with a little flutter, "I have something I'd like to add."

The archbishop's smile tightened.

"Go ahead, Professor," Paul said, as the camera swung toward Dr. Marley.

Marley's eyes shone as he looked into the camera. "Archbishop Bright is wrong," he said. "We're no longer left merely with speculation." He paused and seemed to tremble with excitement as he continued.

"Pollen and faint images of flowers found on the Shroud now indicate that it was located at some time prior to the medieval historical record in the area of Jerusalem."

The small muscles at the corners of Wesley's eyes and mouth flexed.

"How can images of flowers tell us that?" Paul asked.

"It sounds like someone has a vivid imagination to me," Wesley said with a stiff smile.

With a dismissive look at Wesley, Dr. Marley turned to Paul. "The pollen and flower imprints were initially discovered on the cloth years ago. Recently a professor at Duke University, Dr. Alan Whanger, identified several species of plants—the crown chrysanthemum, rockroses, and others—from high quality, enhanced photographs." He paused for a breath and went on in a rush before Wesley could jump in.

"Now the foremost expert today on Israeli botany, Professor Avinoam Danin from the Hebrew University of Jerusalem, has confirmed the presence of the flower imprints, as well as images of a thorn plant, *Gundelia,* which blooms in Israel from February to May."

Paul glanced at the producer and turned to Dr. Marley. "Hurry, Dr. Marley. We're almost out of time."

Marley nodded and his voice took on a hint of urgency as he went on, almost running his words together as he spoke. "Dr. Danin observed the imprints not only in the enhanced photographs," he went on, "but also directly on the Shroud.

He compared the imprinted plants on the Shroud to the pollen and to a database of more than ninety thousand sites of plant distribution, and found that 70 percent of the species were located in areas between Jerusalem and Jericho, some quite near Jerusalem. His conclusion was that it is clear the Shroud was located in the environs of Jerusalem, contradicting the medieval written history."

Paul leaned back in his chair. "That sounds like pretty good detective work to me," he said.

Jonathan Marley exhaled his next words with a glance at Wesley. "Dr. Danin's conclusion is particularly persuasive given the two independent botanical methods of confirmation, the imprints and the matching pollen."

Wesley heaved a sigh and screwed up his face. He could use up some of the time left for the show just by objecting. "Because plants are *typically* found in one area of the world doesn't mean they can't grow in another—France or Italy, for example," he said, leaning back. He looked down and focused his attention on stretching out his long legs beneath the table and crossing them at the ankles, as if bored.

"You didn't let me finish, Archbishop." Marley's face flushed red. "Dr. Danin also identified one of the plant images as *Zygophyllum Dumoson.*"

"What was that?" Paul interrupted, with a grin for the camera.

"The bean caper," Marley explained. He paused and looked off, as if collecting his thoughts. "It's popularly known as the bean caper, and it grows exclusively . . ." He paused again, emphasizing the word, "*exclusively* in Israel, Jordan, and Sinai. Because of that the presence of the bean caper on the Shroud doesn't even require independent verification by pollen to place it in that area."

Wesley smothered a yawn.

"But most important," Marley went on. With an intent look to the camera, his voice took on a breathless, excited quality. "Dr. Danin has also recently concluded that the flowering bean capers on the Shroud were picked in the springtime, in April or May, the time that we celebrate as Easter and Passover."

"Easter and Passover?" Paul let out an abrupt laugh. "Explain yourself, please, Professor Marley," he exclaimed. "How can anyone possibly know precisely when the flowers were picked?"

Beside the main camera the producer was holding up his hands, signaling. Wesley adopted a noncommittal expression, ignoring the stir that rose from the various assistants working near the set at Marley's words. It wouldn't be much longer now, he hoped.

"Yes, yes! Let me explain," Marley replied with his eyes on the producer. Ignoring the camera, he turned to Paul. "The bean caper is most intriguing because the leaf pattern is unique. The imprinted leaf image on the Shroud indicates the specific state of growth found with that flower only in the spring."

Paul's eyes opened wide. "Is this certain?"

"Yes." Marley paused and his eyes slid to Wesley. "Given Dr. Danin's conclusions and the fact that the Shroud's location near Jerusalem occurred prior to the medieval record—" He paused, picked up some papers that Wesley hadn't noticed before and held them before him. "—it's unmistakable. The

Shroud originated in the Near East, and the flowers were placed on the body that it covered during the springtime."

For the first time since he was a boy, Wesley could think of nothing to say. Dead time ensued, television's nightmare—a stretch of silence that is lost time—while he sifted through his memory for words, for a response, for some mention of those flowers in Emily's research. Nothing came to mind.

As she stared at the bright monitor listening to Marley, a quick thrill of anticipation came over Emily. She recalled what Leo had said just before she'd left him. "The Shroud represents hope."

Cameras rolled back, people began moving around the edge of the set just outside the range of lights, and she caught herself. When she turned her attention back to the show, Paul was inviting Jonathan Marley and Wesley to finish the discussion with him next week.

Wesley regarded Paul with a bleak look and nodded. He was exhausted but trapped. Yet another week of this, he groaned to himself.

Paul looked at the set of papers that Jonathan Marley still held in his hand. "Perhaps you could share those articles you mentioned with Archbishop Bright," Paul murmured to Jonathan Marley.

"I'll be glad to," Dr. Marley said in a cheerful tone. "I have copies with me."

"Well, this is certainly a dramatic turn of events," Paul said, turning to the camera. "Flowers from the first century might reveal the origin of the Shroud of Turin!" His eyes danced as the music rose, and he raised his forefinger, shaking it at the viewers. "Be sure to tune in again next week, folks. You're not going to want to miss this one."

The producer made a furious winding gesture and Paul glanced at Wesley, speaking quickly. "Wish we had more time, Archbishop. But we'll look forward to hearing your thoughts on this new development next week."

Wesley smiled his famous grin, but when a commercial appeared on the monitor and the set came to life, the smile died. He reached down to disentangle the mike from his jacket lapel and squinted to find Emily beyond the lights. It was time to finish this thing, and he knew exactly how to get started.

In his small apartment across the city, Leo flicked off the television set and stared unseeing into the darkness. Little Guy hadn't changed a bit, he concluded. But the boy he was and the man he had become were distinguished by one important fact. The archbishop now held tremendous power. He held the bully pulpit.

Once again Emily picked up the botany articles that Marley had left with Wesley. She could hardly believe her eyes. One of the articles contained detailed photographs and drawings of the plants. On the original photographs taken from the Shroud, the imprints of the flowers were faded. But when enhanced by the sophisticated photography used by the researchers, they were clearly visible. According to the botanists, just as Jonathan Marley had claimed, some of the plants grew *only* near Jerusalem, and the leaves of the little bean caper were in a state of bloom found only in the spring, the time reported by each one of the four Gospels of the New Testament for the crucifixion of Jesus.

"Astounding coincidence!" the archbishop said in a sarcastic tone when she handed him the articles. He glanced down and quickly set them aside.

"Possibly," Emily agreed. But she was puzzled at his reaction. He had become stubborn lately, refusing to examine any of the evidence, refusing to accept any conclusion regarding the Shroud of Turin other than that it was a thirteenth-century fraud, a forgery at best.

"I don't know what's come over you, my dear," he said, giving her a severe look. His eyes narrowed. "*Of course* it's coincidence. What else is there?"

Her stomach went into a spasm. She steeled herself to urge him to look at the information she'd gathered. Even more, she longed to tell him of the spark of excitement the botany reports had kindled when she'd read them. But his expression stopped her. Suddenly, Emily was struck dumb by the limitations of words, of the walls they create to rise around us, closing us in with things we understand, things we can describe, and shutting out the unknown, the elusive, the inexplicable.

Sometimes silence is best. What else is there, indeed?

Emily veiled her eyes, and with a self-conscious shrug she stood. "I'm off," she said, keeping her tone casual as she shifted her purse to her shoulder and picked up her briefcase. "See you tomorrow. But you might want to take a look at those articles," she said to him over her shoulder. "They're very thorough—some are illustrated."

The archbishop raised his brows, and she felt his eyes on her as she headed toward the door. He was disappointed, perhaps even angry, she knew. After all, it was unlike her not to agree when he'd made his opinion on a subject like the Shroud very clear.

Emily's steps slowed as she left the cathedral through the great doors and walked down the front steps toward Fifth Avenue. Suddenly she thought of TeeBo and this cheered her. She'd made a habit lately of going out of her way to see him, even when she found only a minute or two to spare, but he hadn't been there for the last few days. Turning, her step quickened as she began to walk down Fifty-first toward his corner.

Near Lexington Avenue Emily spotted the small mound of muted color that was TeeBo, visible between a sea of moving legs. She maneuvered her way through the five-o'clock crowd to his spot at the wall. His eyes were closed, and his chin rested on his chest. He was asleep.

"TeeBo?"

His eyes sprang open, and his face tilted up as he squinted into the sun. The grooves on his forehead smoothed when he recognized her. "Hey, hey, hey!" he said, shifting himself away from the wall into a sitting position. "It's the sad-eyed lady of the lowlands."

"Dylan?" Emily squatted down beside him.

"Yeah." He stifled a yawn, stuck a piece of straw between his teeth, then leaned over to the cigar box and peered in. He picked up a dollar bill that lay on top of a small pile of coins.

"I saw him once. A few blocks from here." He stuffed the bill into his shirt, then picked up the coins and began to count them. "Gotta put these away. People see money in the box, they stop worrying about me."

"How much?" Emily asked, looking at the coins.

He finished counting before answering. "Three dollars and fifty-five cents," he said.

Emily opened her purse.

"No." TeeBo shook his head. "Just sit and talk for a while."

"What kind of beggar are you, TeeBo?" she teased, pulling out a dollar bill and dropping it into his box. He picked it up.

"Part-time, mama," he answered, tipping an imaginary hat. "Besides, I've decided I'd rather look up your skirt."

Emily smiled and slid from her heels onto the sidewalk. "You haven't been around for a few days. I thought you'd gone missing," she said as she settled into a comfortable position against the wall, confident now that no passerby would notice her down here.

"Worried about me, were you?" He looked at her with amusement.

"Yes. I suppose I was." Smothering a touch of resentment still lingering after the conversation with Wesley, she asked, "Don't you ever think that life's unfair, TeeBo?"

"I just make the best of things."

She slanted her eyes at him. "Are you telling me the glass is half full?"

"I suppose it depends on whether you're pouring or drinking, Babe," he answered in a laconic tone, plucking the straw from his mouth. He gave it all his attention, rolling it between his thumb and forefinger. "How's that mystery coming along?"

She laughed at the diversion. "It's research on the Shroud of Turin. It's on exhibition at the Met. You know anything about the Shroud?"

TeeBo nodded. "Sure," he said. "My mama was a good Catholic. Before she passed, that is." A fleeting smile crossed his face. He sighed. "That was a few years ago. But Louisiana's still full of mackerel snappers who won't eat meat Fridays. We celebrate St. Joseph's feast day, All Saints Day." He shrugged one shoulder. "Things like that."

Emily was intrigued. "Then tell me what you think of it."

"What? The Shroud? I don't think anything about it." He gazed past her at the moving legs.

"Well then," Emily said, "what is it you think about all day?"

TeeBo leaned back and looked at the sky, a patch of blue between the buildings. "Hmm. That's a hard one. I think about the old days. My mama. She was so pretty and smart and sweet. Came from Baton Rouge." He glanced at Emily. "City girl, she was." The sun blurred for an instant, and with a covert movement he swiped a corner of his eye. "Worked hard all her life. Never let things get her down. Always wore an apron, her hair pulled back, you know, like in a pony tail, and always laughing."

"She sounds nice."

He nodded, looking off. "And I think about the fishing boats going out from Empire, past Pilottown at the mouth of the Mississippi, and through the South Pass while the moon's still hanging in the sky like a big ole moon pie, and the air is fresh and cold." He glanced at Emily. "And looking for the rip," he went on as a smile grew across his face. "Little flurries of fish in the current, the Gulf stream down from Nova Scotia—and hooking up, casting out, setting the drag when a big one hits."

With a short laugh he slapped his hand down on the edge of his cart. "Good times," he said under his breath. "Good times."

"Moon pie?"

When he looked at her again, his eyes danced. "Yeah." He drew a circle in the air with his finger. "You know, those big flat round cakes? They're usually covered with orange or white icing, or chocolate sometimes, with marshmallow inside."

"Ugh!" Emily made a face. "I can't imagine eating such a thing."

"You wouldn't believe the things we eat in Louisiana, lady."

"I know. Awful crayfish things."

"Crawfish, please. Mudbugs."

Emily laughed. After enduring Wesley's obvious disapproval for several days, it felt good to laugh.

Teebo stretched, then reached across and gave her forearm a light pat before he folded his hands behind his head and leaned back against the wall watching the ebb and flow of urban life and thought about Empire, and it seemed like no time at all before the sun went down.

CHAPTER EIGHTEEN

Wesley took Marley's articles home with him that evening and tossed them on his desk in the study. After a satisfying dinner of roast beef, medium rare and seared—just as he liked it with a tinge of pink at the center—a spinach salad, and a small helping of scalloped potatoes, he sipped his cabernet while Miss Honeman cleared the table. When she had gone, he put down the glass, leaned on his elbows, and ruminated over the problem of Emily's strange behavior that afternoon. Finally, reluctantly, he rose, picked up the wineglass that was still half full, and strolled into the study to read those articles about the flowers.

They were just what Jonathan Marley had claimed. Strange as it seemed, some of the pollen and plant images on the Shroud *had* actually been matched to flowers that only grow near Jerusalem and bloom in the springtime. But according to the historical written record of the Shroud, that was impossible. Every movement of the relic since its first appearance in the thirteenth century had been carefully recorded, and that record indicated that it had never been in Jerusalem, or anywhere outside of Europe for that matter. Owned first by various families of the French nobility, the Shroud was exhibited in France and was finally moved to Italy in 1578, where it remained.

He gazed at the photographs of the flower imprints that Marley had described. It was the timing of the thing that bothered him the most. Just as he'd said, some of the imprint images evidenced an early state of bloom, indicating that they were picked in the springtime, according to Dr. Danin. Wesley shook his head. This was the exact season described in each one of the four Gospels for the crucifixion of Jesus, the final act culminating in the great myth of the resurrection. How *convenient* it all was, he thought. Too convenient.

A door closed somewhere in the rectory near the end of the hall, and he glanced at his watch. Ten o'clock. That would be Miss H, closing herself into her room for the night. He wanted to examine the photographs of the flower images again, but he was tired. Setting aside the articles, he gazed blindly at the wall across the room, resolving to take another good look at the pictures first thing in the morning. After a few minutes he rose, finished off the glass of wine and headed for his own bedroom.

Ghostly figures emerged from the gray mist, and Wesley groaned in his sleep. The faint outlines filled with light and shadow and gradually pictures emerged, forming like a spinning top's patterns separate as it slows. At first he could see a tree and someone standing in the mist. But when the lines sharpened and shapes formed, he could see a little girl. She stood in a clearing under several twisted trees. At last the shadows turned to colors, brightening the pictures, transforming the dream.

Was it a dream? It seemed so real—more like a memory than a dream.

She wore a long, blue dress, a tunic that fell to just above her ankles. Dark hair was caught at the nape of her neck; and when she turned, peering back through the trees, he could see that her hair was woven into a braid that hung to the middle of her back. She looked familiar. Could he know this child? Wesley tried to call out to her, but the sounds wouldn't form. The girl swiveled as if searching for something or someone. After a moment she began walking with slow, careful steps toward what appeared to be a rocky cliff.

Through the drifting mist he strained to see. Was that a cave? He watched as she moved toward the entrance. Light flickered through the opening, illuminating a small bouquet of flowers that she held in her hand. She seemed to hesitate, bracing her free hand on a large stone, a boulder, as if frightened. Then with a slight lift of her shoulders, she entered the cave. Again he strained to see. It *looked* like a cave.

Inside the cave suddenly Wesley found himself just behind her, floating, moving forward with the girl. It was a free sensation, as if he were part of the mist without form—there yet not there at all. Over her shoulder he saw two men kneeling before something, a long slab of heavy stone, perhaps; it was rough and uneven. And on top of the slab was the body of a man lying still, clad only in a loincloth. He couldn't see the face, but somehow he knew the man was dead.

Terror gripped him. *Sam?*

No.

The girl moved toward the body, and he came gliding with her as if they streamed through viscous liquid. As she grew close, one of the men raised his head. He gasped and started to rise, but the other stopped him. They seemed to see the child but not him. Did he know these two? They also looked familiar. The child halted and he stopped with her. She stared, transfixed by the corpse stretched across the stone. He followed her gaze.

Colors in the dream grew vibrant now: yellow light, dark red blood the color of garnets, and the damp gray of glistening stone, a stark white burial cloth. In the circle of light thrown off by the torch, the features of the dead man were sharp. He could see that the body was ravaged. Dark rivulets of blood streaked the face, but the blood was thick, appearing already almost dry, not clear and bright and new like Sam's blood had been.

The dead man's hair reached to his shoulders, and Wesley had the thought that it was arranged that way for burial. Hands were crossed at the groin, and huge gashed punctures just above the wrists and near the ankles were also caked and smeared with blood. The flat head of an iron nail protruded from flesh and bone just above the foot. A large side wound gaped—a raw gash of torn, bloody flesh. A sense of gloom, of great tragedy, struck him as he stared down at the dead man whose name hovered on the periphery of consciousness, just out of reach.

But the thought flicked away when the girl bent over the still body. As he stared, she stretched out her arm and gently placed something on the corpse. When she straightened and stepped back, he looked down. Scattered across the bloody chest were the flowers she'd held. With growing dread he examined the flowers, first one, then with a rising sense of urgency, another and another, their colors and shapes, the forms of the petals, the stems and stalks, until finally the images were burned into his mind. A terrible suspicion pushed to the surface of his mind, bubbling as it slowly transformed into a raging torrent of fear.

He twisted, trying to pull away from the child and the flowers and the dead man. But the girl turned and seemed to see him now. Her large, grave eyes, the color of blue ink—*those indigo eyes*—caught his own and held them. As he stared back at her, the scene dissolved—the yellow light, the corpse and men, the cave—until at last only the child's face hovered in the smoky mist.

Indigo eyes. The words struck him again as she too disappeared.

Wesley flinched violently and woke, drenched with sweat. His muscles were taut and strained, and his chest hurt. Conscious of his own ragged, uneven breath, he fought for control, trying to ignore the terror that gripped him. He stared at the ceiling above, locking out thoughts of the dream, concentrating until his breathing had slowed. Finally he let his gaze scan down the far wall of the bedroom until it settled on a pane of glass that reflected the glow of lanterns in the courtyard. The light had a calming effect, and he felt the tension seep from each aching muscle one by one.

It was a dream, Wesley told himself. Only a dream. He reached across to the table beside his bed and turned on the lamp. But even as the bright light filled the room, the child's eyes floated before him. He fell back upon his pillow and stared once again at the ceiling. Strange the things a mind can do, he mused. But those eyes. Where had he seen them before?

After a moment he shook his head and rolled onto his side, preparing to rise. It was then the thought flashed through his mind; and suddenly, with terrible clarity he remembered those eyes and the grave little face. The realization jolted his nerves as an electric shock. Impossible! The dream child looked exactly like the girl selling flowers at the foot of the cathedral steps some weeks ago. The little flower girl, Emily had called her.

It couldn't be! he told himself. Eyes wide, the archbishop bolted upright, swung his feet over the side of the bed, and, bracing himself, looked to the nightstand where the vase of flowers stood, the ones given him by the little flower girl.

Yes, there was the vase, and there were the same strange flowers—still alive, still vibrant, almost glowing with color. Slowly, he sat down on the edge of the bed and drew the vase toward him, studying the small bouquet that stood in the water, the flowers as fresh as if they'd been picked just this evening. He quizzed himself—how many weeks had it been? Three? Four?

The thought crept in: *these flowers should have died long ago.*

Wesley sat motionless as images danced in his mind, pieces of a puzzle that rearranged themselves over and over until a thought formed. Once again his heart began to pound.

Somehow—although he knew this to be impossible—somehow, the child in the dream and the flower girl from the cathedral were one and the same. The flowers placed upon the dead man's chest in the dream were the same as the flowers in the vase. And the flowers were all too real.

The name came to him all at once. *Yeshua.* Jesus. The dead man's face was the image on the Shroud.

Throwing aside the duvet, the soft, silky feather quilt that covered him in winter, spring, summer, and fall, the archbishop stood. Mechanically he slipped his feet into the worn flannel slippers placed by Miss H each day with wonderful regularity on the floor near the foot of the bed. His thoughts spun. The flower girl. The flowers. The Shroud. Pictures flashed through his mind like arcs of fire that burned for an instant, then disappeared into the ether until, finally, only one question consumed him.

Pulling on his dressing gown, the archbishop hurried through the hall, walking softly so that Miss H would not awaken. Down the corridor he rushed and into the study where he flipped on the light and crossed to his desk. The articles containing pictures and illustrations of the flowers, their stems and stalks and leaves, their petals, lay open on top just where he'd left them.

Without taking time to sit, he grabbed the report and flipped through it, trying to ignore the growing fear. He found the photographs near the end of the article as he remembered, the flower images photographed from the Shroud. Running his eyes down the page, he found the pictures he sought.

It couldn't be. But as he stared, the archbishop confirmed what he already suspected. They were one and the same.

Photographs of the rockroses, crown chrysanthemums, and bean capers displayed in the article were identical to the flowers still blooming in the vase by his bed and the flowers in the dream. His eyes stopped on the image of the bean caper, the one that bloomed only at Easter, only at Passover—at the time of the crucifixion of Jesus described in the Gospels.

He closed his eyes, picturing the bouquet in the vase by his bed. *They were the flowers of the Shroud.*

Wesley sank into the chair beside the desk and dropped the report onto his lap. The coincidence was too great. And those indigo eyes. Impossible! But he knew it was true. A menacing roll of thunder sounded in the distance. The flowers were living proof, a key to the truth that could destroy him.

The thought exploded in his head. The Shroud was real. He *knew* at that moment beyond a shadow of doubt, almost as if he'd known all along, that the Shroud was real and that this could destroy him.

Wheelchair. Wheelchair.

Emily clenched her jaw and repeated the word in her mind as she held the phone while the clerk at the Veterans Administration looked for TeeBo's military records. His current record, that is. They'd lost—*misplaced,* she'd corrected in a tart voice—the original ones when TeeBo had tried to transfer his file from Louisiana to New York. It had taken Emily four hours merely to find out what office to call to get this information.

"Lost?" Emily repeated.

"Happens all the time," the clerk said.

Wheelchair. Wheelchair.

"Still there?" The clerk chirped into her ear.

Emily glanced at her watch. She'd been on hold for twenty-two minutes. "Yes," she answered, drawing the word out.

"Listen," the clerk said. "We've got a backlog on claims, if you know what I mean." Emily heard the crack of gum. She gritted her teeth and waited.

"I found a file for Mr. Thibideaux," she pronounced the *X*, "but we got nothing from before—before, you know, when he actually moved up here. U'mmm, his *service* record."

"He needs a wheelchair." Emily paused and sucked in her breath. "The man's a veteran. Do you understand? And he has no legs. He fought for this country, and now he has no legs, and he has to push himself along on the ground on a giant skateboard."

"U'mmm."

Emily tried to suppress her exasperation with the young woman. She could picture her on the other end, rolling her eyes—heard it all before—*whatever*—curling her fingers to inspect her nails.

She gripped the phone. "What do we have to do to get him one?"

"You could put in a new claim."

That had possibilities. "How long would that take?" Emily asked. "A claim for a wheelchair. *One single* wheelchair," she couldn't help adding.

"Don't get snippy, Miss. It's not my fault. This is just the claims *processing* office, you know. Have to have a claim to process to do my job." She paused. "Used to be eight months. Now it's about, oh, five—say, five and a half. Depends."

"Depends on what, please."

A sigh drifted through the phone. "The VA has to have the military records to process a claim, you know. We can't operate around here without those papers, and they have to be located and then shipped when the request is made, then it goes to the review board for a disability rating." She snapped the gum and paused again. "You know, 10 percent, 50 percent, 100 percent? Do you want to make that request or what?"

Emily closed her eyes and pressed the phone to her ear. "Yes, please. Believe me, he's 100-percent disabled. Just tell me what I have to do to get one lone wheelchair."

"Just a minute. I'll have to transfer you." The gum snapped, and the phone disconnected.

The dial tone buzzed. "Oh no!" Emily's head dropped to the desk. Maybe the church would spring for the wheelchair. A creak of wood made her sit upright. The archbishop stood in the doorway glaring at her. His face was flushed with anger, and she forgot all about the wheelchair.

✣ ✣ ✣

Emily bit her tongue. For the first time ever that she could recall, she was furious with Wesley. She looked down at the botany articles on the flowers he had just tossed on her desk with such contempt, and her eyes blurred. *Why?* she asked herself. His rage over the Shroud was completely incomprehensible. Was this the man she'd thought she loved?

"I've counted on you, Emily," she heard him say in an unfamiliar, heavy tone. "And you've let me down." Red patches flushed his cheeks, and she watched color streak up his neck.

"It's almost beyond comprehension that you could give credence to such rubbish, and we're going no further with this nonsense." His expression was tight and angry. "I have responsibilities to uphold." He seemed to stifle a shiver, and his eyes grew hard. "This report about some silly flowers is the last straw. I will not dignify it by discussing it on a national television show. You'll call and cancel my appearance at once."

"We *can't* do that," Emily said, interrupting the tirade. "You'll look foolish. I've checked the botanists' credentials, and they're impeccable. The articles do nothing more than set forth certain facts." She cocked her head toward her shoulder and raised her brows. "What is it that worries you so?"

He appeared to catch himself, then drew up his chin and looked down at Emily. "As archbishop of the Apostolic Church, I cannot—no, I *will not*—treat seriously superstitions and relics like the Shroud of Turin." He glared at her. "Do you have *any idea* what would happen otherwise? Why, my dear, every crank in this country would crawl out of the woodwork."

Emily jumped as he slammed the flat of his hand down on her desk.

"We'd spend all our time examining pieces of the cross and bleeding statues and such," he continued in that staccato tone. "I've spent my entire life working to abolish this shabby sort of thinking, and I'm not about to indulge it now."

Emily thought for a moment. Working to keep her tone soothing and conciliatory, using all of her powers of persuasion, she said, "You have to keep your commitment and appear on the show, Archbishop Bright. But you don't have to take a position on the conclusions of the botanists." She avoided his eyes, still not certain that she understood why this was suddenly so important.

The archbishop continued to glower.

"Just brush it off if you don't want to discuss it," she urged. "You can make the point that the pollen and flower images are only one small piece of circumstantial evidence to be weighed. But you can't *ignore* the information," she warned. "Jonathan Marley won't let that pass." She stared back at him. His agitation was so surprising.

"*Circumstantial evidence!* What are you, a lawyer? Since when have you been admitted to the bar, my dear?" He gave her a hard look, then turned on his heels. "I'll think it over and talk to you later."

She stared as he stormed from her office.

Emily slumped after he'd gone, exhausted from the fierce confrontation. Her hands trembled as she tapped her fingers on the desk and stared at the articles in front of her. Noise from the street below intruded, interrupting her thoughts. Slowly she pushed away from the desk and picked up her purse. A walk might help. Emily hurried down the corridor, through the great doors at the front of the church, and down the stairs. When she began to walk, she looked inward, unthinking, seeing nothing.

"Sad-eyed lady of the lowland." Emily looked down to see TeeBo leaning against the wall that he'd staked out on his corner.

He laughed when he caught her look. "You sure weren't thinking of me. What's happening, sad-eyed lady?"

Emily was surprised at how glad she was to see him. "Not much that's good," she said. She lowered herself to the sidewalk beside him.

"You need to get a life," he said in a gruff tone, maneuvering his cart to give her room to sit.

Emily grimaced. "How do you stay so calm, TeeBo? Why aren't you angry for what's happened to you?" Without thinking, she glanced at the stubs of his legs. A wheelchair could change his life. She wouldn't tell him yet, though—get his hopes up ahead of time. She'd talk to the archbishop after he cooled off. But curiosity got the best of her. "Why don't you have a wheelchair? You're a vet. You've sure earned it."

It was a moment before he answered. "I had one once. But after Hurricane Katrina hit our part of the country everything changed." He blinked, looked off, then shrugged. "Mama had passed, so I came up here thinking things would be easier, with the veterans bureau being right here and all." His voice grew tight. "I found out different when a punk stole it one night."

"Your wheelchair?"

"Yep. After that I got tangled in red tape at the VA, had to learn to pull myself along on the ground." He was silent then, still leaning back against the wall.

Emily glanced at the large muscles in his arms and shoulders, his strong hands that he used to get around, and thought how hard his life must be. "My God. I'm sorry, TeeBo," she murmured. "Really I am. I don't understand why you aren't bitter."

TeeBo shrugged, leaned back and closed his eyes. "I just think of the good things, I guess, like moon pies. Mama always said we have to set our course with a compass—turn toward the good things in life."

Emily thought about his words. "It's not always as simple as moon pies, you know." When TeeBo didn't answer, she sighed and slumped against the wall. "Your mama sounds wise, but the archbishop would put it another way, I suppose. We don't have a compass. It's all just a matter of perspective."

"Self-pity's for losers. You see this thing?" Without opening his eyes, TeeBo nodded lazily down at the wooden crate that supported his torso.

"The cart?"

"Yeah. About a year ago," he continued, "this kid made it for me." He opened his eyes with a sideways look at Emily, and his voice softened. "Cute little kid in a shelter. He worked on it for days, used wheels from some skates. His mom told me those skates were the only toy that kid ever owned."

Emily swallowed and looked away.

TeeBo watched her from beneath hooded lids. "Your archbishop's wrong, Emily. It's not a matter of perspective. Good's good, and bad's bad; and it'll always be that way, just like squares are squares, and two plus two will always be four. That's the way it is. Never mind how you feel about it. That punk did something purely bad. He didn't need that wheelchair. And the kid with the skates, he did something purely good. So now it's my turn to make it worth his while."

That was exactly the opposite of the archbishop's teachings, Emily realized. With him it was how you saw the thing that counted. Emotion. How one feels. Perspective. Suddenly she realized that nothing in the archbishop's world was absolutely good or absolutely bad; nothing transcended the *self.*

"You see?" TeeBo chuckled. "I told you it's as simple as moon pies."

CHAPTER NINETEEN

Wesley knew that he must remain calm. He'd been too hard on Emily; he must have seemed slightly hysterical. His heart raced and his head hurt. He'd returned to her office yesterday afternoon to apologize, but she had already gone. Just as well. He had no reason to offer for his behavior, no explanation. He didn't even understand it himself.

Wesley stood in the cathedral nave and looked at the altar before him. More precisely, he looked at the blank space above the altar where the crucifix used to hang.

The Shroud is real. The coincidence of the dream and the flower girl, the flowers by his bed, and the botanists' articles linking them couldn't be overlooked. Considering all of this together with all the other information in Emily's report, there was no use pretending otherwise—at least not to himself. All the bits and pieces fit together. It was like waving a string of sparks through the air. Wave fast enough and one thin gold line emerges from the blended sparks. All the old stories—the Christian teachings, the myths and legends of Jesus—they were true!

He closed his eyes as he felt his credibility and the budding power and fame slipping away. He must face the fact that the Shroud was real, and this would make a fool of him. It contradicted everything he'd taught and written about for years. It could destroy him. He'd be a laughingstock in his own church.

He sank onto a pew nearby, gazing again at the spot over the altar. What to do? His mind seethed. Ideas rose, and he knocked them down. Thoughts spun out of control. The flower girl's dark eyes formed, then disappeared. He spread his palms, examined them for a minute, and dropped his head into his hands. What to do?

Tears threatened, but he swallowed the angry sobs. Wesley prided himself on self-control. Crying over the thing wouldn't make the problem disappear. He shuddered, drew a deep breath, and held himself deathly still. In just a few days he had to face Jonathan Marley and Paul Johnson and millions of viewers knowing that the Shroud was real.

Power comes from within. Wesley raised his head and began a relaxation technique that had always calmed him. Concentrating, he let his muscles soften one at a time, releasing tension until at last he felt weightless, light and refreshed.

Refreshed. That's a good word, he thought. The cathedral was cool and silent. He chuckled to himself; already he felt better. He sat motionless, gazing at that spot above the altar. Then Wesley began to thrust and parry against his conscience over the problem.

Reason may separate man from animal, he mused, but there's a time to move beyond logic, to *expand* the process of thinking. Wesley sorted through the issues he would face on *Target Zero,* listing to himself the pros and cons, the debits and credits as he tallied the cost of truth. Should he tell the world what he had learned—that the Shroud is authentic? Could he reverse himself so completely, admit that he'd had a great *revelation?* His lips puckered with distaste; he disliked that fundamentalist word. Could he admit that the Shroud was genuine and that the words of the man on the Shroud spelled out in the Gospels of the New Testament were also true?

No one else knew what he had learned. He frowned and slowly shook his head. No. It was impossible.

For hours Wesley balanced on the precipice, on the razor edge of an abyss. The cathedral turned dark and damp, and he felt a chill. As he mulled over his options, the terror grew. Fear crawled through his body, up from his toes, into his groin, gripped his bowels, knotted in his chest, numbing his mind as he calculated the price of truth.

For starters he would lose all credibility. His glorious reformation would disappear in a heartbeat if his constituents learned that the Shroud was real; they'd return to the old ways without him. He'd spent his life, his entire career, teaching that only here and now matters. The Shroud would prove that wrong. They'd burn him as a heretic if *Saturday Night Live* didn't get him first.

And no one would buy his books; they'd be discounted down to a cent. He'd lose the national pulpit on the evening talk shows. Forget Paul Johnson. Larry King and Bill O'Reilly would count him as just another loser, like those televangelists that ended up in jail a few years ago. What were their names? Big hair. Pay for prayers, for intercession. He'd be ridiculed by Letterman and Leno.

Wesley squeezed his eyes shut at the thought and tried once again to calm himself. Start over; relax, fingers first. From the fingers to the forearm . . .

Outside the sky turned gray, and the atmosphere grew heavy. Thunder sounded in the distance. Ominous and low, it rumbled over the city; a long, continuous roll, like the old sound of drums moving closer. He'd heard these drums all his life. Mist condensed, forming translucent drops on the stained glass windows above the altar. Inside the great cathedral the archbishop felt the sudden drop in temperature. Then in the silence he heard a sound.

A voice came from deep within and all around him at once; thin and silver it came with the hollow timbre of a flute: *You have the power to choose.*

He froze but now heard only silence and the light rain that began to fall.

Free will. Wesley opened his eyes as the two small words entered his mind and held there, repeating again and again. He had the power, the right to choose unfettered. This much he knew was true. This is the human condition, the right or burden to choose.

This was reasonable. But did he have the courage to fight for what he'd earned?

Wesley sat, listening, but the voice was gone. As he waited, staring at the altar, slowly the answer formed: if we have the power to choose between two things, then it follows that one choice *must* be as good as the other. Nothing else made sense. Forget the flowers, the child, the Shroud. He was free to choose the lie. The realization shook him. Could this be right? He trembled with the thought and averted his eyes from the empty place above the altar.

I'll think it through, he told himself. Slowly, tentatively, he rose and stood for a moment, looking around the cathedral, his cathedral, as if seeing it for the first time. Images formed in Wesley's mind: his mother's face shining with pride on the day of his ordination; the title of his first book at the top of the list, the *big* list in *The New York Times*; the parties, limousines, lights, appearances on national television shows, pictures and interviews in major newspapers, private consultations with the President, with other heads of state. He had the power to choose to keep all this. But all of it would disappear if he told what he knew about the Shroud, if he told the story of the flowers and the child. If he told the truth.

I'll think it through, he resolved again.

Emily signed off the Web. No response yet on her question about the three-dimensional aspect of the image on the Shroud. Conscious of a deep sense of disappointment that threw her somewhat off-kilter, she shuffled papers on her desk, opened a book and ran her eyes down the page, then closed it, picked up her notebook, and put it down. A question popped into her mind, startling her. Did she really want to find that the burnishing process or some other artistic technique could explain the image on the Shroud? With an irritated shake of her head, she banished the thought.

Emily was waiting to see Wesley, to try to reinstate the bond she'd sensed growing between them before this conflict over the Shroud of Turin had surfaced, to reassure herself that he was the man she'd thought she knew—brilliant, courageous, and outrageous, a rebel at heart like Dad, unique. Wasn't that how he really was, her Wesley?

But she'd been waiting all morning, and time seemed to drag. What was happening? she wondered. Margaret had said he was on his way, running late. Emily looked at her watch, then pushing aside an uneasy feeling, walked down the hallway to the archbishop's office. Margaret was at her desk in the anteroom. She glanced up for an instant when Emily walked in but continued typing.

"Morning, Margaret," Emily said in an offhand manner. "Is the archbishop in yet?"

"Nope," Margaret answered, continuing to pound away on the computer. Emily watched as her fingers flew over the keyboard. Click, click. Click, click.

"How on earth do you do that?" Emily asked.

"Do what?" Click, click. Margaret appeared to be hypnotized by the monitor over the keys.

"Type so fast without looking."

"It's basic word processing, Emily. Anyone can do it." She grinned. "Even you."

"I doubt it." Emily wandered to a window and looked out. The sky was bright blue today, clear and cold. "Do you know when he'll be in?"

"Any minute now," Margaret said in a new brisk tone. "But you got here just in time."

Emily turned with a quizzical look. "Oh?"

Margaret stopped typing. She looked at Emily and her voice turned wheedling. "I need to run an errand. A manicure, actually." She flushed. "I wouldn't ask, but I've got a date tonight. Could you possibly man the fort for about half an hour?" She nodded her head toward Wesley's inner sanctum. "He should be in shortly, and I can't have him walking into an empty office."

"Sure," Emily said. Margaret had a date. Suddenly she realized that Martin had not called after the Paul Johnson show last week. Her spirits dropped even lower at the thought, and she waited in silence while Margaret slipped on her coat and picked up her purse. It had been a long time since she'd thought of such things as dates. No time. And anyway, there was Wesley. Maybe.

When Margaret was gone, Emily ambled around the desk and took a seat in Margaret's chair, swiveling it from side to side, feeling bored and restless. She picked up a pen and wound it through her fingers, remembering Martin's eyes—the green color of those eyes, the way he'd laughed when he'd said maybe their meeting was a miracle. She smiled to herself. Perhaps she'd call him if she could find that card of his. But catching herself, she dismissed the daydream. *I'll think about him later*, she resolved. *When I have more time.*

Glancing down, she saw an open manila folder lying before her on the desk. Inside a letter lay face up atop several sheets of paper stapled together at the corner. It was the bold letterhead for Brown Investigations that caught her eye. Automatically she dropped her eyes to the subject line and saw written there the name: Jonathan Albert Marley, Ph.D., Stanford University.

She hesitated, staring down at the name as a current of suspicion shot through her. With a quick glance at the closed door to the hall, she scanned the page and flipped to the stapled pages underneath. The words leapt out as she began to read: a DWI arrest, messy divorce, problems with his university transcript. But there was more.

She gasped and leaned back in the chair. Jonathan Marley, the national hero, *had never served in the war in Vietnam.* But he'd been awarded medals for his courage in that war, she remembered. Paul Johnson had said so. Newspaper and magazine articles said so. She had to read the words again before the knowledge took root.

The professor had lied. From start to finish Dr. Marley had lied about his past—to the press, to the university, to everyone he'd come in contact with for the last thirty-plus years, it seemed. The Purple Heart was invented. During the time that he claimed to have been in Vietnam, he was a student attending university in Toronto, Ontario. In Canada.

No wonder he'd seemed nervous on the show. She slammed the folder shut. How had the professor managed to maintain a lie on such a scale? Emily wondered. And then, why had he embroidered upon it for years and years? She opened the folder again.

Because no one had ever questioned his story, the investigator speculated. Why should they, after all? The falsehood had begun as a small one, a casual remark to a reporter in

Los Angeles that appeared in a story on page 5 of the evening paper. But over the years as Jonathan Marley made a name for himself at Stanford, a gloss was added with each repetition, until finally the embellished biography took on a life of its own that was impossible to contain.

In ten minutes Emily had finished reading the entire report. Closing the folder, she stared down at it with disbelief. Marley must have been beside himself when things careened out of control, she reflected, conscious of a stir of pity. The professor had been living on the brink of disaster for years. He must be terrified of exposure.

But as she looked down again at the folder, a new thought rose; there it was, indicting Wesley, the archbishop. Feeling suddenly nauseated as she gazed at it, she closed her eyes and opened them again to face the truth. Wesley, the archbishop, whom she'd loved, *thought* she'd loved, admired. No, of course the word to use was *loved.* He had obtained this report.

In the empty office Emily sat motionless, staring blindly at the far wall without moving until Margaret returned. Then, composing a pleasant smile, she escaped from the office as quickly as possible.

Returning from lunch, which she didn't want and couldn't eat, Emily saw TeeBo ahead, parked on the sidewalk in his usual spot. She was in a hurry, and besides, she wanted to be alone right now, needed to mull over this new discovery. So she quickened her pace, giving him a friendly wave.

"Hey!"

She hesitated. She trusted TeeBo. Maybe it would be good to talk to him about this problem with the archbishop. She glanced down at her watch. It was already two o'clock, and she had a pile of work on her desk. Needed to check her e-mail to see if there was a response from that STURP photographer. Needed to follow through on the wheelchair.

Same old problem. "No time right now, TeeBo," she called, feeling like the white rabbit as the light turned green. "I'll catch you later."

Emily stepped onto the street from the curbstone without looking back and started across. Coming toward her was a woman holding a small boy by the hand. She glanced at the woman's tired face as they moved toward each other. The child dragged behind, and the woman pulled him forward with a series of tiny jerks. As she reached Emily, she stopped to wait for the child to catch up. Emily hurried past them.

TeeBo watched Emily step into the street, only vaguely aware of the young woman and small child beginning to cross from the other side. As they passed each other in the middle, he noticed absently that the woman was taller than Emily. Her child, a small boy, reached only to her hips. The boy's hair gleamed in the afternoon sun like a young child's will, and TeeBo had a sudden picture of himself, a small boy just like this one looking up at Mama on a hot summer day. He shivered and glanced at the sky. The clouds were high white cirrus, and even though it was cold, the sun shone on the city.

One block away a large white van turned onto Lexington, rounding the corner too fast. The tires squealed on the pavement from the skid, and TeeBo's head turned toward the sound. His back straightened as it came into clear focus. The van was gaining speed. TeeBo waited for it to slow.

The subterranean thought began to form. *The van wasn't slowing down at all.*

With the squeal of the careening van's wheels still in his ears, TeeBo turned his head and saw that the woman had halted in the middle of the street with her child, in the path of the van. She turned and bent over her boy in a slow graceful motion. As TeeBo looked at them, the realization surfaced and crystallized: *the van would not stop in time.*

A rush of energy surged through TeeBo. Without thinking he lifted himself straight on the wooden cart, balancing on the heavy stumps of his legs as he pulled up and out of his torso. Then, as the van came on, in one smooth movement his hands flattened on the wall behind him, and he pressed them hard against the cement.

In that split second he glimpsed this child—the child in the street with soft silky skin, round eyes trusting in his mother as he holds onto her hand. TeeBo saw him grown, smiling on a porch swing with children of his own. He saw the mother, old, surrounded by her grandchildren, standing on a smooth green lawn near flowers that were tended with love over the years, and she laughed as she looked off into the distance.

TeeBo heard Mama's voice calling like she used to do when supper was on the table, and he saw her shining face. She seemed to smile, but the smile was wistful, and just before she disappeared, he wondered why. A symphony of crickets and wild birds rose, fading to the marshland near the South Pass. Beneath his feet the old boat hummed and churned on through the water till the river met the Gulf. A pelican rose nearby and caught the drift, soaring off. He felt the sun warm his skin, and in the distance he saw the silver flutter in the dark blue rip that told a school of small fish was passing by.

Emily had stepped up onto the curb at the far side of the street when, suddenly, she was conscious of something large and white racing toward the intersection. She turned her head, looking back over her shoulder. In the middle of the street, she saw the mother and her child standing directly in the path of the oncoming van.

As the blur of white sped toward the woman and the child, a shrill scream pierced the air. In that instant TeeBo pushed himself off from the wall on the rolling cart with the bull strength built from months of dragging himself along the ground one inch at a time. As he shot forward, his great arms flailed in arcs, powerful whirling circles that propelled him toward the street as his hands hit the pavement with smacks and the wheels of his cart spun. TeeBo flew straight across the sidewalk and, as Emily watched with horror, launched himself into the air from the curbstone.

Emily opened her mouth to scream as her eyes took in the scene. Later she recalled the moment as if the universe had split in two and all the fury of life rushed toward her in that second: the white van speeding toward the woman and child, the boy looking up at his mother, and TeeBo flying toward them through the air on his wooden cart. She had a brief glimpse of TeeBo's cart crashing to the cement and his truncated body hitting the woman and child, knocking them aside.

Just before the silent darkness descended, Emily's brain recorded the image of the van as it hit, shattering the heap and the cart that were TeeBo in a furious blaze of harsh white light.

CHAPTER TWENTY

Emily could hear the voices but kept her eyes closed. Something hovered in the back of her mind, but she couldn't make it out. Her body was pillowed, stretched over a long and soft thing, and she felt boneless, languid. She must be lying on a bed, she decided. The voices murmured, and finally, out of curiosity, she cracked her lids just enough to peek from underneath.

Something bad had happened; she strained to remember what it was. Through half-closed eyes she saw Wesley sitting in a chair nearby. Behind him Miss Honeman was engaged in conversation with a woman dressed all in white. She thought about that—the woman all in white must be a nurse. With this her eyes sprung open, and Wesley met her gaze. Emily struggled, trying to push herself up from the bed, but her arms were weak and gave way. Wesley disappeared and the nurse's face loomed over her.

"Don't try to sit just yet, Miss Scott," a cheerful voice said. The nurse slipped her hand under Emily's neck and lifting her head slightly, adjusted the pillow. Emily watched her face for clues, trying to determine what had happened.

Someone took her hand. Wesley, she realized; but she couldn't remember a time when he'd held her hand before. Turning her head to him, she managed a weak smile and raised her eyebrows. "Am I all right?"

He nodded, understanding. "You're fine," he said. "The doctor says you'll be okay."

Behind him the nurse reached up, adjusting a line of clear plastic tubing. Tracing it with her eyes, Emily saw that it led to a syringe that was planted in her arm and taped.

The nurse glanced up just then. "We're taking it out soon. The IV's just a precaution."

Emily turned back to Wesley. "What happened?" she asked.

"You tell us," he said grimly. "You fainted on the corner of Fifty-first and Lex. Hit your head on a curb, apparently." With a relieved smile, he patted her hand. "It gave us quite a scare, my dear. I was just about to leave the office, and Margaret took the call. Apparently you were out cold, and an ambulance brought you to the hospital."

She gave him a blank look.

"It was a wreck, an accident," he explained.

That shadow drifting behind her thoughts, just at the edge of consciousness rose. She saw a blur of white, and a small body flying through the air. "The child?" she asked, exhaling the words. "Was the child hit?"

"No, no," Wesley soothed, patting her hand once again. "The child is fine. So's his mother. They're very lucky though. From what we've been told, a speeding truck just missed them." He gave her a consoling smile. "It did hit a beggar, though. Probably a homeless person."

With a small, spasmodic jerk Emily withdrew her hand as the image of TeeBo flying through the air assaulted her. Her chest caught fire, and she gasped to fill her lungs with air. The nurse, walking toward the door, turned back to her. "Are you all right?" she asked in a sharp tone.

Emily nodded without speaking. As the scene came rushing back, she squeezed her eyes together to blot it out. Wesley released her hand, and his chair scraped the tiled floor as he shoved it back from the bed. "Nurse!" she heard him shout, as if from a distance.

Someone grabbed her wrist and probed it. A cool hand stroked her forehead.

Emily steeled herself and, knowing that she must, opened her eyes, gazing first at the nurse and then at Wesley's puzzled face through a blur of tears. "I'm fine, I'm fine," she said, waving the nurse away. "It's just . . ."

Wheelchair. The wheelchair! She'd never gotten him the wheelchair. Again she saw TeeBo flying through the air. "TeeBo!" she blurted.

"TeeBo?" Wesley asked, bending over her. "Who's that, Emily? Someone you know?" His voice was gentle, soothing.

"It wasn't luck," Emily said in a faltering voice. "The child wasn't just lucky. TeeBo saved his life. I saw him." Her voice rose and broke. "I saw him!"

✣ ✣ ✣

Emily looked at the investigator's report on Jonathan Marley that she'd just finished reading and tossed it down on the floor beside her. She had asked to see it again and Wesley had obliged. She was stretched out on a couch in the living room of her apartment, and Miss Honeman had put a pillow under her head and a light blanket over her. Emily made an exasperated sound; Miss Honeman had bustled around when they'd brought her home as if she was an invalid. Her head still ached. They were worried about a concussion for a while, Wesley had said. But the doctor had pronounced that she was fine now, on the mend. No concussion. Nothing was broken.

Except TeeBo, she thought.

She pushed off thoughts of TeeBo. She would think about him later. No time now; she had to concentrate. Wesley's appearance on *Target Zero* was only forty-eight hours away, and the thing was rapidly turning into a disaster. Remembering the e-mail she'd sent to the STURP photographer, she tensed. Loose ends unnerved her. The archbishop needed all the information she could gather before the show. For some reason he'd suddenly decided that the Shroud was important after all; surprises would not be well received.

Oh well. Nothing she could do about it right this minute. She turned her mind back to the investigator's report and grimaced. Brown Investigations had given Wesley the ammunition to destroy Jonathan Marley, the great American war hero. The report was scurrilous, sickening. And Emily knew that it would be effective. The camera loved the lanky, smiling archbishop. He could look into the lens and say just about anything, and people listened and agreed. After Wesley finished with Marley, viewers would accept as final authority anything the archbishop had to say about the Shroud.

Emily closed her eyes, feeling tired. Why was Wesley going to such extreme measures over the Shroud of Turin? The phone rang, interrupting her thoughts. The noise was irritating, and she could think of no one in the world whom she wanted to talk to right now, so she let it ring. When the answering machine came on after four rings, she heard a familiar voice. Martin Allen's voice.

"Emily. Martin Allen, here. I've been thinking of you." Emily's heartbeat quickened, and she lifted her head from the pillow to listen. "Please give me a call back when you have a moment," he said in that stilted voice people use for answering machines. "Here's my number, in case . . ." Quickly she threw one leg from the couch, but it tangled in the blanket. Then she heard the sound of fumbling in the background . . . a door slamming, another voice. "Do you have a minute, Professor?" Then Martin's voice, lower now: "I have to go. Call me!"

She fell back onto the couch. Her head pounded as she stared at the telephone. He hadn't left his number, and Emily wondered where she'd put Martin's card. Suddenly she needed Martin's card, and it was probably in her purse, and the purse was all the way across the room, near the door. She sighed; it was just too far away. And she was tired, too tired to move. *Melancholy* was the word that came to mind.

Her gaze roamed on past the telephone, lighting at random on one thing after the other in the gloomy room. There was that piano she never had time to use. There was never any time for things like that. Thanks to the archbishop. Wesley? Overcome by a wave of self-pity, her eyes slid to the investigator's report on the floor beside her that Wesley had procured. No, definitely, from now on he was the archbishop.

Time, time, time, time, time—the words wheeled through her head, developing a cadence that annoyed her. *No time, no time, no time.*

No time for such things as finding a wheelchair. The accusation rose, and a sob welled, filling her chest, tightening her throat until it ached. *The wheelchair.* She'd never had time to give TeeBo even one day in that wheelchair.

She stopped the thoughts, feeling lightheaded and dizzy, too weak to move. Her stomach growled, but the idea of food turned her stomach. Nausea rose. And how could she think of food when TeeBo is . . . no . . . she wouldn't think of that. She searched for something safe to ponder, something that would calm her. *The archbishop?* Bowels twisted. No.

Her limp body sank into the cushions. She stretched out her arm to the coffee table that Miss Honeman had moved close and pulled her research notebook over toward her. Listlessly she lifted it, gazed at it, and dropped it onto her chest. A minute passed while she studied the ceiling overhead. At last she picked the notebook up again, opened it, and holding it straight-armed over her head began to read, forcing herself to focus on the words.

For forty-five minutes she read. She read her notes on the exhibition at the Met. She read what she'd been told by Martin and Amy and Leo Ransom, and she read her summaries from the botany articles. After absorbing all of this, she started over—read it all again. When she'd finished, she dropped the notebook onto the floor with a thud and looked off.

The cumulative effect of reading all of the information in the notebook together at one time made a powerful case that the Shroud was real—that it originated in Jerusalem, or nearly, centuries earlier than the official radiocarbon date, that it contained ancient human blood, and that the image was created in a mysterious way not yet understood by science.

Glancing down, she spotted the investigator's report on the floor beside the notebook. Bracing herself on one elbow, she reached down, retrieved it and held it, weighing it. If the archbishop used this against Marley on the show, the Shroud would never have the fair hearing she'd promised Leo Ransom. But why would he do such a thing?

Holding onto the investigator's report, she leaned back against the pillow. *Why is the Shroud so important to Wesley all of a sudden?* she asked herself again, and TeeBo's words came back to her. TeeBo would have said, "Walk back the cat." Look for the first cause, the reason behind the archbishop's strange behavior.

Thinking of TeeBo, she closed her eyes. The morning papers had been full of the terrible event. TeeBo was described by the reporter as a hero. Witnesses spoke of seeing him roar past them on the ground, transforming into a streak of color as he soared over the curb like a human cannonball. Because of him, the child and his mother were alive.

"I've made arrangements for your friend's body to be sent home to Louisiana," Wesley had told her earlier. He'd seemed somewhat confused by her friendship with TeeBo, but nevertheless, she had to admit that he'd been kind.

"Thank you," she'd said. "I didn't know he even has . . . *had* . . . family left." Her voice had broken as she'd remembered the look on TeeBo's face when he'd spoken of his mother.

"Evidently he had an uncle who cared a great deal for him." Wesley consoled. "His mother's younger brother, I believe the man said. The police located him for me. I promised to send him copies of the stories. The young man was quite a hero."

"Yes," Emily said, fighting back the tears.

"Do you think he knew them?"

"The child and the woman?"

"Yes."

Emily shook her head. "I don't think so. He didn't seem to have many friends."

Wesley puffed out his lips and looked off. "Extraordinary. I wonder what made him do it?"

"I don't know," she'd told him.

Now Emily looked around the room; and when her eyes fell on the telephone, she focused on it to banish the depressing memories, willing it to ring. Still the obstinate thing was silent. She considered Martin's card again and grimaced at the purse, taunting her from across the room.

No. Her purse was too far away, and she was too tired, and besides, her head still hurt.

Archbishop Bright was avoiding Emily. He heard her voice in the anteroom to his office; he heard Margaret put her off once again, for the third time today, following instructions.

I must think! He told himself. Emily can wait.

The Paul Johnson show was only twenty-four hours away, and he knew the time had come to make a decision. The investigator's report lay on the desk in front of him. The man had done his work. Marley had been lying for years. Unbelievable. Wesley opened the file and fingered the report. He'd read it several times, almost knew it by heart. Defamation wasn't a problem. The facts were a defense. And Marley was a little crude, reserved and standoffish, he mused. He'd probably left a trail of acquaintances who vaguely disliked him and were happy to discuss his failings with the investigator.

Wesley slipped the report back inside the folder. Of course, he still had some thinking to do, but, on the other hand, it was comforting to know the balance of power had shifted his way. How to use this information was the question.

He drummed his fingers lightly on the desk. Shoving back his chair, he stood, walked to the window and looked out, seeing nothing, then walked back to his desk. He glanced down at the folder, tapped it lightly, then turned and ambled back to the window. A lot was at stake. He frowned to himself; in fact, as he now saw it, the Shroud was an attack on his own personal credibility.

Margaret stuck her head in and said good-bye for the evening. The archbishop nodded to her in a distracted manner and continued pacing—back and forth, desk to window, window to desk.

Finally he lowered himself into a comfortable chair in the corner of the room. Settling back, Wesley let his gaze wander over the office, judging his possessions as he always did, as a stranger would seeing them for the first time. He studied the oversized mahogany desk polished and gleaming, the silver and brass appointments laid out neatly on top. He liked that word, *appointments*—the gold pen upright in the onyx stand, the rows of books lining the walls. Many were bound in fine leather with thick gold lettering on the spine. And he'd read every one of them; no uncut pages in these books. Some were first editions that he'd collected over the years.

His eyes scanned down to the expensive Persian carpet, thicker than most, yet still fine with intricate patterns worked through the crimson wool. Dust in a stream of light from the window caught his eye, and his gaze trailed it to the window. The light outside was growing dim. He was surprised to see how late it was. *Funny,* he thought, *the sepia tone that light takes on just before the sun goes down in winter.*

Suddenly he looked up and blinked. A shadowed figure stood in the open doorway—a man, slightly stooped. The hall light shone an aureole around his silhouette.

"Hello, Wesley."

Where had he heard that voice before? It was low, harsh, oddly familiar. He strained to see. "Who's there?" he whispered.

As he braced his arms to push up from the chair, the figure stepped into the room. Wesley froze and, after an instant, dropped back down into the seat.

Leo Ransom stood gazing down at him. "Don't you recognize me?" he asked.

Wesley stared at the frail priest with white hair and parchment skin dressed in an old-fashioned clerical black suit that he hadn't seen worn in years. For a moment he saw only the outline of the man, like a stick figure of Leo Ransom—flat and unreal but grim, as if he'd jumped right out of the Old Testament—an avenging angel! Wesley blinked and Leo smiled, but his eyes were chips of ice.

"Mind if I sit?" Leo asked, pulling a straight-backed wooden chair over beside Wesley's and taking a seat without waiting for the answer.

"Does it matter?" Wesley answered after a moment, spitting the words. He rose and crossed to his desk, wanting to put it between Leo and him. He sat down and turned to the old man. "Same old Leo," he said. "Nothing's changed I see." For some reason his stomach constricted, and unaccountable images flashed before his eyes in rough, stilted sequence: Sam falling; Sam lying on the ground; the judge at trial; Leo at the ball game; Jesse in the park. The old hate simmered, crawling through him as he worked to keep his face expressionless.

"It's been a long time," Leo said.

Wesley shifted his gaze to the top of the desk, then cleared the space in front of him as if it were a battlefield, shoving aside pencils and paper. When he had finished, he folded his hands on top to steady them, took a deep breath, and looked up. "What brings you here?" he asked mildly.

"Emily visited me a few days ago," Leo replied.

Wesley lowered his eyes and watched Leo beneath hooded lids as he rolled a pencil back and forth on top of the desk with his fingertips. Emily. His little Emily. With Leo? Suddenly he burned with envy at the thought. He couldn't bear to think of Leo near Emily. "Oh?" he murmured.

"She was doing research for a report on the Shroud of Turin."

Wesley looked up at that. "What do *you* know about the Shroud?" he asked, motionless now.

Leo gazed at the last light filtering through the window. "I've studied it for years." He shrugged and his eyes slid back to Wesley. "She wanted information and I gave it to her."

"Does she know about Sam?" The thought of Emily discussing little Sam and him turned his blood cold. He heard Jesse's voice again: *You said to let him go.*

"No. She's not even aware that we're acquainted." Leo paused. "We only talked about the Shroud. I thought that maybe you were really interested. She said you'd give it a fair hearing."

Wesley released a sigh of relief, then failed to suppress a chuckle. "I take it you saw the Paul Johnson show last week?" he asked, lifting his chin as he spoke. "What did you think? Did you believe there was the slightest chance that I'd become an advocate for that old relic?"

"No. But I hoped that you'd be evenhanded, present the evidence fairly. I expected that an archbishop of the Apostolic Church might consider letting other people decide the truth for themselves."

"Truth!" Wesley gave Leo a deliberate look of contempt. "Since we're alone, Leo, let me put it to you bluntly."

"Please do."

"Personally, I think truth is irrelevant to any given situation. I'm fairly pragmatic, you may remember. I prefer expediency." He laced his fingers together on the desk in front of him and studied them. "The question I ask myself about truth is what real difference does the thing make to my own life?"

Leo stared out of the window. "That must be a bit unnerving," he said. "Circumstances change." Stone-faced, he turned back to Wesley. "I'd add a caveat. As you implied on the show last week, a house built on sand won't survive a storm."

Wesley unlaced his hands and spread the fingers of one hand up before him. He needed a manicure, he observed. "Even if I believed that the Shroud was authentic," he murmured, dropping his hand, "I don't think I would bring myself to make a case for it, Leo. You see," he looked up, "between you and me, I don't really care whether it's real or not." His lips curled, but his face was set. "Call it my bargain with the devil, if you like."

Leo's eyes narrowed. When he spoke, his voice was harsh and low. Wesley bent forward to catch his words. "I wondered how far your narcissistic rage would take you," Leo said.

Wesley pulled back as if struck. "You're just the same Leo—so, so righteous," he said, shaking his head. He slowly inspected the priest from head to toe. "I'd almost forgotten why I dislike you. Do you want to know?"

Leo nodded. "I never did understand."

Drums pounded inside. Wesley dipped his chin and pressed his fingers to his temples. "It was you, the judge at Sam's trial, my father—every one of you let me down." His breath was shallow and the words came out a hiss. "It's from each one of you that I learned there's no such thing as truth, no such thing as justice. Promises all broken. Self-righteous arrogance." He clenched his jaw, wishing the old man would leave.

"You were a liar and a manipulator when you were a boy, Wesley. But you're a *destroyer* now," Leo said with vehemence. "You've betrayed the oath you took to uphold Christian faith when you were ordained, the promise to uphold the basic ideas of Christianity; and *most important,"* he lingered on the words, "the resurrection of Christ that the Shroud represents."

"Oh please," Wesley said, fighting a sickening stab of fear. Of course Leo didn't know about his dream. About the flowers and the Shroud. How could he? He gave Leo a thin, tight smile. "The resurrection? The Shroud? You put that as though those stories are facts. Let's just try, for once, to hold a conversation based on reality." He wondered if he could just toss Leo out of his office.

Leo went on, ignoring his words. "It's one thing to have a personal opinion on a matter like the Shroud. But you!" His eyes raked Wesley as if seeing him for the first time. "You stand in the shoes of the apostles, but the only thing you're consecrated to is your own ambition."

"Why is it," Leo asked in the ensuing silence, "that you are *so* relentless?" Gazing at Wesley, he slowly shook his head.

"How do you justify using the power of your position to destroy the church, and faith, and hope?"

Wesley studied Leo in the half-light. For an instant he almost weakened as he thought of his mother, of Father Leo holding his hand as they walked together into the courtroom. But then he thought of Sam. Fiercely he drew himself back from the memories that could deflect him from his choice and his goal.

"You told me once that faith is nothing more than trust," Wesley said, remembering the broken promises, the lies. His voice hardened as he spoke.

"And I failed you with that answer, Wesley." Leo studied his shoes. "I should have understood that trust must be based on something solid. Not everyone has the gift of faith."

He gave Wesley an intent look. "For some people that's the importance of the Shroud," he said. "It's tangible proof that there's more, something beyond this physical world that we muddle through each day. It tells us that absolute truth and goodness exist, even when we're feeling lost."

Wesley's lips pressed together, and the crease between his eyes deepened.

Suddenly Leo slumped and looked around the opulent room, knowing that he was defeated. He turned his head and met Wesley's eyes—the eyes of Rebecca's son, looking back at him with hatred.

Wesley's eyes flashed. "Look where faith has gotten you, *Father* Leo." He stood, shoving back his chair and glaring down at Leo. "Look at you," he said in a low, ominous tone. "You're all dressed up like a priest with no place to go. Everything you stand for is dead. Just as dead as Sam."

Leo closed his eyes. "How can hatred last so long?" he murmured.

Wesley wheeled around and stared out of the window, looking down on the courtyard, now almost hidden in shadows. He braced his arms behind his back, working to banish images of Sam. "Hate is stronger than love," he finally said, turning back to Leo. "It has more staying power." His eyes fixed on Leo's white-rimmed collar for an instant and flicked away.

"Besides," he added, lounging back against the window frame and folding his arms over his chest. "The old church was finished years ago. I've invested my life in renewing the corpse." His eyes glowed through the dusk like burning ash. "How many millions of people have wasted their lives because they were terrorized by religion? I rid them of that."

"You have it backwards, Wesley," Leo replied. "People are driven by hope, not fear."

Wesley snorted with disdain. "You're a fool, Leo," he said, in a dismissive tone. "Look around you." He waved his arm at his possessions. "I don't need your promises any more. I have power, money, fame. Presidents and diplomats ask for my advice. And you're here to suggest that I give it all up?"

His face hardened with a look of determination, and he gave Leo a cold smile. "No thank you. I stand alone. I've looked into the abyss; and to paraphrase Nietzsche, once you've looked into the abyss, it's already too late."

He dropped down into the chair behind his desk and leaned back, folding his hands over his stomach. "Now get out."

Seconds passed while Leo braced his hands on the arms of the chair and with all of his effort pushed himself up. He stood swaying and reached for the back of the chair. After a moment he turned and looked down at Wesley. "I believe that it was also poor, mad Nietzsche who said nothing can originate from its opposite, Wesley. Including evil."

Wesley sat in the dark without moving long after Leo had gone, knowing that he would never see the old priest again. Jumbled images formed in his mind out of all sense of order. At first they were happy thoughts that brought him comfort: his mother laughing at his antics when he was small, the bees—he almost smiled at the thought of the bees, the years at Yale. But then the old hauntings rose as they always did, sucking at his soul, if such a thing exists. Sam, dangling from the edge of the roof and his own cry, raw with anguish: *Let him go!* Sam falling through the air, slowly at first, drifting, then suddenly careening toward the earth. And a small boy running down the dirty narrow concrete stairs as fast as he could run, gasping for breath, holding back his tears.

He wished that he could cry right now.

There's no time to cry. Just *run!*

Run!

He'd not really seen Sam fall, Wesley realized, even though he'd pictured the moment every day for over fifty years. His heart began to hammer. Once again he heard the drums, pounding, pounding. Nietzsche had said something else too—something he'd buried, refused to think of since the day he'd first read the words at Yale. Now they burned forth in his mind.

Terrible experiences pose the riddle whether the person who has them is not also terrible.

With both hands he pushed back from the desk and crumpled. *Father. Son. Holy Ghost.* The haunting, unfamiliar words that he'd learned from Leo crashed through his mind. *Why weren't you there? Why weren't you there?*

Suddenly, without warning, anguish that had simmered, lain dormant for all those years, burst forth, exploding with a force that rocked him, carried him with it. Hunched, he planted his elbows upon his knees and hid his face with a fierce, almost uncontrollable desire to free the tears, to sob. With all his strength, he struggled to contain it.

God the Father, God the Son, God the Holy Ghost. The words slipped out instead. *Where were you on the day Sam died? How could you abandon him . . . and me?*

Finally, with a great effort Wesley raised his head, exhausted and drained. And in that instant a last gleam of the dying sun flashed from the pointed tip of the gold pen on his desk. As it caught his eye, Wesley grew still, watching the light glitter before him, remembering for some strange reason the silver dollar his father had given him just before he'd left. Odd thing to remember. But he knew that he'd already made the choice.

Why should he give up all that he'd worked for over the years?

The flickering golden light held his eye. So what if his success was built on a lie? Sometimes truth must adapt to circumstances—whether a lie is bad or good depends on the time and place and events. Look at all the little white lies people tell every day to get through this swamp of life. The future is always uncertain; what happens now is concrete, real. And we have the power to choose.

He jutted out his chin. The Right Honorable Archbishop Wesley Bright, leader of the Apostolic Church, counselor to presidents and diplomats, recognized coast to coast, darling of the intelligentsia, darling of the media, *Little Guy,* would have his treasure now, on earth.

I choose NOW, he almost shouted into the empty room.

And Emily? What if I lose Emily?

The archbishop gave a knowing smile, one that he'd practiced many times; but the smile wavered. Nonsense. He could sort things out with Emily. She was his protégé. The woman loved him, respected and trusted him. Emily would understand. And slowly the thought emerged: she was all he had to love.

CHAPTER TWENTY-ONE

The air was fresh and cold as Emily hurried down Fifty-first Street toward the cathedral. As she approached TeeBo's corner, tears threatened. Averting her eyes, she continued. It had to be done sometime, she knew. She couldn't go through the rest of her life avoiding the corner of Lexington and Fifty-first.

Nevertheless, she was relieved to see the light turn green as she reached the corner, and without slowing she hurried across. It was still early, but Emily wanted to speak with Wesley about the show. She needed to hear him tell her that he wasn't planning to expose Professor Marley on national television, that the detective's report was nothing more than an exercise of some sort. She had called him at the rectory last night, but Miss Honeman answered the phone and said the archbishop had asked not to be disturbed.

Emily ran up the cathedral stairs, but when she pulled on the side door that led to the offices, it wouldn't budge.

Impatiently she knocked, pounding on the door until finally she heard a key turn, and it opened. Mr. Cundrell, the elderly janitor, looked out and, when he saw Emily, opened it wide for her.

"Morning, Miss Scott," he said without a smile. "You're early today."

"I suppose so," Emily said, waiting until he had closed the door behind him. "Has the archbishop arrived yet?" she asked, when he turned back to her.

"Not yet, Miss," he said, pocketing the key. He picked up a mop leaning against the wall near the door. "It's a bit early for His Grace though, I'd say."

"Yes, well . . ." Her voice trailed off as he turned, bent down again for a pail of water, and trudged off. She watched his back for a moment, then hurried to her office. Turning on the computer, she checked e-mail to see if the STURP photographer had responded to her question about the three-dimensional aspect of the Shroud image. Not yet.

It was late afternoon before Wesley could see her. When she entered his office, he was seated in a chair in the corner rather than in his usual place behind the large desk. *Strange,* she thought; he looked pensive, different somehow. Harder. He sat bolt upright with his feet planted on the floor instead of lounging back in his usual, almost lazy slouch.

He glanced up and his lips stretched into a smile. "Well now," he said, looking her up and down, "you're looking fit today. Thank goodness." He shook his head as he rose. "I must say, Emily, that you had us all a bit worried for a while." Coming around his desk to greet her, he stretched out his arms, rested his hands on her shoulders and peered down, inspecting her. "Are you feeling well? Any leftover aches or pains?"

She gave a nervous laugh and drew away. "I'm fine," she said. "I want to thank you again for taking care of things." She dropped into the nearest chair. "It was very kind of you."

"He must have been a fine young man."

"He was." Emily gave him a steady look. "Let's talk about tonight."

Wesley colored. "Yes. Well, that's all under control, Emily, and you're not to worry. You've other things on your mind right now." His words came out in a rush as he retreated to the chair behind his desk where he sat and busied himself with papers stacked in a box on the corner of the desk, marked "In."

Emily rose and stood, touching the edge of the desk with both hands. Her heart raced. "Your Grace."

Wesley raised his eyes to her. "Yes?" he replied in a cautious tone.

She took a deep breath. "Please tell me that the detective's report on Dr. Marley is not something you intend to use on the show this evening." Her voice was hesitant. Looking down at him, she waited for his answer.

He tilted back in the chair and gave her a wry smile. "One must never go into battle unprepared, my dear."

"Battle?" she repeated, surprised.

He shook his head, as if flustered. "That might not be the right word. Let's just say that it's background."

"Nothing more?"

He blew out his cheeks and studied her. "That remains to be seen," he said after a moment, lifting his chin. But seeing her worried expression, he softened. "Don't be naive, Emily," he said, smiling. His voice was intimate as he rose and came around to where she stood.

He took her hand in his and held it as if it were a precious thing with a look that told her he had something more to say. But he seemed to check himself instead and, dropping his arm to his side, perched on the corner of the desk facing her. "It was Marley who made the mess of his life," he said. "Not me; not the detective. If you're uncomfortable with what you've read, remember the stakes. If necessary," he added with an intimate smile, "think of it this way: the end will justify the means."

As she listened to his words, Emily turned cold. She hugged her arms against her chest while the archbishop stood and herded her toward the door. "I think it would be a terrible mistake to bring it up on the show tonight," she heard herself say, as if from a distance. "This television show isn't a battle. It's only a discussion about the Shroud of Turin."

"Oh, you're quite wrong about that, Emily," the archbishop retorted. In the anteroom, Margaret's desk was empty. She'd gone for coffee, as he'd encouraged her to do so that she wouldn't overhear. His eyes darted past Emily, and she turned, hearing a door open and close at the other end of the hall. "The discussion tonight is about *much* more than the Shroud of Turin," he said, holding her shoulder as he steered her toward the outer door.

Emily stopped, turned, and waited for him to say that the real issue was truth. But his next words made her stare.

He maintained his grip on her shoulder and looked down at her as Margaret's footsteps sounded in the hall. "The real point of the show tonight is power."

"What did you say?" She wondered if she'd misunderstood.

His fingers squeezed her shoulder. "What I ask you to think of is this." Dropping his chin, he gave her a deep, grave look, remembering his mother's words years ago. "Power is the difference between happiness and misery, Emily. And it has been abused by people like Marley who've made supernatural religious claims for thousands of years—claims like this hoax, the Shroud." He hesitated and forced himself not to think of the dream, the indigo eyes.

"What does that have to do with destroying Jonathan Marley?" she asked, in a low, fierce tone.

"He's a fraud, like all the rest. I'm here to expose them for what they are," he went on, masking his unease with a blank expression. "I'm going to call them all to account, these cheats who preach, then let us down. I'll show them all." Something stirred as he said the words—a vague feeling that he'd said them before—I'll show them all.

Emily shrugged him off in one smooth motion. "What if it turns out to be true?" she asked, walking toward the door. "What if the Shroud really is the burial cloth of Jesus?" She paused, turned back to him, and lowered her voice, steeling herself, struck by the new spark of courage that she'd found.

"It seems to me that the question of the authenticity of the Shroud is open," she said. "It has nothing to do with Dr. Marley's situation. That report reads like a tabloid. How do you think you'll appear if you use the information?"

The archbishop gave her a mild look. "You misunderstand. I merely intend to hold Marley to account," he said under his breath. Behind her Emily heard Margaret hesitate just outside the open door. When she entered the room, Wesley's face transformed, softening as he greeted her, smiling. His eyes crinkled first at Margaret, then at Emily.

"We'll discuss this later, after the show," he told Emily, patting her shoulder before he wheeled around, following Margaret to her desk. Ducking his head, he retrieved a stack of mail from the desk and began sorting through the envelopes.

A long e-mail from the STURP photographer waited on the computer monitor when Emily returned to her office. She looked at the disarray on the desk and glanced at her watch. Only three hours were left before she was to meet the archbishop at the television studio across town. She still had a hundred things to do, and it was rush hour. Should she take a taxi? No, impossible to get one right now. She'd finish up here and walk.

With a sigh Emily turned back to the computer and printed out the e-mail, plucked it from the printer, and stuffed it into her purse. Rush hour. What an appropriate term.

Emily came into the television studio with Wesley and greeted Jonathan Marley, who stood alone just inside the door. The archbishop stopped to speak with him. Emily paused, but at a frown from Wesley, she left them, entering the studio to take a seat just behind the center camera near a viewing monitor. Paul Johnson stood in the middle of the set studying some papers as someone adjusted the lighting, conferring with him in a low voice from time to time.

The room was cool and quiet, and Emily leaned back in her chair to wait for Wesley to reappear. The clock on the wall said ten minutes to go, and she tried to calm herself. The show had stirred things up, and the morning paper carried a long article about the archbishop, Jonathan Marley and his exploits in Vietnam, and the Shroud. Even the director at the Met expressed surprise at the new level of interest sparked by the lively discussion on the show last week. He had spoken with Margaret earlier in the day to let the archbishop know that the exhibition was being held over.

Emily glanced over her shoulder, looking for Wesley. Still he didn't appear; and after a moment, remembering the e-mail in her purse, she dug it out. It was a copy of a printed article several pages long, she saw. The e-mail was crumpled, and she smoothed it on her lap, then picked it up to read.

After reading it through twice, she put the e-mail down. Small beads of perspiration formed on her forehead. The Shroud image could not have been created by an artist.

According to the article, the STURP scientists had used a VP-8 Image Analyzer to study the three-dimensional properties of the Shroud. The VP-8 was a device originally designed for NASA in the 1960s to create topical relief maps from photographs of the moon; it converted light and dark areas into an accurate vertical relief. In 1976 scientists at Los Alamos National Laboratories put the famous Enrie photograph of the Shroud into the VP-8 and were startled to find that unlike an ordinary photograph or a painting of an artwork, the image had true three-dimensional properties; that is, the image densities measured by the VP-8 on the photograph were directly proportionate to the actual distance the cloth was from the body at any point.

Emily summarized what she'd just read to herself. A normal photograph analyzed under the VP-8 results in a distorted mix of light and dark shapes rather than a true dimensional image; she understood, because the light or dark shading in the photograph is due solely to the amount of light originally reflected by the subject onto the film and not to the actual *distance* of the subject from the film. Under the VP-8 a painting or drawing or any other known artistic technique would obtain the same result.

But the Enrie photograph taken in 1934 was unique. Unlike any other, with the Enrie photograph the VP-8 displayed a precise and accurate dimensional relief of a human form, indicating that the Shroud had actually covered the body of the man in the image. The VP-8 took the destiny of the image and converted it to vertical relief, as in bas relief. The closer the Shroud was to the nose or the cheekbone in the Enrie photograph, the proportionately darker the image appeared in that spot, and the farther away the lighter the image appeared. In other words, there was an exact mathematical relationship between the distance of the body from the cloth and the light energy from the Shroud image.

As she reread the e-mail, Emily's heart began to race. From a practical point of view, this spatial data "encoded" into the image on the Shroud eliminated the possibility that it was created by any method of reflection, as in a photograph, or by any type of painting, drawing, rubbing, chemical contact, thermal image, diffusion image, bas relief, dry powder contact, or scorching process. And additionally, because of the three-dimensional properties, STURP concluded that regardless of the process of creation, *the Shroud image was formed while the cloth was draped over an actual crucified human body.*

There it was. There was no way a forger could have recreated the precise mathematical relationship of the body to the Shroud that was revealed under STURP's VP-8 analysis.

A warm feeling flowed through Emily, surprising her. Martin was right. There was no explanation for the image on the Shroud; it remained a mystery.

But in the next instant, her reverie dissolved and Emily froze. Wesley had to have this information before the show aired. This would change his view of the Shroud. It changed everything. She jumped at the sound of a voice nearby.

"Where are our stars, Miss Scott?" Paul Johnson's young producer asked.

"Emily, please," she said, still preoccupied. She looked around. Where *were* they? Glancing up at the clock, she saw that time was growing short. "I'll go find them," she told him.

"Thanks." He disappeared in the direction of the set.

Emily tucked her purse under her arm and rose. Working her way through the cameras, cables, boxes, chairs, and lights that now surrounded the set, she went in search of Wesley and Jonathan Marley. As she neared the door that she'd entered, she heard angry voices rising and falling on the other side. She pulled the door toward her and peered out into the hallway. The archbishop wore a grim smile as he looked down at Jonathan Marley. Neither man spotted Emily.

"This is outrageous! It's slander! How did you come across this information?" Marley rasped. Emily's eyes grew wide as he made a fist and then lowered his hand. Suddenly his back seemed to give way as his shoulders hunched. He'd figured it out. "A detective! You've hired detectives!"

"You have my assurance . . ."

"I have children."

Emily coughed, and both men turned their heads toward her. "Sorry to interrupt." She gave Wesley a furious look. "But we've only a few minutes before the show," she said. "I've been sent to find you."

"Our discussion is finished," Wesley said smoothly, putting his hand on Jonathan Marley's shoulder in a friendly manner as if to steer the man before him. "As I was saying though, you have my assurance."

"I don't *need* your assurance," Dr. Marley said, shrugging him off angrily. Wesley stared at his back as the professor ducked around Emily and pushed through the door into the studio.

Emily arched her eyebrows. "Please tell me that you're not going to mention the information that detective dug up on the show tonight."

"Of course not, my dear," Wesley said, strolling to the door. He opened it and moved aside, motioning for her to enter. "That's exactly the assurance I was trying to give the idiot." An almost imperceptible smile played at the corners of his mouth and vanished.

Paul was waiting on the set when they walked into the studio. With a jovial call to him, Wesley broke away from Emily.

Paul looked up with a relieved expression and waved him up.

"I have to talk to you," Emily blurted, grabbing the sleeve of Wesley's sweater.

He turned and halted, glaring down at her. She'd never seemed so aggressive before. "What is it, Emily?" he said impatiently, nodding toward the set. "Can't you see that I'm late? The shows about to start."

"I know. It's just . . . it's about the image on the cloth. Remember?" She waved the printout of the e-mail before his face, and he gave her a questioning look.

"We talked about the idea that the image on the Shroud could have been created by an artist—a forger. Well, it's impossible. The thing is three-dimensional."

Wesley narrowed his eyes and brushed her hand from his sleeve. "So what?" he said, clipping his words as he glanced at the set. "So what if it's three-dimensional? You mentioned that in your research; it's nothing new."

"No, you don't understand." She forced herself to go on as he gave her an impatient look. "I didn't take it far enough before. This new information's so detailed, so precise, it's . . ." she paused, at a loss. She'd almost said that it was inexplicable, too convincing to ignore.

"Archbishop Bright!" The producer appeared at his side with a frantic look. "It's time, sir."

Wesley smoothed the sleeve of his sweater where Emily had grasped him. He wore his best cashmere crewneck; the casual look was best, he always thought. Grinning down at the producer who stood a good six inches below him, he chuckled. "No time like the present, eh?" he said, throwing his arm across the young man's shoulders and turning away.

"Don't worry about that little item, Emily," he called back over his shoulder in a matter-of-fact tone.

"But . . ."

"It doesn't matter now. Makes no difference."

Emily watched them hurry away. The cameras, furniture, people, all seemed to fade into the darkness of the room as they passed until only the bright lights shining down on the set were visible. Wesley stood still as the microphone was clipped onto his sweater. Again she had the thought that he seemed different tonight—brittle, almost ruthless.

With a profound sense that things had altered between them in the past few minutes, she lowered herself into a chair in front of a monitor and watched Wesley take his place at the table across from Jonathan Marley. From the darkness she could see the professor's hand trembling as he picked up a glass of water and sipped it. The archbishop bantered with Paul and the producer.

Marley's face was flushed red, she noticed, and already he perspired under the hot lights. He slumped in his chair, looking small, exhausted, and older than before. Wesley had terrified the man, she realized, and it occurred to her that perhaps this was his intention all along.

Advertisements ran across the monitor, and shortly after they began, sound from the set was audible in the studio. Emily slid back in her chair with a tight feeling in her chest as she watched Wesley. This was a side of the archbishop that she'd never seen before, she realized. Had he always been this person, so ambitious, so grasping and self-absorbed?

As Paul opened the show and introduced the guests, Jonathan Marley's face was gaunt and shadowed. His skittish eyes darted from the camera to Wesley and back again. In contrast, Emily observed, Wesley seemed at ease, in top form. His manner of tilting his head with a thoughtful look at a spot just above the camera gave the impression to viewers that he was engaged in an intimate conversation with each one. He'd practiced that look, she knew, as he'd been taught by that media relations person—the lizard.

Paul began the discussion tonight with the bloodstains on the Shroud, reserving the intriguing questions of the flowers and the creation of the image for the end of the show—a hook, Emily suspected, to hold the viewers.

When Dr. Marley began describing the results of chemical testing on the fibers of the cloth, a quirk of the archbishop's lips was visible just long enough to permit the cameras to capture his almost hidden amusement. Each time the professor began making a point, with perfect timing Wesley interrupted. Ten minutes into the show, Wesley dominated the discussion.

A heavy feeling descended on Emily as she watched the two men. Wesley exuded contempt. He sparred openly with the professor, glazing every word, every look into the camera with his knowledge of Marley's secret. Emily was stunned at his new energy and zeal, the ridicule with which he tore into each shred of evidence offered up by Marley.

She saw it coming—the professor's collapse—an instant before it happened. Crimson with rage, Jonathan Marley exploded. His lips tightened and stretched back across his teeth as he frowned, jutting his face across the table toward Wesley and punctuating each word with a small jerk of his chin. "How can you, a man of the cloth, the spokesman for the Apostolic Church, take such *pleasure* in destruction?" he burst out.

Paul and Wesley each looked at him in surprise, taken aback by his emotion. "Well, Archbishop Bright?" Paul finally said, turning to Wesley. "I suppose you'd like to respond?"

Wesley's brows flattened, lowering over his eyes. His lips curled into a half smile, and he gave Jonathan Marley a quizzical look. "Please enlighten the viewers," he said in a breezy tone that carried more than a touch of sarcasm. "What is it exactly that you think I've destroyed?" He gazed at the professor with his slight smile for a beat.

Dr. Marley opened his mouth to speak, but Wesley had already turned to the camera. "What is it you're hoping to find in that old cloth?" he began. "Clues to an invisible paradise?" He chuckled softly, sharing his amusement with each viewer. "It's the same old sucker story, isn't it? Martyrdom now in exchange for something better later on."

He looked off into the distance, as if considering the question. The camera moved in so that his face filled the screen. "But tell me," he went on, turning to Jonathan Marley, "which paradise should we seek? Eden? Nirvana? The garden of Paradise? Perhaps Elysian Fields?"

His voice was thick with sympathy as he shook his head. "Look around you. What you see is real; you can touch it, feel it; you can count on it. It's tangible, and it's all we have."

Wesley gave Marley a piteous look. "Everything's relative, Dr. Marley. If you're thinking that the Shroud authenticates the words of Jesus, makes them somehow divine, you're wasting your time and ours here tonight." He spread his hands and shrugged. "Life's full of rough spots. We each have to deal with that knowledge alone, on our own terms."

Paul pressed his lips together and looked down as if considering whether to say anything. After a beat he raised his eyes to Wesley. "Many intelligent people would disagree," he said.

Ignoring him, Wesley leaned toward the camera and curled his fingers into the palm of his hand in a supplicating gesture. His voice rose. "I'd say it's somewhat childish to pretend the Shroud of Turin—or the words of any ancient sage, for that matter—can provide an intelligent, modern society like ours with a moral compass. There is no such thing." He lounged back and, spreading his arms over the chair, tapped the edge of the table with two fingers, emphasizing each word as he said, "The hard thing is that each one of us has a responsibility to decide what's good for ourselves."

Still smiling, he glanced at Jonathan Marley, the war hero. "We can't weasel out of that."

"But the Shroud," Marley began.

"You may have thought that sort of thing was clear during your years in Vietnam," Wesley interrupted, speaking softly. At the mention of Vietnam, Marley paled. He shot Wesley a look of pure hatred, and the camera delivered it across America.

"It's said there are no atheists in foxholes, of course," Wesley went on, glowering back at the professor. "But in the civilized world, outside those foxholes, moral order is governed by human nature, our will to survive."

Taking a deep breath, Jonathan Marley seemed to come to a decision. He swallowed. "I beg to differ," Marley said, leaning forward. "What happens to the survival instinct when a father gives up his place in a lifeboat for his child?" he asked.

Paul for once was silent. He turned to Wesley and waited.

"That's Philosophy 101, I believe." The archbishop gave Marley a sympathetic smile, one that said, "Come child, let's be reasonable," and shook his head. "It's a trade-off, of course, a choice between two things of value, Professor Marley. In the case you mention, the father has valued the child's life above his own." He shrugged, as if bored. "It's human nature to act from motives of self-gratification."

As Emily stared at Wesley on the monitor, his face dissolved, and TeeBo's image formed instead. TeeBo flying through the air in front of the white van. The voices in the studio receded, and in the silence she had the certain thought: *Wesley was wrong. TeeBo couldn't possibly have made a conscious choice from self-interest when he'd saved the woman and the child. There wasn't time.*

And something else struck as she turned the idea in her mind. TeeBo couldn't have been motivated by any thought of reward either. Unlike Professor Marley's example of the father and his child, TeeBo hadn't even known the woman or the child he'd saved. The courageous act had just roared from the center of his being. He'd made an instant decision to do the right thing regardless of the cost. *What drives that sort of courage?* she wondered.

"It is *agape.*" Dr. Marley's voice intruded.

"What's that?" Paul asked.

"*Agape* is the ancient Greek word for an act that is absolutely good," Marley replied. "It's the act of making a sacrifice that outweighs everything else, even the strongest self-interest." As the professor turned to Wesley, Emily saw that his back was straight; he'd regained his proud bearing. "Courage comes from character," he went on. "It comes from a sense of right and wrong that exists outside ourselves." Marley's face set with resolve, seeming to dare the archbishop as he spoke.

Wesley just stopped himself from rolling his eyes. The professor was insufferable, he decided, and using the information in the investigative report was the correct thing to do after all, under the circumstances. Emily was wrong.

Marley took on an obstinate air as he went on, ignoring Wesley and turning toward the camera. "*Agape* is what carries our soldiers through battles, regardless of personal cost," he said.

He leaned forward, raking his fingers through his hair as he spoke. "The heroes are men and women who leave their families at home to fight for freedom and our beliefs—like the Marines on Iwo Jima in World War II, and our other battles—like the soldiers and airmen at Normandy and Bataan, the young sailors risking their lives on carriers, submarines, patrol boats." He paused and looked off. "Remember those little PT boats darting behind enemy lines in the South Pacific night after night like relentless mosquitoes?

"And think of our firefighters and police," he went on, looking at the camera again. "All the ordinary citizens during times like 9/11 who've risk their lives helping strangers."

Marley's voice grew strong as he drew a long breath and seemed to pull strength from some inner reserve. Neither Paul nor Wesley spoke. Emily, watched, holding her breath, stunned by the professor's passion, his sudden transformation. "That's what makes this country great," he said.

From the monitor his eyes seemed to penetrate Emily. He took a deep breath, and his face set with a determined look as he turned to Wesley. "Instinctive goodness does exist, and it transcends science and even our own selfish desires, no matter the cost. That's the meaning of the Shroud."

An uneasy frisson stirred Wesley as he sat listening. Images of the flowers near his bed, of the child's eyes—indigo eyes—formed in his mind, but he forced them aside. He had chosen. The man's arguments must be devastated, he knew, if the question of the Shroud's authenticity were to be ended once and for all. Otherwise, his life's work would be destroyed, a career invested battling the old religious view of a divine messiah, each one of his books that sold well because they were controversial, because they dared to ridicule the stale, old-fashioned ideas of absolute good and evil, right and wrong, and made life easier in the bargain. He'd published hundreds of articles on the subject. They'd all be discredited if the Shroud and the idea of the resurrection survived this show. Now every particle of his being focused on the destruction of Marley, on winning.

"Those are fine words for a man who's never had to make such a choice," the archbishop said softly when Marley paused.

The camera swung to the professor. Seconds passed as he stared at Wesley without blinking. Filled with pity, Emily watched as he began to tremble. Slowly his face contorted as he seemed to realize that he'd gambled and lost. Leaning forward, Jonathan Marley dropped his head and buried his face in his hands before one hundred million viewers.

The camera shifted abruptly to Paul Johnson who gaped from one guest to the other.

Emily rose without taking her eyes from the monitor.

"The Shroud of Turin is a fraud," the archbishop said in a quiet voice, with a touch of sorrow that rang false to Emily's ears. "No intelligent person could possibly give it credence."

Paul, ignoring Wesley, bent toward Marley and touched his shoulder. Receiving no response, he straightened; and while the camera swung to Wesley, he signaled the young producer, who nodded. Wesley's eyes turned down, his brows drew together, and his mouth puckered as he took on a look of astonished compassion.

"Well, folks," Paul said in a subdued voice, shifting his gaze to the camera as the music rose. "It looks like our time for this discussion is up, but," he paused with a hopeful look at each of his guests, "perhaps we should continue next week?"

"Certainly," Wesley said, leaning back and heaving a sigh. "If Dr. Marley feels it's necessary."

Paul's head swiveled toward the professor who had straightened in his chair. His cheeks were red. Jonathan Marley stared back at Paul with a blank expression.

The camera swung back to the host. "Right," Paul said, with a quick nod. "That's all the time we have for tonight, folks. We'll just have to leave it at this for now." He gave the viewers an uncertain smile.

Standing before the monitor, Emily saw only TeeBo's body flying through the air, the child looking up at his mother. She crumpled the e-mail that she held in her hand and let it fall to the floor, knowing that her life had changed. Emily didn't know how it happened that she felt this way, or why, but, as TeeBo would have said, some things are certain: two plus two will always be four, and what is good will always exist *outside* the self. TeeBo had shown her that much. He'd been driven by the universal law, the simple rule that the man on the Shroud had taught: *Care for others, as you would have them care for you.* He gave his life, like all the other heroes Marley described, not for any reward, not for fear of punishment, not out of self-interest, but merely because it was the right thing to do.

Gazing at Wesley on the monitor, Emily saw the shell of a man. *Wesley was wrong,* she realized. *Truth is not abstract, it's the law within the law.*

And the Shroud? She turned away from the monitor. It wasn't necessary to have all the answers. For now, the questions, the possibilities, were enough.

She walked through the dark studio, leaving Wesley behind. Opening the door, she entered the hallway and pushed the button to summon an elevator. When the elevator arrived, she stepped in, turned, and studied her reflection on the shiny brass wall in front of her while it descended. Glancing at her watch when the doors opened on the ground floor, she caught herself and made a wry face.

Plenty of time now, TeeBo.

As she walked from the building out onto the sidewalk, hoping that a taxicab would cruise by, she heard a whistle.

The night was cold and clear, and streetlights bathed the area around her. Before she could catch herself, her head turned toward the sound of the whistle. Lounging against the corner of the building, hands in his pockets jingling change, was Martin.

Emily stared as she took in the lean body and confident grin, and suddenly she laughed, feeling free and alive and tingling with the excitement of beginnings.

"Got time?" he asked.

"Yep," she said.

CHAPTER TWENTY-TWO

His hand slammed down and swept the vase from the table. Glass shattered on the bedroom floor and water seeped around his slippers. He looked down at the flowers strewn across the room and felt a renewed surge of the old hatred. A feeling so powerful, so strong and physical that it knocked him back, and he fell onto the bed.

He hated the flowers and all they stood for: Leo Ransom and the old church, with its hypocrisy, its empty platitudes as dry as dust, with its God who wasn't there on the day that Sam had died.

Wesley sat on the edge of the bed, and for the tenth time this evening, since he'd stepped down from the set to look for Emily and found that she had gone, he was conscious that he missed seeing his reflection in her eyes, her adoring smile. What good was it to win a battle when no one was around to care, to tell him that he'd been magnificent? If his mother was around, she'd . . . oh well. He wondered why he felt this way. Empty. Hopeless. Depressed. Lonely. Perhaps even terrified.

Terrified! He gave a sharp bark of a laugh at that last thought.

Why should he be frightened? He'd done it. After the show Paul told him the switchboard was jammed with callers. Highest ratings ever was a certainty, the young producer had said. Marley had disappeared.

He'd done it. His position was intact. After tonight the Shroud of Turin would be a nonevent, a relic of superstition. Things could return to normal. In fact, he mused, he was even stronger than before. He held the power of the church in his hands. He, Wesley Bright. Little Guy. The *Right Honorable* Archbishop Wesley Bright.

His conscience stirred as he glanced down once again at the flowers strewn across the floor. He had *lied.* Lied to the world. It was a Faustian bargain, he knew—fame and power in exchange for the lie. Wesley was conscious that he may have crossed a line of some sort now, but no one else would ever know—other than Emily, perhaps, if he ever told her. How could they know?

And Emily?

He pushed thoughts of Emily away. She'd be back. Even she couldn't know for certain that he'd lied. He hadn't told her what he knew about the flowers, of the dream. She had no way of knowing. He might discuss it with her later. Sometimes, as he'd told her, the ends justify the means.

Liar! whispered an inner voice.

He checked the thought and forced himself to smile until gradually his spirits rose. But still he felt restless. Impulsively

Wesley kicked off his slippers and, stepping around the spilled water and flowers and bits of broken glass, he went to the closet for shoes. Grabbing a coat from the nearest hanger, he shrugged it on and yanked a wool hat down over his ears. He needed fresh air. With an afterthought he rummaged through the bottom drawer of his bureau. After a moment he located the silver dollar that his father had given him and jammed it into his coat pocket.

Wesley Bright walked down the street trying not to think of Emily and Jonathan Marley and Paul Johnson and the Shroud, determined to enjoy the night's victory. The evening was cold, and he pulled his coat tighter so that it was snug around him. He was grateful for the warmth of the woolen hat. He'd read somewhere that 90 percent of body heat escapes through the head.

Finding himself in front of the Met, Wesley grimaced and turned left, walking briskly down Fifth Avenue toward midtown, fingering the coin in his pocket. Across the street on his right, Central Park was all shadows, reminding him of the garden in the dream. No! He refused to think of the dream right now. This should be a wonderful night; he would not think of the little girl, of the flowers that she held, the flowers on the table by his bed—the flower images on the Shroud.

He forced his thoughts to something happy—tomorrow morning's newspapers! The print reporters had been waiting after the show. The interviews had gone well, he knew. He felt it. Couldn't wait to see the photos.

But a vision wormed its way into his thoughts, spoiling the moment. It was the man in the dream, the prisoner lying on the stone slab in the tomb. He pressed the coin in his pocket hard against his palm with his thumb to deflect the image. *No! No! No!*

The sound of his own voice stopped him. He glanced around, but the street was empty. No one heard. Besides, he told himself. It was only a dream.

But . . . still, there were the flowers.

All night he walked through the streets of the city. Even after he grew fatigued, exhausted in fact, still he walked. So long as he kept moving, he wouldn't have to think of the flowers or Emily. He gazed up at the buildings made of glass and steel and concrete that surrounded him. They stretched to the sky, and it crossed his mind that the energy man once put into creating monuments to God, the great cathedrals, was now used to create buildings like these instead, temples to celebrate commerce—financial institutions, hotels, corporations, shops full of expensive things to own.

Well? What's wrong with that?

His step slowed. The chilling thought slipped in: *What had he done?* He tried to dismiss the hateful question, but each time it came creeping back, slithering around in his mind until he thought he'd go mad. He grew cold when he thought of the dream. The girl, the flowers. The man, lying on the cloth. Lying on the Shroud. The Shroud was real, and he'd lied to destroy it.

Suddenly the archbishop halted in his tracks and listened. A sound in the distance, a deep rumble through the night like the roll of drums unsettled him. Desperately his eyes scanned the scene before him, searching out an anchor for his thoughts. He found himself almost back where he'd started, near the park not so far from the hotels, the Plaza. City lights reflected on long sheets of glass, glittering; windows filled with things that wouldn't last. He looked into a small boutique and stared at the display of clothes and shoes and jewelry, each thing to be purchased for a price that could feed several villages in third-world countries. Turning, he gazed about, taking in the bright lights, the lines of cars near the hotels, the hansom cab just rounding the corner of the park, two people walking close together.

He studied them all, suddenly swept by a wave of desolation. Emily! Where was Emily? Squeezing his eyes shut for an instant, he wished that she were here.

She'd simply disappeared after the show. He shivered and pulled his coat tight. Cold air seemed to penetrate his bones these days, not like when he was young and strong. He refused to accept that Emily was gone, but the thought slipped into his consciousness again and again. And Mother was gone. And Sam.

He waited for the light and crossed the street in the direction of the park. "I'm alone," he said out loud, and the realization made him dizzy. He reached out his hand and steadied himself on the edge of a wooden bench. It was pushed back from the sidewalk, against the stone wall that ran along that section of Central Park.

The moon was high, and he realized that he'd been walking for hours. The night was dark. He looked up. Funny thing about the moon—without the sun it had no light. *But I can do it all alone!* he cried. *I don't need anyone. Not even Emily!* His thoughts churned as he looked at the moon and remembered words from some poem Emily had quoted.

Love is lost; the moon burns.

The world spun, and suddenly he had the sensation that he was falling, sliding through a tunnel of dark and empty space. Disoriented, Wesley fell onto the bench, closed his eyes, and dropped his head into his hands.

In silence he waited, trying to empty his mind of thoughts, trying to float in the weightless drift of black that seemed to envelope him. He was cold and tired. And then, from far away again he heard the drums, and once again they were familiar. It was a muffled, dull, distinctive sound, a rhythmic cadence. *Drums?* At this time of night?

His head jerks up and his eyes fly open. Sunlight floods a narrow street. He stares straight ahead at a wall built with heavy blocks of rough-hewn stone, then turns his head in wonder. "Where am I?" he demands, but the words are lost in the din of a jeering crowd and the sound of drums reverberating through him as they draw close, ever closer; fierce, loud, demanding drums that seem to call for him.

He's standing in bright sunshine with a group of restless, rowdy men. The stench is overpowering but familiar. Sweat and dirt and fear. Many of the men are bearded; all wear tunics or long cloaks wrapped at the waist with rope belts and sandals on their feet. Something presses against his legs, and he looks down to see the top of a small child's head, a little girl, he realizes in the instant before he hears a raw, harsh cry. A man's voice, wrenched with pain.

Not here. He doesn't want to be here. Desperately he looks around. Where are the buildings, the electric lights, steel and glass? Where are the automobiles and paved streets?

The drums and cries and screams of pain submerge all thought, and as he waits, they grow louder than before. The crowd jostles him. Glancing down again at the child, he's surprised to find that he cares for her; and he pulls her close, holding her against him. He bends over her, peering through the crowd in the direction of the noise. There. He sees them now—just there, to the right.

The drumbeat crashes through the street as a small cadre of soldiers round the corner. He straightens, willing himself to remain calm, telling himself that this is the dream again. But still it's different now—how *real* everything appears. He blinks and opens his eyes, but nothing's changed—the crowd, the child, the stone walls. And the drums. Strange. It's as if at once he occupies parallel spaces in the universe, as if he's watching himself from two different points in time and place.

The soldiers come on, ringed around three men, surrounding them. They're Roman soldiers from the fort, Antonia. *But how can I know this?* he wonders. The three men in the middle of the soldiers must be prisoners; they're stripped almost bare of clothes. Two wear only loincloths. One wears the tattered remains of a filthy, blood- streaked robe. He stares as they make their way down the narrow street toward him and rests his hand on Hanna's shoulders.

Hanna? Her name is Hanna?

He feels her press back against him as the soldiers grow close. Someone laughs and he glances over to his right. A soldier is advancing on the crowd; he's pushing and the rough crowd shoves back. Hanna trembles and he grips her now, hunching over her to deflect the crush of humanity. He's swamped by the odor of bodies and perspiration. It's difficult to breathe.

He sees . . . feels . . . the child tense, and suddenly he realizes that she is pulling away from him. He jerks her back against him once again. She tilts her face up to him and smiles.

It's all so real. Where is the park and his bench and the city? Emily!

This is no dream. Wesley shakes his head, struggling to escape, but instead the drums come on with the pounding, throbbing beat. As the procession draws near, he sees that the prisoners carry something on their shoulders, heavy wooden beams. Whips crack through the drumbeat, slashing across their bare backs and shoulders. His eyes fix on one of the prisoners, and he stares with growing dread. It is Yeshua.

His heart pounds wildly as he watches Yeshua move toward him. The light around him fades, and all at once the crowd dissolves. He ducks and pulls the cowl over his head, letting it fall across his face.

It's dark now, nighttime, or perhaps it's almost dawn. He's sitting on the ground, and the dirt beneath feels hard and cold. From underneath the cowl he peeks around, holding his head very still so as not to draw attention. He's frightened, confused, but relieved to have escaped the crowd and noise and the soldiers.

Where am I? he wonders. All around him are walls frescoed and painted with colorful symbols. It must be a courtyard, it comes to him, an inner courtyard in a house in the city of Jerusalem. Somehow he knows: this is the home of Caiphas, the chief priest.

Four men lounge on the ground nearby in the center of the courtyard. They're stretched out close to a fire, and the warmth draws him. But he holds back, knowing somehow that these men are dangerous. Sometimes they glance toward him. They're dressed in the tunics worn by temple guards, thick cotton trimmed with embroidery. There's something ominous about them. He's waiting, repressing the desire to flee. Yeshua is inside; he's been taken there by soldiers.

"This man was with him too. With the Galilean."

The voice is sharp, malicious, and it startles him. He raises his eyes to see a servant girl standing over him with a sneer, arms akimbo, sandaled feet planted wide apart. Her words ring through the courtyard.

Slut.

The murmuring around the fire stops, and the men turn to look at him. He's conscious that they're waiting for his answer.

His mouth is dry. Barely glancing at the girl he composes a look of disdain. "Woman, I don't know him," he says roughly.

The girl's mouth twists. She gives him a sly look, then shrugs and swings away.

He forces himself to remain where he is, not to get up and run. The guards near the fire commence their murmuring once again, glancing at him as they talk. Suddenly, one of them catches his eye. He freezes as the guard stares back at him with a reflective, accusing look.

"You *are* one of them," the man growls. "I heard you speak. You're from Galilee." The guard shifts his position on the ground, as if to rise. The others have turned as well, and they study him, waiting.

He swallows and, despite the cold, feels dampness on his back. "Man, I am not!" he says, working to hold his voice even.

For a moment the guards watch him; then they glance at one another and settle back around the fire. Minutes pass while he waits for Yeshua to reappear, uncertain what to do, how to act. How much time can he have left? The murmuring commences once again among the guards, low urgent tones that chill him. He holds rigid, not daring to move.

A flash of light startles him. *Emily!* he cries to himself. *Thank God!* He moves to rise, glimpses buildings in Manhattan, the sky streaked with lavender at dawn. He stretches out his arms, and darkness blankets him, pulling him back into the courtyard. The serving maid now stands near a doorway. The temple guards still huddle by the fire.

Confused, he passes his hand before his eyes. Pictures explode in his mind, flashes of light containing Emily and Hanna, the silent park at night and the ancient courtyard, an automobile moving slowly down Fifth Avenue and soldiers jostling the prisoners, pushing them toward Golgotha. Yeshua at the center of the sorrowful procession.

Overcome by the jumble of thoughts, the hellish confusion of time and space, he pushes himself up from his place on the ground, stumbling with the weakness brought on by fear.

As one, the guards turn their faces to him.

"This man was certainly with Yeshua of Nazareth. He is a Galilean too," the servant girl calls from across the courtyard.

As one, the guards stand with slow, deliberate movements, eyes riveted to him. A hand grasps a knife worn at the hip.

Ice slips through his chest. "I am not!" he insists, cowering.

He is falling through a dark and heavy mist. From somewhere far away, long ago, he hears the small voice calling from the garden.

Uncle? She sounds frightened.

Hanna stands at the entrance to a tomb bathed in moonlight. Her indigo eyes pierce his, and once again she calls out: *Uncle?* Her voice is urgent now, an echo from eons past, a hollow, haunting sound.

He wills his eyes to open. Morning light filters through the trees, and across the park he sees the tops of tall buildings. He struggles to rise from the bench, but his limbs are heavy, and he finds he cannot move.

Once again Hanna calls. Through space and time he sees the child, searching. Wretched, distraught, her uncle hiding in the forest, struggles to his feet. Tears spill down his cheeks; and as he turns to her, moonlight strikes his face.

Then from his bench near Central Park, Archbishop Wesley Bright rises and cries out, staring into the face that mirrors his own in the distant garden. At once the union is complete. The veil of time lifts as he raises his hand to Uncle's flesh and feels his own, brushes the tears from Uncle's cheeks and his own, and stares back at his reflection.

In the half-light of dawn, from somewhere far away—from the courtyard, from the garden, from deep within the park in the middle of Manhattan—a cock crows.

Once, then twice.

Cathedral bells toll from down the street . . . *betrayal . . . betrayal.*

Like light flashing off the facets of a prism, memories return. In anguish Wesley drops onto the bench and sits motionless, closing his eyes as once again he hears Yeshua's warning. The words surround him, sinking through him, burning: "Before the cock crows, you will deny me three times."

Pain shoots through Wesley as he recalls . . . no . . . *hears* again the immortal, terrible words. They drove him then, two thousand years ago, and judge him now. He sits motionless in the past and present, suspended in a timeless space between two worlds, waiting.

He feels the presence in the instant just before he lifts his eyes. His chest aches, and the drums that called throughout his life now seem to pound within him as he stares. Before him stands the Man of the Shroud, straight backed, expectant, as he'd looked in those happy days when they'd walked the fields of yellow sunshine near the sea.

Seconds pass and at a nod Wesley's eyes slowly move from the face, to the chest, to the small bundle cradled in the arms. Sam's silken hair gleams; his skin shines with an incandescent light. His tiny hands curl against the chest. Overwhelmed, Wesley sees the child move, nestling close, tucking his small head beneath the bearded chin with a contented sigh.

The drums have stopped and Yeshua smiles. The smile streams to Wesley as he lifts his face, releasing him from years of guilt and pain and sorrow as it shimmers through his flesh, entering his heart and spreading through his veins limb to limb, surging effervescent through his blood. When it bursts into his mind, he reaches out for Yeshua, longing to touch him, and little Sam.

But in that instant something holds him back. His hand, stretched out midair just before him hovers there. Somehow he knows: first, he has hard work to do.

When Yeshua speaks, his voice is life itself, the sound of many waters:

Do you love me, Peter?

AFTERWORD

Emily

Boston—March 2010

The snow's melting in the rain and everything here in Boston has turned to slush, but I'm thinking of the months to come, and that gives me chills, dear reader, and a humble feeling that almost drives me to my knees. But . . . first things first.

Will you join me in a cup of coffee?

Great. Sit right there. Nothing like a steaming cup of coffee on a cold, rainy morning, right? Sugar and cream?

Right. Me too.

Ahhh. This tastes good. I feel the pleasure of this room down through my toes while I sit with you and drink hot coffee. This is the warmest part of the house—the yellow walls brighten up a dark day, don't you think? That was my idea. After Martin and I married and I moved in, that was the only change I wanted to make. Yellow reminds me of sunshine. Ha! Sunshine was a scarce commodity this winter.

Where's global warming when you need it?

Reader, when I think of all that's happened since last we met, I don't know where to begin. But the baby's asleep and once he wakes . . . oh well, you know the rest. At least, statistically, 50 percent of you should know the drill.

It's been, what . . . three years . . . since last we were together? I haven't seen Wesley Bright, the Archbishop, since that final Phil Johnson Show when I walked out of his life. Wesley was headed down a path to destruction, determined for some reason to nail Dr. Marley to the wall, and suddenly . . . somehow, as I sat behind those cameras and watched, everything came together in my mind. I thought of what those flower images on the Shroud really meant, and of TeeBo, and of Wesley's Faustian choice—his lie—and I knew with certainty that he was wrong about everything.

Yes, I agree. It was all so sad. What happened to him afterward?

Hmmm. Wish I knew. It's quite a mystery.

Then there's Margaret. You remember her, don't you, the Archbishop's gatekeeper, his secretary? Yes. Well, I spoke to her a few months after I'd left. I called to ask about the Archbishop, out of curiosity more than anything. She said he'd just disappeared. Poof! And no one's seen him since!

Strange, I know. Margaret says he returned only once to the office after that show. It was two days later and he looked haggard, she said, solemn and curiously detached. Seemed completely unaware of all the commotion he'd caused in the press. So unlike him not to revel in the attention. But there was a backlash of sorts, Margaret said. He'd gone too far, denying the Shroud, tearing Marley down in public like that. The Cathedral offices had been inundated with furious e-mails afterward.

You're asking about Miss Honeman, what did she know? Hmmm. Oh yes, the housekeeper. Well, she was a tough one. I didn't call her—we didn't really get along. But Margaret spoke with her several times, said she was quite distraught over his disappearance. He'd shattered a vase of flowers after the show that night, she told Margaret.

Funny thing about those flowers though—I still get chills when I think of the botany reports that Dr. Marley passed on to us, me and the Archbishop. Remember those? Doctors Whanger and Whanger first noticed the images. Then Dr. Danin, one of the world's foremost botanists, from Hebrew University of Jerusalem, confirmed their observations, and after a lengthy study he concluded that three species of the flower images on the Shroud grow only around Jerusalem, and were in a state of bloom found only in the months of Easter and Passover.

Whimsy meets science, Martin says.

But reader, after that last conversation with Margaret, Martin and I followed the trail of those flowers through the next four years. Not long after the Archbishop disappeared, in 2007 more information emerged. When a computer expert, B. Galmarini, transformed a two-dimensional photograph of the Shroud into a detailed 3D image, he noticed depressions around the face area of the Man of the Shroud, on the forehead and right cheek. After studying earlier 2D photographs of flowers in those areas, several scientists concluded that the flowers on the body made the depressions, and that the flower images were obstacles that interfered with the transmission of the 3D information between the body and the linen cloth.

Yep. I know it's complicated. But the bottom line is a matter of building the chain of proof, confirming the evidence. This was one more way to show that the flower images were not imagination. They'd now been observed using two different photographic techniques. Plus, as you'll remember from my conversation with Leo, pollen on the cloth matched these species too.

And that's not all. In 2007 five more species of plants and flowers that bloom only in the spring were found on the Shroud by Dr. P. Soons, and one grouped species of *Anthemis*—in the sunflower family—was placed on the body in a careful arrangement, perhaps like a bouquet.

Perhaps the little flower girl put them there, I told Martin.

He merely laughed. Whimsy or not, science does have its limits.

Another cup of coffee? No? Well, I think I'll take a refill. I do wish this rain would stop. This coffee helps, though. It's nice and hot.

Now, where were we? Oh yes.

So. If you add all of this new information to the fact that the radiocarbon dating has now been fully discredited . . . oh yes . . . Dr. Raymond Roger's findings published in *Thermochimica Acta* in January 2005 have been substantiated. Do you remember? Rogers proved that the radiocarbon dating in 1988 was performed on samples of cloth woven onto the Shroud during the medieval period with invisible stitching.

He died shortly thereafter I was sorry to hear. But his work at Los Alamos National Laboratories is carried on by Dr. Robert Villereal, and it's all been independently verified now by several scientists. I know—*invisible stitching*? That's how Dr. Marley described the technique, and the Archbishop sneered, as I recall. But that claim's been proven too. Dr. Villarreal recently discovered not only threads of cotton in the area of the test samples—cotton doesn't appear in the original cloth, you remember—but he also found threads of cotton and linen intentionally spliced together, and guess what! The threads were covered with a surface resin, similar to starch, that was used to hide the work of the medieval restorers.

You know, that 1988 radiocarbon test was just fatally flawed. Dr. Villarreal and Barry Schwortz, the STURP photographer, were interviewed on a Discovery Channel Documentary on the Shroud not long ago, in 2009. Dr. Villarreal put it this way: "The 1988 age-dating process failed to recognize one of the first rules of analytical chemistry that any sample taken for characterization of an area or population must necessarily be representative of the whole . . . Our analyses . . . showed that this was not the case."

What's all this mean, you ask?

It means that the Shroud is no longer viewed as a medieval fraud. It opens the question up for discussion again. *Is* this the burial cloth of Jesus?

No. No. No! I'm sorry, but your argument is off-base. The question of the Shroud's authenticity doesn't hang solely on the invalidity of the radiocarbon dating. In fact, as Leo told us, historical evidence, paintings, written references to the sacred cloth, certain folds in the linen—things like that—

place the Shroud back as far as the first century, regardless of radiocarbon dating.

It's clear that the Shroud's long journey through history has exposed it to contaminants that would affect any radiocarbon dating. Even the current director of one of the laboratories performing the official test in 1988, Christopher Bronk Ramsey of the Oxford Radiocarbon Accelerator Unit, seemed to agree. In a recent BBC interview he announced that the more advanced technology today could bring the 1988 radiocarbon results on the Shroud into question. Quite an admission from the director of one of the testing labs.

Martin was convinced the Shroud was real before we met, but as you probably remember, I was a skeptic at first.

And now? Well, it's an almost unthinkable conclusion.

But what do you think of this, dear reader: In 2008 Pope Benedict XVI announced an entirely unexpected exhibition of the Shroud of Turin to take place from April 10, 2010 through May 23, 2010. Until that announcement, the next public exhibition of the Shroud had been scheduled during the 2025 Catholic Jubilee year. Public exhibitions are rare. There've have been only four others since the fiftheen century when the Shroud was first moved to the Cathedral in Turin. The last one was in 2000.

So, in May Martin and I went to Turin to view the Shroud, and we walked through those quiet, somber rooms to the darkened one. I said my prayers in a quiet place before going in for the viewing. The real mystery to me now is the timing of things. Why now? Why now is all of this information emerging from the Shroud—in this time of great peril and turmoil, when perhaps more than any other period in history, we need a reminder of why we're all here?

Lean close, reader.

Closer, and I'll tell what's in my heart.

It's such a private thing, this statement, difficult to share. But at the foot of the cross after Jesus died two thousand years ago the Apostle John said, and later wrote: "He who has seen has borne witness, and his witness is true; and he knows that he is telling the truth, so that you also may believe." Those words have been preserved to give us courage today, and the Shroud bears witness to eternal life.

So, after I prayed, I walked into the dark cathedral in Turin—and I believe I looked upon the face of the Messiah.